She sto

the flowers

"Why did you bring them?"

"Why does any man bring a woman flowers?"

"Maybe you know how important it is to me to have some visible proof that you're not ashamed to be seen with me."

Eric's jaw tightened at the old argument. "I've never been ashamed of you, Chrys. Never."

"I hope that's true." Chrys's fingers trembled as she touched the petals. "I decided to wear this sari because it's the most flamboyant thing I own. I wanted to be seen with you."

"Oh, Chrys, have I hurt you that much?" Eric caught her hand in his and lifted it to his lips, flowers and all. "I want to be seen with you, Chrys. And not just because you're a beautiful woman."

Chrys's smile was slow in coming, but it was soft and warm. "I always did like carnations."

"And I always liked you."

ABOUT THE AUTHOR

Alysse Lemery should know enough about romance—she claims that when she met her husband it was love at first sight! Alysse began spinning stories when she was very young, keeping her sisters amused every night after their mother turned off the lights. She is now living in Florida and writing full-time.

Books by Alysse Lemery

HARLEQUIN AMERICAN ROMANCE

46–TWILIGHT DAWN
98–WISHING STAR

Winter's End

Alysse Lemery

Harlequin Books

TORONTO • NEW YORK • LONDON
AMSTERDAM • PARIS • SYDNEY • HAMBURG
STOCKHOLM • ATHENS • TOKYO • MILAN

For Danny, my one and only

Published May 1987

First printing March 1987

ISBN 0-373-16199-9

Printed in U.S.A.

Chapter One

Eric thanked the caller once again and dropped the telephone receiver back in its cradle. His polite mask slipped out of place for a moment and the fingers of his right hand snaked through his hair in agitation. It didn't seem possible, but Joe Beniki was seldom wrong.

Walking over to the color television set, Eric switched the channels, looking for the Cable News Network. If the old man was really dead, then CNN would carry a story eventually. Talbot McLean had been too much of a political power to go out without a word from the media.

While the newscaster droned on about the fate of the Mideast, the slippery road conditions in Minnesota and the latest drug scandal on the sports scene, Eric went into the apartment's small kitchenette. His actions were controlled and even, almost methodical in nature.

He took a thick, squat tumbler out of the cupboard over the sink and put it down on the wide Formica counter-bar. Next, he reached up to open the small cupboard over the refrigerator, took out a bottle of Southern Comfort and poured himself a stiff drink—neat.

Going back into the front room, Eric dropped morosely into a large, overstuffed chair. Slouching comfortably, he put his feet up on the ottoman and hung his arms over the sides of the chair. The drink, as yet untouched, dangled from his hand.

Within an hour and a half, the news he'd heard on the telephone was confirmed. Giving a disjointed sigh Eric leaned forward and flicked off the television with a snap. He studied the contents of the tumbler thoughtfully, then downed the liquid in a single gulp, grimacing at the raw bite of the bitter spirits.

He returned to the kitchen. Tonight he would get morbidly drunk. *And maybe,* he thought to himself, *that will keep the memories at bay.*

But it didn't. Not even one.

ERIC SNAPPED OFF the car radio in disgust. Right now he didn't need to hear anyone extolling the virtues of going home for Christmas. Neither the thought of the monstrous house where he had grown up, nor the community where he had spent so much of his youth, warmed his heart. Platteville was simply the town where his parents had lived—incompatible, but unwilling to divorce—until his mother's death fifteen years earlier had ended the incessant bickering once and for all.

The winter weather fit his mood exactly. The sky was a gloomy gray. He had forgotten how unwelcoming a December sky could be in this part of the country. It was obvious that the snow wasn't going to hold off too much longer.

"Well, if you're going, get going." He tried talking out loud to himself, to see if it would make the interior of the rental car more congenial, but it didn't seem to make any difference at all. Instead, his voice echoed hollowly and only served to point out how alone he was.

Clenching his jaw with steely determination, Eric thrust the car into gear and made a cautious left turn at the last stop sign in Belmont. The shiny Citation picked up speed slowly, more because the driver had reservations about finishing his trip than because of the slippery, snow-covered road.

Was he making a mistake? He'd asked himself that a dozen times since catching the plane early this morning. He wasn't happy about returning, but he hoped the trip would take some of the bitterness away.

It was funny, he mused silently; the phone call Thursday night had taken him completely unawares. So much so that he'd forgotten to ask Joe how he had managed to locate him. But what had surprised Eric even more was the fact that hearing of his father's death had really upset him. If someone had asked him a week ago, he would have said: "I couldn't give a damn."

He had spent Friday nursing a monstrous hangover and telling himself that he had owed no allegiance to his father while he was alive, and that now he was dead, he owed him even less. He had lain awake most of Friday night, too, telling himself that he could use this trip to put the last of his past behind him. Then this morning, well before sunrise, he had started making travel arrangements.

"Maybe I'd have been better off just forgetting the whole thing," he muttered.

The changes were unsettling. For some reason, he hadn't really expected things to be any different than they had been eight years ago. Yet this entire trip had been filled with changes. Madison, Verona, Mount Horeb, Blue Mounds, Barneveld, Ridgeway, Dodgeville, Mineral Point, Belmont, each city showed change. He didn't know if he was actually ready to accept the fact that things had changed.

Platteville, he thought, sighing, would have changed, too. But in what way? Would the changes be for the better? Could his father have changed too?

A mile or so outside Platteville, the Evergreen Trailer Court flashed by. The trees had grown tall, no longer hiding the trailers from view. And, once more, change seemed to be the order of the day. In fact, Eric told himself wryly, if it hadn't been for the population marker outside town and the slope of the hillside, he wouldn't have recognized Platteville.

Gibson's, once a fairly isolated department store, had a new name, if not a new image, and its parking lot was now surrounded by the trappings of other flourishing businesses. To his right, there was a deep gully, with tufts of dried cornstalks clumped sporadically in the old snow—and a house he didn't remember. In the distance he could see the local dairy and several other small businesses. The milk trucks were shiny bits of silver wending their way along the icy roads. It almost seemed as if he were observing a toy town.

Cresting the final hill, he applied his brakes cautiously as the road dipped steeply. At the bottom, looking completely out of place on the craggy hillside, a huge sign advertised the city's historic Mining Museum. Eric slowed the Citation, hesitating briefly.

In the distance, by the main crossroads, he could see more evidence of business growth. To the right, a small side street beckoned. Virgin Avenue. How many students had stolen those highly prized street signs over the years? Eric wondered. There was probably one in his old bedroom now, if his father hadn't had all his things thrown out.

"Damn!" He cursed out loud, forcing from his mind the beginning of a memory that had nothing to do with his father. He slid the rental car into gear with an abrupt lurch. He had come back in order to put the past behind him, not to dredge it up. Especially not that part of it.

It took less than five minutes to wind his way through the hilly streets and reach the massive structure that had once been his home. The large limestone building stood only a few feet from the northernmost boundary of the University of Wisconsin. And, as he had remembered, the house and grounds were every bit as immaculate, impressive and impersonal as they had ever been.

The stately edifice was truly majestic in appearance, standing as it did in the middle of a one-acre lot. But unlike the university buildings it so closely resembled, no trees shaded it, no ivy had ever dared to climb its stone walls. It was cold, bleak and almost sterile. Deep drifts of snow were piled high along the drive, and not one single footprint marred the white expanse of lawn. The windows were unlighted, giving the house a vacant, unlived-in air. It lacked life. It lacked warmth. And, as always, it lacked love.

Eric sighed regretfully as he got out of the car and headed toward the front door. *This is one thing that hasn't changed.*

Standing on the stone porch, Eric wasn't sure if he should knock or just walk in. Hunching his shoulders against the wind, he decided not to wait for someone to answer the door. Instead, his long, brown fingers closed around the handle of the old-fashioned latch. It bit coldly into his flesh but moved easily beneath his hand. There was not even a hint of a creak or a groan from the hinges.

"Something else that hasn't changed."

He had admired his father's housekeeper almost as much as he had disliked her. She had been one of the few people who possessed the ability to look down her long, thin nose and make everyone—even his father—shift uncomfortably and think twice about making a fuss.

Opening the door wider, Eric saw that the foyer and main hall were as dim as ever. Many people would have been intrigued with all the nooks and crannies. Yet when he was living there, the house's gloomy interior had only served to emphasize his filial inadequacies. No amount of expensive furnishings, no amount of brightly hued flowers had been able to lighten the atmosphere.

Taking a deep breath, he squared his shoulders, bracing himself for the first step that would lead him down the length of the depressingly opulent hall. Even though the house had been decorated by one of the finest firms in southwestern Wisconsin and was filled with a fortune in original art and polished antiques it wasn't a home. It wasn't even a comfortable house. He had always felt that if someone warm and loving ever came into the house the cold facade would be destroyed just as surely as touching a reflection in a pool of water destroyed its image. But nothing and no one had ever cared to try. Not in Talbot McLean's household.

His fraternity brothers had kidded him about living in the frat house when his own home had been available. It had been easier all around to let them think that he, like most other young men, craved privacy away from a watchful parental eye. Back then he hadn't been able to share the lonely feeling of isolation, nor the debilitating feeling of inadequacy, with anyone.

With anyone but Chryssie.

Eric muttered a gritty expletive, but there wasn't any real feeling in the curse. Chryssie was a part of his past and he would have to deal eventually with the memories she evoked. And eventually meant during this trip. Even though she had never set foot in this house, her memory was tied in with this place in his mind.

It had been a mistake to insist on a relationship that neither of them had been adult enough to handle. He'd known that long before she had, but he'd been unwilling to admit it—even in the end. In those days, he'd been far too stiff-necked to admit to mistakes. And he'd been too insecure, even with her, to try to explain how he felt. At one time he had even wondered if he might not have been in love with her. But nearly a decade of hindsight had shown him clearly that he wasn't capable of loving anyone. Not then, and not now.

Chryssie had accused him of knowing that his father would disapprove of their relationship because her background was neither socially nor politically powerful. He hadn't bothered to deny it. It had been the truth.

His mistake had been in never being able to explain that he actually feared Talbot's implacability. Feared him for himself and for her as well. When she had broken off with him, he had let her go without a fight, knowing that at least she would be safe from the sharp, cutting edge of his father's tongue.

For the first time in years Eric allowed himself to speculate on what might have happened if he had made different choices. Then abruptly he shook his head, clearing it of the past. Speculation after all this time was a complete waste. He'd do better to try to locate someone in the kitchen. It was only a few minutes after one o'clock. He was certain to find someone there.

"Wrong again, McLean." He spoke under his breath, but his words echoed hollowly throughout the empty kitchen.

The only sign of activity came from a coffee maker that gurgled contentedly in the corner. Mrs. Hill, it appeared, had finally succumbed to the blandishment of an automatic coffee maker salesman. In the past she had been a stickler for the "old way, only way" school of thought.

Not up to working out the strange new twist of the housekeeper's mental processes, Eric shrugged out of his coat. The fresh aroma of the coffee was well-nigh irresistible. He hadn't had anything to eat or drink since early morning, so he helped himself to a cup of the black brew. Inhaling deeply, he perched on the far corner of a large, free-standing chopping block, letting one booted foot swing idly.

Not bothering to let the coffee cool, he sipped it slowly. His eyes were pensive and his expression thoughtful as he surveyed his surroundings. The kitchen seemed to have taken on a personality of its own. In fact, it was almost inviting. And that was nearly enough to make him wonder if he really had the right household.

"Now wouldn't that be a laugh," he murmured to himself. "Prodigal returns: right town, wrong house."

"Well!" A feminine voice filled with disgust and a thick brogue cut sharply into his musings. "Just make yourself to home now, why don't you, cowboy."

Eric grinned. He had forgotten how out of place his Western-style clothing would appear in this community. Standing up, he politely doffed his hat in acknowledgment of the sharp words. He didn't recognize the stocky woman with the blue-rinsed hairdo and snapping brown eyes. But then again, that was not particularly surprising. Mrs. Hill had not been known for keeping her help. Especially not the cooks.

"Thanks, I will." He grinned engagingly. "Do you know where Mrs. Hill is?"

The cook stopped in surprise. "Mrs. Hill? She lives on Market Street, I think."

"Didn't she come to work today?"

"Work? Mrs. Hill? She hasn't worked here for three years. Now who are you that you wouldn't be knowing that?" Her eyes narrowed suspiciously. "Are you some nosy reporter? For I'm warning you Senator McLean's assistant won't hesitate to call the police and have you put out."

Eric set down his half-finished cup of coffee and straightened up to his full six feet two inches. "I'm Eric McLean."

The blue-haired woman's look of suspicion turned to consternation. Shuffling uncomfortably, she stammered a bit, then looked away. "Were you knowing about your father, lad?"

"Yes." Eric had to bite back a smile. "Lad" wasn't a term he'd have thought anyone would apply to him again. "I know. Is the new housekeeper around? I'd like to find out what arrangements have been made."

More than a little flustered by the prepossessing young man in front of her, the cook stammered some more. "It's her day off. But Mark Henshaw, your father's assistant, is upstairs."

"You don't mean to tell me that Spencer quit, too?"

"He retired about a year ago. Said the work was getting to be too much for him."

Eric could hardly believe what he was hearing. Spencer, like Mrs. Hill and, more importantly, like his own father, had seemed immune to the normal wear and tear of life. They were people apart. Indomitable. Unaging. Impervious to change.

Unaware of Eric's thoughts, the older woman bustled forward and gathered up his discarded coffee cup. "You'll be wanting to have a word with Mark now that you're here, I'm sure. You might try the study on the second floor. There've been so many phone calls yesterday and today that I'm bound to think that you'll find him there."

"Thanks." Eric nodded briskly and headed up the back stairs. He took the steps two at a time, moving easily and quickly through the halls, not having to stop and wonder where anything was. Without any hesitation, he opened the door to a small suite of rooms. Then, just as quickly, he stopped on the threshold of the apple-green room.

A woman's back was turned to him. Her left hand was braced against the open file drawer for support as she stretched upward with her right hand. Her face was partially hidden by her raised arm and by the long brown hair that swirled across her shoulders and fell down the length of her back. A wide, gold band glinted metallically on the ring finger of her left hand.

Eric's breath caught in his throat. For a moment, one very brief moment, he wondered if he was hallucinating, if somehow he had managed to conjure her up in his mind's eye. But there was no mistaking her physical presence for the half-formed image of a dream. She was real.

And he would have known her anywhere. Even after eight long years.

"Mark?" The young woman didn't bother to turn around but continued reaching for the thin journal just beyond her fingertips. "Have you found those papers yet? I've found several references, but not the actual documents themselves."

"Chryssie?" Eric's voice was deep with wonder. "Chryssie Gallagher?"

Chapter Two

A voice from the past. Words without warning.

Chrys closed her eyes briefly and held herself very still. She had known it would happen—and that it would happen soon. She'd thought she'd be prepared. She'd thought, foolishly it now seemed, that she'd be completely unaffected. Completely unaware.

Her hesitation was brief—so brief that she hoped it would go unnoticed; but she needed a moment to sort out the rush of memories that sped from the past. It wasn't that she had dreaded their meeting. She'd gotten over him years ago. It was just . . .

Chrys's lips twisted briefly. Mockingly. That was the trouble with being rather circumspect. She just didn't have any experience in greeting old flames.

Deliberately she forced herself to finish reaching for the journal on the shelves just over her head. Once her fingers closed around it, she drew it down and tucked it securely in her left arm. It felt real and solid. It gave her strength and purpose, a reason for being in his father's house.

Turning, she gave her skirt a modest, hem-restoring tug before extending her right hand and smiling pleasantly.

She didn't intend to let Eric guess just how discomposed the sound of her name on his lips could make her feel.

"Hello, Eric." Her voice was low and steady. The normal, natural sound of it both pleased and reassured Chrys as she waited for Eric to cover her palm with his.

Yes, she'd been taken unawares, but there was nothing else between them when their hands met. No frisson. No special feeling. No awakening of emotions from the past.

Chrys smiled, and this time, her smile was far more genuine. It was easy to put her earlier feeling of unease down to surprise at hearing herself referred to as Chryssie Gallagher. She hadn't answered to Gallagher since her marriage and she'd outgrown "Chryssie" years before.

"I'm sorry you aren't returning under happier circumstances. How was Jerome able to contact you so quickly? When I saw him yesterday afternoon he was still pulling his hair out in frustration." She grinned. "And if you've seen him lately, you know he really can't afford to keep doing that. Hmm?"

When he didn't comment, Chrys released his hand and stepped back, feeling a little foolish for chattering so. But once again, she managed to dismiss the feeling, putting it down to an understandable—and acceptable—bout of nervous tension. After all, Eric had once been a part of her, and she a part of him. It was hard to know how much had changed and how much had remained the same.

Head tilted to one side, she eyed his muscular frame with honest curiosity. He had changed. A great deal if her eyes were to be believed. His form had filled out considerably. His shirt stretched tightly across his broad shoulders and his jeans clung snugly to his narrow hips. Chrys took in his hand-tooled belt and Western boots with only a hint of a laugh flickering to life in her eyes. His clothing was a little unusual for Wisconsin, but it seemed to suit him more than his hand-tailored suits or cashmere sweaters ever had.

The flame in his reddish-brown hair had darkened several shades so that its glinting highlights were like the sheen of rich copper. His blue eyes, too, seemed more brilliant than ever next to the teak of his tan. It was a little surprising to realize that he was even more attractive than she had remembered, for he'd always been pretty potent stuff.

But what really surprised her was his face. It was more mature now—definitely not a boy's face. It was the face of a man, composed of lean cheeks, a high broad forehead, heavy brows and a long, straight nose. There was strength as well as maturity in the squared jaw and she couldn't help wondering if it reflected his environment or his heredity.

There had been a time—a rather long time—when she had resented him bitterly. But Ken had helped her put most, if not all, of her youthful pain and resentment behind her. Chrys's lips moved easily to form a warm smile that had nothing to do with Eric McLean. Dear Ken, he had taught her so much about life and living.

Eric was startled by the degree of warmth in Chrys's expression. Slowly his eyes dropped, scanning the length of her body, then returning to her face. What was she doing here? Had he conjured her up? His fingers ran uneasily through his hair in an unconsciously disturbed gesture.

She was real enough.

Too bemused to do more than wonder at the coincidence, Eric slowly raised his eyes, tracking each of her features, each of her curves. He found it hard to believe that she was only two years his junior. She looked little older now than she had at eighteen. Her face was still serious, but touched with elfin charm. Her delicately arched brows and thick lashes were the same warm shade of mink-brown that he had always remembered. Her nose still had a suggestion of a tilt at its tip. But what he remembered the most was the gentle curve of her mouth. She had had the sweetest kisses imaginable.

But she has changed, he told himself, taking a closer look. There was something about her... a sense of serenity... a sense of identity. She was so calm. So poised. As if he was simply an old acquaintance.

Was that possible? Could she really think of him as little more than an old friend? Granted, their affair had ended a long time ago but it had been passionate and intense for the entire duration. Nor had it fizzled out to an anemic conclusion. The parting had been painful, intensely so. Neither of them had wanted to put an end to what they felt. He would have sworn to that.

He studied her face carefully, seeing nothing but polite interest. Surely she must be feeling some of the same things he felt. A tinge of awareness. A hint of regret. Or, at the very least, a touch of curiosity.

Unnerved by his intent regard, Chrys shifted her stance, bringing the journal up to her chest, holding it with both arms. She didn't know if she was glad they were meeting or not; but, she reasoned pragmatically, she had known that they would have to meet at some point. After all, it was a logical assumption. Eric McLean was Talbot's only son and heir. She, on the other hand, was the archival librarian who had been assigned the task of collecting, inventorying and appraising the collection of political memorabilia Talbot had bequeathed to the University of Wisconsin's Area Research Center.

"Have you spoken with Jerome yet?" She didn't like the quaver that had infiltrated her voice. But the way Eric was looking at her made her uncomfortable. He seemed to be waiting for something, some sort of sign. But she couldn't oblige. She simply didn't know what he expected from her after all these years. It was hard enough knowing what she expected from herself.

When her arms tightened protectively in front of her, Eric noticed the wedding ring once again. The young girl he had known had been too much of a woman to offer anyone pretense or sham. Her commitment had been heart, mind, body and soul. He slapped a lid on his confused emotions, telling himself that he couldn't possibly be feeling anything like envy. Still, he concluded silently, the man whose wedding band she now wore had to be one very lucky guy.

Eric's smile was both wry and rueful. It looked as if he had been well and truly replaced. Only an absolute fool would have expected anything else. He was trying very hard not to be a fool.

The trouble was that Chryssie had always been much too vibrant to fade into the background. Perhaps that was half his problem. He had never completely forgotten her—not even in the arms of other women.

When Chrys repeated her question for the third time, with a sharp note to her words, Eric finally shook off his apparent trance. His voice as he answered was low and rich, tickling the memories of her ears. Yet his response had nothing to do with her question.

"It's been a long time, Chryssie."

Suddenly Chrys remembered another time and another place when he'd used the same words and that same husky tone. The time when she'd returned from Christmas vacation to the small cabin that had been their hideaway, their secret place. She also remembered her own passionately abandoned response, and blushed. The kindling of a strange new fire in his dark blue eyes told her that he, too, was remembering the taste of things that were better forgotten.

She was older now, and wiser in the ways of men. Wiser in the ways of this man in particular. He had no hold on her, and he had no right to try to make her remember things she had once tried so hard to forget.

"I've missed... talking with you, Chryssie."

The gentle flush subsided quickly. Her head lifted proudly, but her eyes couldn't hide the flicker of disillusionment that lurked in their depths. She hadn't completely forgotten the pain. She probably never would. The past few minutes had shown her that she remembered Eric a lot more clearly than she had first realized. It was a real pity. Ken had given her new memories, wonderful, loving memories, but unfortunately he hadn't completely obliterated Eric's memory from hers.

When Eric reached out, touching her wedding band lightly, she frowned in swift confusion. What was the matter with him anyway? Did he get some sort of kick out of making her uncomfortable? For a moment, a glint of fierce defiance darkened her eyes. Then, tamping down her rising ire, she took a firm hold of the situation.

"It has been a long time, hasn't it?" Her smile was pleasant, no more. She turned back to the filing cabinet. Dropping the journal back into place she started sorting economically through the manila folders. "I'm really curious about how you managed to get here so quickly. I thought Jerome didn't know where you were."

Eric blinked, focusing on her words at last. "Jerome? You mean Jerome Weaver?"

Chrys's hands jerked to a halt. She turned slowly, compassion replacing every other emotion. Fate couldn't be so cruel as to send him back intent on reconciliation just days too late, could it?

"Oh, Eric," she said softly. "I'm so sorry. Talbot died in his sleep early Thursday morning."

He nodded curtly. "I know about my father's death. That's why I came back. Does Weaver want to talk to me?"

At first Chrys was surprised that he already knew of his father's death, if Jerome had not been the one to contact him. Then, assuming he had maintained contact with some of his old friends, she didn't question him further. "Yes. He's been quite anxious to get in touch with you. Why don't you give him a call now?"

"Yeah." Eric moved forward toward the telephone. A tiny muscle twitched erratically in his jaw. He reached out for the receiver, then turned to her instead. His strong fingers closed firmly around her elbow. "Chryssie, what are you doing here?"

She held back, not wanting his touch, but she couldn't prevent him from holding her lightly. Nor could she prevent the admiring light that came into his eyes as he studied her navy-blue dress with its white lace cuffs and collar. She could, however, let her own eyes reflect her disdain at his unwarranted actions.

Strange, he thought silently, completely unaware of her annoyance. *This is only the third or fourth time I've seen her in a dress.* In college, her clothes had seemed old-fashioned and dowdy until she had discovered that blue jeans and T-shirts had been the order of the day.

"Do you work for my father?"

"No, I'm a librarian with the university. I work in the archives. Your father donated a lot of his papers and books that dealt with local history and his own political years to us," she replied evenly.

"When I explained to Jerome that it was essential that we have access to the entire collection before anyone attempts to weed out any of the unimportant papers, he, as the executor of your father's estate, offered to let me start compiling the inventory immediately. That's why I'm here."

Eric's eyes narrowed just a shade as he released her. His hand rose to snake distractedly through his hair. His booted foot tapped silently against the plush carpeting as he tried to assimilate her statement. At the moment he really wasn't all that interested in Talbot's estate. "I thought you'd moved away." He paused, adding guardedly, "To stay."

"So did I," Chrys replied evenly. She was determined not to let him make her feel more ill at ease than she already did. She had a perfect right to come and go as she wanted. "I moved back when my husband took a job with the university's Industrial Technology department."

Eric dropped her arms abruptly. Turning away, he stepped closer to the desk phone. "Have you been married long?"

"Ken and I were married eight years ago."

The same year I left here for good. "Your husband must be very special." Eric's voice was thoughtful. He'd seen the soft light in her summery eyes when she spoke of her Ken.

"Yes." She nodded toward the phone. "Hadn't you better call Jerome?"

"Yeah, I guess I should." He picked the receiver up, then replaced it carefully. "Chryssie? Are you happy?"

"Very." She reached for another journal, glad that he couldn't see the confusion she felt at his questions. Surely he wasn't going to act as if there was still something between them after all these years? He hadn't cared enough when they had been lovers, why should he pretend now?

She turned slowly, her eyes widening as she met his questioning gaze. His face was a dead giveaway. He felt sorry for her. Her lips tightened. She had no use for his pity and no need for his concern. He had failed her when she needed him desperately, when she had needed him most; and now, when she needed him least—

"I'm twenty-eight, Eric. And I'm Chrystal or Chrys, not Chryssie. Chryssie was a foolish, impetuous child. I've left her and all her memories behind me. What we had was over a long time ago. A long, long time ago."

He started to interrupt, but the cold look in her eyes stopped him. He didn't want to see her eyes turn cold and gray. He liked it best when they were warm and blue like the summer sky. "How did you end up working for the university?"

She shrugged, accepting the change easily. "When Ken and I moved back here, I started as a volunteer. Fortunately for me, there was an opening within a few months and I had an edge on the other applicants since I was already familiar with the system. After a year or so I took some advanced training in archival management and worked my way up." She grinned. "Or down, rather. The regional archives are housed in the basement of the library."

"You got your degree then?"

"Don't sound so surprised, Eric." Her immediate response was completely natural, and showed a hint of temper as well as a touch of complacency. "I always was smart. Scholarships go to women too, you know. I got a master's in library science."

"You should have taken the money I offered you when we—" He broke off abruptly, leaving the sentence unfinished.

Damn! He knew he'd blundered badly bringing up the subject of money. Toward the end their every encounter had included at least one fight over the money he'd wanted to give her. She had seen his offers of financial assistance as both insulting and demeaning. He hadn't meant them to be, he'd just wanted to help her. She'd never had enough and he'd always had too much.

Chrys ignored his blunder. To even acknowledge his comment would resurrect terribly ugly and bitter scenes in both their minds. She changed the subject adroitly, hoping to divert him from any further inquiries into her private life. "What about you? Do you have your own law firm now?"

"No. Other things got in the way." Now it was Eric's turn to shrug. "Being a lawyer was Talbot's dream, not mine."

Once again Chrys noticed that he ran his hand through his hair in an oddly uneasy gesture. She frowned thoughtfully, but he continued, breaking into her half-formed thoughts.

"I—uh—had a lot of time to think about where I was headed after I left here. I found I preferred the classroom to the courtroom. I wanted to be outdoors during more of the year, so I moved to New Mexico a couple of years ago. I picked up my master's in history and started teaching. I'm working on my doctorate now."

"Mmm. That explains the tan." Chrys didn't probe any further. "I thought you looked awfully brown for Wisconsin. Do you like the weather down there?"

"Sometimes I miss the changing seasons. Where I live we don't see much snow. Or rain either. But it's worth it, knowing that I don't have to spend seven months of the year alternating between hibernation and snow shoveling."

When the silence lengthened uneasily Chrys searched for something else to say. "What's your dissertation about?"

"Mining law." He knew she wasn't really interested, but he answered anyway. "I'm especially intrigued with disputes involving ecology and land use. It's a good field to be in."

"Now you sound like a politician." She spoke lightly, unthinkingly.

A shutter came down over Eric's face and his expression appeared pinched. "No. Politics aren't for me."

His hands clenched tightly. He drew a long deep breath, then let it go in a slow raspy sigh. "You said it first, Chryssie—Chrys," he corrected himself quickly. "It's been eight years. We've changed a lot."

"Eric—"

He held up his hand for silence. "*I've* changed a lot. Not always for the better, but not always for the worse, either. Coming back here was . . . very difficult for me. Don't make it any worse than it has to be."

"I wasn't trying to needle you, Eric." Chrys's explanation was sincere; her fingers rested lightly on his strong arm. "If I'd stopped to think about it I wouldn't have said anything at all."

"Chrys! I've found—"

Both Chrys and Eric turned to face the short blond man who stuck his head in the doorway.

"Oh, sorry," Mark Henshaw apologized cheerfully. "I didn't mean to interrupt."

Chrys was glad for the interruption. "Don't be silly, Mark. You're not interrupting anything but the tail end of a 'do you remember when' session."

When she laughed Eric was startled once again by the change in her face. Her whole expression softened and warmed as she smiled at the newcomer. She was so free of shadows. He envied her that.

"This is Eric McLean," she continued. "Talbot's son. Mark Henshaw, your father's assistant and right-hand man. Why don't you two get acquainted while I give Jerome a call. He'll have a conniption fit if someone doesn't let him know Eric's arrived."

Mark Henshaw stuck out his hand, momentarily distracting the younger man. "Sorry about the senator. He'll be sorely missed."

Eric mumbled something polite and noncommittal and allowed himself to be led away.

IT WAS NEARLY FOUR-THIRTY when Chrys, enticed by the rich, aromatic scent of a flavored coffee, entered the mansion's kitchen. "Hi, Janet. Is there a cup to spare?"

"To be sure." The older woman grinned and started to get to her feet.

Chrys waved her back down. "Don't bother to get up, Janet. I can help myself."

"Are you done for the day, then?"

"Mmm. Eight to four on what should have been my day off is enough, I'd say." Chrys grinned over one shoulder. "I'd be on my way now, but Mark promised to give me a ride home."

The cook settled back into her chair, her voice thick with the burr of her native country as she propped her feet on an empty chair. "Chrys, have you seen Eric McLean?"

"Earlier." Chrys nodded and blew across the steaming coffee before adding a half a teaspoon of sugar. "He and Mark and Jerome have been cloistered in Talbot's upstairs office since early this afternoon."

"Would you be knowing if anything's been said about my job?" Janet was concerned; well-paying jobs were hard to come by.

"Sorry. I don't. Although I'm sure they'll let you know just as soon as possible."

"Mmm." The older woman frowned, her stout features scrunching in concern. "Do you suppose he'll be wanting to keep the house open for a while?"

Chrys pulled out two kitchen chairs. Then, like Janet, she sat down on one and put her feet up on the other, crossing her legs neatly at the ankles. She would have liked to be able to offer the other woman some hope, but from what she knew of Eric's past she found it highly unlikely that he would consider keeping his father's house open for any length of time.

Still, she couldn't quite bring herself to crush the expectant look on the older woman's face. Instead, she shrugged. "Anything I said about what Eric McLean might or might not do would be sheer speculation, Janet. You know I'm only here to make sure that nothing that looks as if it might be of value to the regional archives gets thrown away before we get a chance to evaluate it in terms of our collection."

The cook grimaced. "He doesn't look like he's from around here, does he?"

"He mentioned that he's living in New Mexico now." Chrys smiled to soften the blow. "I don't think he plans on coming back to stay."

"Maybe Mr. McLean took care of it in his will?"

"I couldn't say, Janet. Even if I did know, which I don't."

"Aren't you working on Mr. McLean's estate?"

Chrys chuckled. "I'm a librarian, remember? The only thing I'm doing is protecting the university's interests."

Leaning back, she continued sympathetically. "Aside from the fact that Talbot donated a lot of his papers to the regional archives, the only thing I know about Talbot's will is that Jerome was asked to be his personal representative. He mentioned something about a formal reading on Tuesday of next week. You should have your answers after that."

Janet's face reflected her disappointment. Then, dropping her feet to the floor, she leaned forward eagerly. If Chrys couldn't satisfy her curiosity on one front, she might be able to do so on another. "Did you know the lad before he moved away? You're from Platteville originally, aren't you?"

Chrys hid a smile in her coffee cup. Eric McLean didn't have the appearance of a lad. Physically he'd grown up with a vengeance. "Not exactly in Platteville, Janet. My family was from Benton. However, I did know Eric when I was a freshman. In a small college like this, everyone tends to have at least a nodding acquaintance with everyone else."

Chrys blew gently on her coffee, cooling it. She had known a number of students and an equal number had known her. However, Eric had been very careful once they started dating, and she suspected that few if any of her classmates had known about the two of them. In fact, she wouldn't have been surprised to learn that their relationship had been the county's best-kept secret.

Looking back, she could see that Eric had seldom taken her anyplace where he might have run into his friends, and never, ever, had they gone someplace where they might have run into his father's friends. The places they visited had been, for the most part, unpopulated by humans.

At the time, she hadn't cared. She was in love with love. Eric's desire to keep her secluded away had made it all somehow seem more romantic. Until the day came when she was forced to face reality: Eric didn't want anyone—and especially not his father—to know what they shared.

"Do you think the lad will want me to stay on and fix his meals while he's here? Tomorrow's my day off and Jack and I had planned on going up to see the kids in Montfort. But if he—"

"No, he won't." A deep voice answered, startling both women. Eric walked into the room in front of Mark Henshaw. His eyes traced the slender symmetry of Chrys's long legs. He didn't bother to hide his smile when she hastily dropped her feet to the floor and smoothed her skirt down over her knees. "I can get my own meals, so don't change any of your plans on my account."

"Are you sure, Mr. McLean?" Janet lifted one hand to nervously pat a blue-gray curl back into place. "The kids and Jack would understand—"

"Make it Eric, and I'm sure. I'll probably be in and out all weekend."

"Go ahead, Janet," Mark seconded. "You've put in a lot of extra time this week already and there'll be plenty of work come Monday, what with the funeral and all."

Turning to Eric, Mark explained that quite a few of Talbot's friends and political peers were due in, and that while they weren't expecting any to stay overnight, they had made arrangements to cater a rather extensive buffet after the service. Then, turning back to the cook, Mark continued. "Besides, Eric can always call on either Chrys or myself if he needs anything."

Thanks a lot, Mark, Chrys thought sourly.

Eric McLean might not be able to devastate her senses as he had once done, but she didn't need to go around tempting fate either. Nibbling her lower lip thoughtfully, Chrys frowned. Even if she hadn't known him before she would have found him an attractive proposition. In fact, she mused silently—and with an unusual touch of black humor—if she hadn't known him before she might have found him a good deal more than just attractive. However, there was something about a love affair gone sour that tended to peel the tint off rose-colored glasses with a vengeance.

While Janet was getting ready to leave, Chrys got up, intending to rinse her cup and saucer. Before she could do more than reach for the tap Eric stopped her. "Don't bother, Chrys. I'll take care of it later on."

Chrys's face mirrored her surprise, but only for a moment. When they had shared the cabin, he had never offered to help with the housework. Eric had held some decidedly outmoded opinions on what constituted acceptable work for men and women. "Funny, I never thought of you as the dishwashing type."

"Oh, I'm quite domesticated now," he assured her.

So, he's married. Now what made that thought flash through her head? It didn't matter to her what his marital status was.

"After a couple of years of pigging it on my own, I finally decided I would have to learn the rudiments of housekeeping. Even a bachelor is expected to give a party every now and then. I figured no one would come if I didn't practice at least the minimum chores such as laundry, dusting and dishes."

"I know exactly what you mean." Mark laughed with understanding.

"So do I," Chrys added dryly, and Eric knew from the gentle humor in her eyes and the mocking twist to her lips that it was some sort of private joke between her and Mark.

"Aw, come on, Chrys. Give a guy a break," Mark groaned.

"Not a chance. I've seen how you keep house," she said solemnly, eyes twinkling with remembered mirth. "Are you ready to leave yet?"

"Sorry, Chrys." Mark shook his head. "I know I promised to give you a ride home, but I've still got some calls to make. Can you wait another half hour or so?"

"It's okay, Mark, but I don't think I'll wait. I wanted to get home before five today."

"I can give you a ride, if you like," Eric offered. "My car's just outside."

"Thanks anyway, Eric." She turned him down with a smile. "But I can walk. It's not all that far."

"Well, then, I'll walk with you," he persisted. "I could use the exercise."

"No, really. I wouldn't want to put you to the trouble."

Eric waved her words aside. "It's no trouble. I've been sitting in planes and cars and tiny rooms since four this morning. It'll be a pleasure to get outside, stretch my legs and breathe some clean, fresh Wisconsin air."

Chrys tried to turn his offer down again, but when she noticed the peculiar look Mark sent her way, Chrys desisted. Perhaps she was making too much of nothing.

Still, she hadn't liked the way he'd looked her over when he first came into the kitchen. If Eric McLean was looking for something more than a means of stretching his legs and clearing his head, he was going to be sadly disappointed. Because she wasn't letting him close. Not ever again.

Chapter Three

When they left the large yellow limestone house, Eric noticed that it was just starting to snow but the flakes were still few and far between. Eyes narrowed for a moment, he watched the tiny particles lace their way lazily through the darkening sky. There wasn't anyone else around. In the past he would have slung one arm casually around Chrys's shoulder, sheltering her. However, it didn't take much insight on his part to realize that she would not welcome the reminder.

Eric tipped his hat down over his brow, stuffed his hands deeper into his pockets and hunched his shoulders slightly, bringing his coat collar up around his ears. Wisconsin winters were not something that he had missed during the past few years.

A sideways glance showed him that Chrys, on the other hand, was impervious to the cold. While her hands, like his, were deep in her pockets, that was the only similarity. Her stride was quick and sure as she moved across the patchy sidewalks. In the past his longer stride would have outdistanced her easily, but after years of living in milder climes, he didn't feel comfortable with the slick walkway.

Letting his glance linger, he noted that her whole appearance reflected her inner pride and sense of self-worth.

Her face was tilted upward, meeting the buffeting breeze with a smile as it pushed her long hair back away from the silvery pelt of her jacket. She looked comfortable and self-assured. A woman of means.

"That coat suits you. The silver-blue sheen—" He shrugged. "It's a good color for you."

"Mmm." Chrys ran her hands lovingly over the silky fur. "When Ken and his mother first gave it to me I objected. But Ken finally talked me into accepting it when he told me that they'd had it cut down from one of his grandmother's coats. Besides," she said, laughing at her own weaknesses, "terrible as it is to admit, I really do love the look and feel of it."

"Where's your husband now? At work?"

"No." Chrys's hesitation lasted only a second. "Ken died a few years ago."

Eric stopped short. "I'm sorry, Chrys. I didn't know."

Glancing back over her shoulder she shrugged. "No way you could have. Look, I really did want to get home by five."

He started walking again, not saying anything for a few minutes. Finally he reached out, running his own hand over the silky pelt, touching her shoulder sympathetically through the fur. "Is your jacket warm enough? It feels cold."

Chrys moved away, not enough to make it obvious that she didn't want his touch, but enough to leave him suspecting that that was the case.

"It's really quite warm on the inside." She raised one hand, directing his attention to a point straight ahead. She didn't want to talk about herself. "They tore Old Main down. Did you hear about that?"

"Yes." He let his hand drop back to his side, adding dryly, "As an alumnus I was offered the opportunity of buying a souvenir brick."

The grin she sent his way was full of good humor and curiosity. "Did you get one?"

"No." He chuckled. "I let the opportunity slip by. How about you?"

She shook her head. "I'm not an alumna from here. I graduated from Madison, but it's just as well. I couldn't see it either. One more paperweight I'd have to dust."

Feeling more at ease, Eric grinned back. "Where are we headed anyway?"

"Across campus, down by Russell Hall."

"Russell Hall?" Eric's brows drew together as he tried to place the building in his mind. "Do you mean the Ivory Tower?"

Chrys laughed at the old, student name. "Pioneer Tower, please. Faculty and staff are discouraged from being disparaging." Her quick grin flashed once more. "Russell Hall is the long, low building in back of the tower."

Chrys pointed in the direction of a tight cluster of buildings. "There've been a lot of changes on campus since you and I first went here. Gardner and all the other dorms along here have been changed into offices now. Just like Brigham Hall was when we first started."

"Is Ottensman still sinking?" Eric nodded toward the science hall.

Chrys shrugged. "I doubt it ever was; but no one's mentioned it lately. Henry Grossen will be able to tell you, though. He's a chemistry professor now."

"Maybe." Eric hunched his shoulders again and frowned. He hadn't really intended to look up any of his old acquaintances but maybe he should. Chances were that he would see a lot of them at the funeral anyway.

After another idle comment or two on the changes the university grounds had undergone, Eric remained silent and thoughtful as they continued across the campus. He found the solitude of the campus strangely peaceful as the sky grew progressively darker. He knew that it was close to the dinner hour, but few if any students were braving the winter weather.

Lost in her own thoughts, Chrys didn't break the silence either until she reached her own home. "Well, this is it."

Eric came to a halt by her side. The house was an older home with a high sloping roof. The pale green exterior and darker trim made it appear warmly inviting. Every available inch of the porch railings were hung with ropes of pine boughs and wide red ribbons. A large Christmas wreath hung in the center of the oval glass of the front door. The snow-covered lawn was well trampled by human and animal alike, but it didn't look messy, only well loved. To one side, flanked by a miniature stand of pine, a madcap family of snowmen—obviously of "Ma in her kerchief and Pa in his cap" fame—guarded the territory.

Eric chuckled, remembering the lopsided snowman Chrys had once insisted that he help her build. "I don't know if I'd recognize your place in the wintertime if you didn't have at least one of those in your yard."

"What's the point of living in Wisconsin if you don't make use of the natural resources?"

Her answer had been much the same ten years ago. Eric removed his Stetson, ran a finger around its inner band, then slapped it decisively against his thigh. There were things that he wanted to know about his father, and she might be the only one who would understand his questions. "If you've got a minute, I'd like to come in and talk. You're the only one I can ask about Talbot."

Chrys hesitated briefly, then shrugged her permission. Her house might not be as impressive nor as expensively furnished as what he was used to, but it was filled with love and spotlessly clean. More than that, no one could ask.

Although the thermostat was set in the mid-sixties, the house seemed quite warm compared to the outside temperature. The smell of chili permeated the air. Chrys hung her jacket in a small coat closet and indicated the free-standing coatrack for Eric's things. Seating herself on the built-in boot box, she started to remove her boots. "Would you like anything to drink?"

"No." Eric knelt in front of her, helping her off with her boots. When the last one was off, he didn't release her immediately. One hand remained around her ankle, the other cupped the heel of her foot.

Chrys pulled gently away and dropped her boots onto a rubber mat. "If you want to talk about your father, you're welcome to stay and do so. Otherwise, I've got things to do."

"I want to talk about Talbot." He sank back on his heels.

"Fine." Getting up, she padded across the hall in her stocking feet to get a pair of comfortable shoes out of the coat closet. Her movements were unconsciously graceful as she slipped on one shoe and then the other. "I think I might have something to drink in the front room, but I'm not sure. Why don't you have a look?"

"No. I really don't want anything to drink." Eric, who had remained kneeling, shook his head. "And I do want to talk about Talbot."

"Well, then." The dusky twilight, combined with Eric's peculiar behavior, was making Chrys nervous. She wanted a moment to herself. "Go on in the front room and have a seat. I have to check on dinner. I'll only be a minute."

Eric straightened up to his full height. The top of his head was only an inch or so lower than the ornate candelabra that was suspended from the high ceiling. "The kitchen's fine with me if you don't mind. My boots won't do as much damage there."

Chrys fixed him with a long, even stare, then shrugged lightly once again. She felt uneasy about his motivation, but she was willing to give him the benefit of the doubt—up to a certain point.

"It's this way." She led him out into the cheery kitchen, indicated that he take a seat at the maple table. When he was seated, she went into the pantry to check on the contents of her Crockpot.

"Smells good," he called softly.

She frowned pensively. Was he fishing for an invitation to stay for dinner? "Sorry, Charlie," she muttered to herself. If that was the case, he was going to have a good long wait.

Coming back into the kitchen, she waved him down when he started to get up. Her expression clearly stated that she was beginning to regret letting him come inside.

"Don't be so suspicious, Chrys," he chided softly. "I didn't invite myself in to drag out the old memories of what we once shared. However, I do owe you an apology and I did want to make it before I left town again."

He caught her hand, squeezing it firmly. The wedding band felt cold against his fingers. "I wish there was more that I could do, but under the circumstances..." He shrugged, letting his voice trail off.

Still not perfectly convinced of Eric's good intentions, Chrys moved away from his touch. Lacing her fingers together, she laid her hands in her lap. "An apology isn't necessary, Eric. What happened between us was a long time ago and only a part of growing up for both of us. What did you want to ask about Talbot?"

Eric shifted uneasily in his seat. His hand rose; then, self-conscious under her steady gaze, he lowered it back onto the table. "I guess I could use a drink after all."

Getting back up, Chrys started toward the front room. Eric caught at her arm, stopping her. "Coffee or tea would be fine, Chrys." He grimaced, remembering his last sentimental bout. "I'll pass on the hard stuff. I spent Thursday night talking to a philodendron."

A mink-colored brow arched in mild surprise. After a moment her expression softened as she realized that Thursday probably would have been the day he heard of his father's death. "Which would you prefer, coffee or tea?"

"Doesn't make any difference." Eric knew that their conversation was stilted and awkward. As he watched her moving around the kitchen he felt as if he was standing on the edge of two worlds. One was the past and familiar—even with its bittersweet taste. The other world was a new one. Few things seemed familiar. His own reactions were the strangest of all. Coming back was very...different from what he had expected.

"Chrys?"

She turned away from the stove, head tilted to one side, waiting.

"Jerome wants to see me again on Tuesday. I'll know more about Talbot's plans then." He leaned forward in his chair. His eyes were brooding as he looked out the windows. He tried concentrating on a tiny sparrow who was busy sorting through the bottom of a bird feeder, looking for just the right seed.

She turned back to the stove. The silence that hung in the air was not an easy one. But the source of the tension was one of his own making and there was nothing Chrys could do but wait.

"There have been a lot of changes, haven't there?"

"Yes," she agreed softly. "But change is often healthy."

"I know." He sighed, not taking his eyes off the tiny brown bird. It was now or never. "What about Talbot, Chrys? Had he changed? Was he different than I remember?"

Placing a cup of coffee in front of him, she resumed her own seat. "I didn't know him well enough to say, Eric. The first time I met him was while Ken was still alive. We'd run into him a couple of times a year, but always in connection with some university-sponsored event.

"I saw quite a bit of him in the library. But aside from him having me scrounge up some obscure book or document that he was looking for, that was about it. We didn't have a lot in common."

"From what Mark and Jerome said this afternoon, I got the impression that he knew his time was short."

"Perhaps." When Eric leaned forward, cradling the cup in his hands, she continued. "He seemed . . . at variance with the ways I remember you speaking of him. No less autocratic, but not as ruthless."

"Did you like him?"

She sighed softly at the wistful note in Eric's voice. This she understood very well. It had taken her a long time to accept that her own father would never give her the affection she craved. And like Eric, she had learned to live with it, but it still had the power to hurt.

"I neither liked nor disliked him, Eric. He wasn't an easy person. You should know that better than anyone."

He lifted the cup to his mouth. "I never made any attempt to contact him once I came back from South America. He wasn't happy about my going. In fact, he did everything he could think of to prevent it. But I wouldn't listen." He shrugged. "I had to get away. I needed that space to survive."

"Talbot never liked being thwarted," she acknowledged carefully.

Eric got up and poured himself another cup of coffee. "Somehow it doesn't seem so important now." Walking back to the table, he set the cup down but remained standing, looking out the windows once again. "Did he ever mention me?"

Chrys went to his side. Her long, slender fingers lay comfortingly over his arm. She pressed firmly, feeling the strength of his muscles beneath her hand. "No, Eric. Not that I know of."

He shrugged. It hurt knowing that Talbot had been able to erase him from his memory—even though he had tried to do the same. "I was as bad as he was. I suppose I should have made some attempt to contact him after I got back, but I let my own stiff-necked pride stand in the way."

He looked down into her earnest face, then back to the darkening sky. "I hated it there. Everything seemed to go wrong from the start. All I intended to do... There was too much pain and suffering... everything was so hopeless. The Peace Corps seemed like another dream gone sour. I was always afraid that he would ask me what it was like. And I was even more afraid that I would tell him about it and that he would gloat."

Chrys would have liked to deny it, but she knew as well as Eric did that Talbot was perfectly capable of holding a grudge and that he had seldom let sleeping dogs lie. She contented herself with pressing his arm once again.

His hand covered hers and his voice softened unconsciously as he used the name he had always associated with her. "What about you, Chryssie? Did your father ever change?"

"No. Not really." Chrys grimaced, remembering a recent trip she'd made to her father's farm. Amos Gallagher was as unyielding as ever. Nothing and no one could touch the man inside. "But I learned to accept it. After a while it wasn't so important. Other things became more fulfilling."

"Like your husband?"

"Like Ken."

"Was he good to you?"

She smiled reminiscently. "Good to me and good for me."

Eric reached out, circling her waist with his arms. "I'm glad. You always did deserve the best."

Chrys stiffened at the strange new note in his voice. She raised her hands to his chest in mild protest. "Eric, let me go."

He didn't seem to hear her. There was a deeply curious light in his blue eyes. Looking up, Chrys suddenly felt his curiosity as though it was a tangible force. Her protestations stilled in her throat and her eyes widened in surprise. She really hadn't thought of him in that way for years, but now she found herself almost as curious as he seemed to be.

Earlier she had noted the changes in his face and body, and, she admitted truthfully, she *had* been curious. It had been a long time since she'd been so aware of a man.

There hadn't been anyone special since Ken's death. Oh, she'd been a little lonely. But what the two of them had shared had been too perfect to have ended with his death. What she had missed the most was companionship and intelligent, adult conversation. But right now, right this very minute, she wondered what it would be like to be caressed by an attractive man. And it didn't matter a whit that the man in question was Eric McLean.

The hands that she had been using to push against his arms flattened over the muscles of his chest. She traced the broad muscular planes with open curiosity. When his arms tightened further and his head lowered fractionally her fingers slipped around his upper arms, tensing slightly in indecision, but the gesture of protest—if, indeed, it was protest—came too late to be effective.

Eric's left arm rose to stretch across her back. She could feel the strength of his muscles as his hand burrowed through her long hair, cupping her nape and stilling her instinctive denial. The words he murmured were soft and reassuring. They made no sense at all.

When he bent to kiss her lips Chrys made one final, halfhearted protest by turning her face away. However, Eric had anticipated her movement. His lips were unerring as they caught at and shaped her mouth lightly.

His first kiss was surprisingly tender, almost hesitant in nature. Eric had always been a gentle lover—but tender? When had he learned that? Chrys felt her breath catch sharply in her throat and her fingers curled in visible response to the hotter, tighter curling in the pit of her stomach.

When Eric kissed her again, his hesitation was gone. He was still gentle, not rushing her, not asking anything, but rather... waiting... waiting.

Chrys's head fell back, letting the palm of his hand support its weight. Her blue eyes were open wide, her expression was somewhat wary, her rosy lips were parted and moist from his kisses. "Eric?"

Cautiously, as though he was afraid she would run, Eric released her waist. His free hand rose to cup her cheek tenderly and she was surprised by the callused, work-hardened feel of his palm. The boy she had known would never have stooped to manual labor.

Sliding his fingers down the line of her jaw, Eric caught her lightly under her chin, tilting her face up to his. His lips were soft as he played with hers. He watched the changing expression on her face through half-lowered lashes. The fingers in her hair tightened while his other hand splayed around her neck, pulling her a fraction closer to his body. Only his hands held her to him. Her breath was sweet against his face.

Chrys's debate with herself was brief. She knew she should pull away. Eric was no longer holding her against her will. She could break free if she wanted. She knew it. He knew it too. But she didn't move away.

His tongue traced her lips, probing delicately.

She moaned low in her throat and her lashes fluttered softly against her flushed cheeks. In truth, she was as curious as he was. What a strange sensation to be held by someone who was utterly familiar, yet totally new.

What funny things she noticed as his tongue slipped between her teeth. Things like the fact that his shoulders were wider than she remembered but that his scent was still the same. Things like the fact that his hair was longer than she remembered but that, as always, it was both crisp and clean. Things like the fact that his mouth was hotter, more passionate, more controlled. Things like...

Eric's hands tightened reflexively around her face and throat as his tongue probed deeper, delving into the warm recesses of her mouth. His chest rose and fell swiftly as his breathing escalated sharply. His heart was pounding unsteadily. He had always loved the soft sounds she made in the back of her throat.

Gently, soothingly, one hand smoothed across her shoulders in a strangely reassuring and compelling gesture. When she took a tiny step forward, pressing her soft body next to his, the hand on her shoulder ran lightly down her back. Pausing at her waist, Eric kneaded the small of her back coaxingly, wanting her to take another step forward. When she did, his fingers slipped a fraction lower.

He could taste her lips, warm and soft beneath his. And he could sense her beginning to tremble in his arms as she finally raised both of her hands to cup his jaw. Her fingers were as soft as the wings of a butterfly as they brushed against his brows, cheeks and ears. He heard his name, like a whisper of silk, on her lips.

God! She was sweet. So beautifully sweet. Her heart was beating like the wings of a bird. He could feel it through the thin material of her dress. She tasted of honey and spice. The soft flutter of her lashes as they dropped farther to hide the darkening color of her eyes was irresistible. He pulled her closer still, reveling in the soft, sensuous feel of her body as it brushed against his.

They drew slowly apart, their lips parted and moist, their eyes wide and wondering. Then, with confusion and longing mixed, they once again came together in a kiss that had no beginning and no end.

Chrys swallowed hard. Her senses were beginning to reel. She felt engulfed and inflamed by the feelings his touch evoked. His strong body sheltered hers. His powerful arms surrounded her, protected her, cared for her. She whispered his name softly, wonderingly, against his mouth. Her arms rose, tightening around his neck. Her fingers tangled in his hair. Her tongue touched his, once, twice. His reciprocation was moistly tensile, and she could hear the sound of a trumpet in her ears.

It was a shame, when she felt so alive and warm, that the horn had to have such a raucous blare. Disturbed by the noise, Chrys murmured a husky protest. Then its import finally dawned on her.

Tearing herself quickly from his arms, she gripped the edge of the sink, taking several deep breaths, trying to clear her senses. What had she been thinking of? How could she have gotten so carried away? How could she let herself respond to him like that? She hadn't responded to anyone like that in all the years Ken had been dead. Maybe Berta was right. Maybe she needed a good roll in the hay—but not with Eric McLean. Never again with Eric McLean.

"Chryssie." Eric was not to be denied. His hands turned her back into his arms.

"For pity's sake, Eric. Don't touch me." She tried to draw away from the hardening hold of his arms, but he refused to release her.

"Chryssie, what's wrong? I—"

"Momma! Momma! Guess what? Berta took me to see the—"

Chrys heard Eric's indrawn hiss of breath just as Mary Kathleen skidded to a halt at the kitchen door. The child's thin, piping voice reflected her curiosity as well as her uncertainty when she saw the man who stood next to her mother. "Momma?"

Eric released Chrys abruptly. A quick glance assured her that Eric wore the same curiously arrested expression on his own face. She groaned silently when she saw that his eyes never left the child.

Mary Kathleen took a hesitant step forward. She eyed the stranger warily. He was awfully big. Almost as tall as Berta, who was, in her opinion, huge. Her eyes darted around the silent room once again. Her mother looked terribly pale, and Mary Kathleen wasn't sure she liked the way the man was staring either.

"Should I go get Berta?" she asked guardedly. If something was wrong and her mother couldn't fix it, Berta could.

"No." Chrys's reply was a bit reedy, but it managed to reassure Mary Kathleen just the same. "This is an old friend. His name is Eric, Eric McLean. He's Talbot McLean's son. You remember Mr. Weaver mentioned him a couple of days ago, don't you?"

Mary Kathleen relaxed her wary stance and came forward to stand next to her mother. Her hand slipped into Chrys's as she looked up at the tall man. She was still somewhat protective, but being normally trusting by nature, she offered a tentative smile.

Chrys put her arms around Mary Kathleen's shoulders and drew the child in front of her. The child's shoulders were thin and bony; but touching her brought Chrys great delight. Her head lifted proudly. "Eric, I'd like you to meet my daughter, Mary Kathleen. Mary Kathleen Morrissey."

Eric squatted down on his haunches, his head still a fair distance up over the child's. Mary Kathleen. She had the look of her mother. A little fey and shyly curious, like a small fawn. But unlike the younger Chrys he had remembered, there were no doubtful shadows in her blue eyes. She was obviously well loved and secure.

He put his hand out, speaking softly. "Hello, Mary Kathleen. I'm pleased to meet you."

"Hi." The man's intensity was a bit unnerving. She looked up at her mother. After a moment's hesitation, she placed her small hand in Eric's outstretched one. It was immediately engulfed and lost in his larger, browner one.

Mary Kathleen stood silently for a moment, then squirmed from foot to foot under Eric's intent regard. "I'm sorry your daddy died."

"Thank you." Eric responded solemnly but still did not release the little girl's hand.

Mary Kathleen fidgeted some more. "My daddy died, too. I don't remember him real good, but Momma gave me a picture once. Do you have a picture?"

"I—" Eric looked up, confused. He wasn't sure how to deal with the curious inquiries of a small child. "I don't know."

Chrys interrupted, knowing from the suddenly intent look on her daughter's face that Mary Kathleen was about to embark on a long list of whys and why nots. "Run upstairs and change your clothes, Mary Kathleen. Supper's almost ready."

"Okay." Mary Kathleen tugged her hand free from Eric's, leaving the room with one last curious glance over her shoulder.

Eric stood watching the child until she was out of sight. When he turned back around, his eyes caught the metallic glint of Chrys's wedding ring as her hand lay against the Formica countertop.

Kissing her had been a stupid thing to do. But he would be damned if he would apologize for that last kiss, for she had been completely responsive. He had not stolen it or forced her in any way. What she had given, she had given freely.

"She's a beautiful little girl."

"Thank you. I'm quite proud of her."

The silence lengthened.

"Look," he said, running his hand through his hair in a tired, defeated gesture. "I guess I'd better leave now."

Chrys's hand rose to her throat, the wide band glinting goldly as it was illuminated by the overhead light. She didn't say anything that might encourage him to stay.

Eric caught her hand, pressing her fingers gently. "Goodbye, Chrys. Take care."

Although she nodded in acknowledgment, Chrys let him go without a word. They would both be better off if the past stayed forgotten.

As Eric rammed his hat on his head and pulled on his sheepskin jacket a tall, black woman shouldered her way through the door, her arms loaded with packages. Eric reached out to hold the door for her. When she eyed him with an appreciative gleam in her dark brown eyes, he grinned wryly, tipped his Stetson politely and left.

Dropping her packages noisily on the kitchen table, Berta poked her head awkwardly around the kitchen door, ogling the handsome man who was walking down the front steps. When he disappeared from sight she let out a wolf whistle that would have put a hardened truck driver to shame.

"Now that's more like it," she enthused optimistically.

"Forget it, Berta. Eric McLean is definitely the footloose and fancy-free type." Chrys started poking through the colorful bags, unearthing a number of gaily wrapped packages. "He always has been."

"Curiouser and curiouser." Berta let all of her six-foot-two-and-one-quarter-inch frame sink heavily into a kitchen chair, ignoring Chrys's playfully pained wince. "Care to fill me in on the details?"

"Nothing fancy. He's just a boy I knew in college."

"Honey—" Berta's gravelly voice was drier than ever "—that ain't no boy."

"Disgusting grammar for an English prof. What have you been teaching my child?" When Berta's brow rose steadily, Chrys shrugged. "All right then, man. And I repeat, he's nothing special."

"If I swallowed that one whole you could sell me a bridge in Brooklyn, too."

"Uh-uh. I've been saving some prime Florida swampland for you." Chrys stopped poking through the packages. Her expression took on a determined air.

She and Berta were as close as two neighbors could be. Since Ken's death, they'd practically lived in each other's pockets. But Berta was also an ardent matchmaker, and Chrys was still too unsettled from her encounter with Eric to want to give her friend any ammunition. "I hope you're planning on staying for dinner. I made plenty and I'll give you your choice of Brussels sprouts or broccoli.

"By the way," Chrys rushed on, hardly giving Berta time to reply, "I want to thank you for taking Mary Kathleen shopping today. We managed to get quite a bit done over at Talbot's."

"Don't mention it," Berta replied dryly, recognizing Chrys's rather obvious attempt to steer the conversation in another direction for the delaying tactic that it was.

"Momma, did the man go?"

Chrys looked up, noticing that Mary Kathleen had changed into a pair of worn blue jeans, but that her long-sleeved turtleneck sweater was brand-new and obviously chosen for the occasion. And the most telling factor of all—her short, curly hair was freshly combed. "Yes. He's gone now. Why?"

"I wanted to show him the new game Berta got me at the mall in Dubuque."

Berta lifted an eyebrow in surprise but Chrys just nodded calmly. If she made a big thing out of this unusual request, it would just make more of an impression on Mary Kathleen than if she treated it as perfectly normal.

"Perhaps another time, pussy willow. He'll be in town for a few days yet. Would you like to set the table for me now? Berta's going to stay, so you can use the good china if you like."

"The Thanksgiving dishes?" Mary Kathleen barely waited for her mother's nod before disappearing into the other room. There was nothing unusual about Berta's staying for dinner, but using the best dishes was another matter altogether.

"Cute trick," Berta interjected gravely, knowing that Chrys had managed to neatly erase the tall man from her daughter's mind. "Shame it doesn't work on thirty-six-year-olds."

"Yes, isn't it?" Chrys grinned amiably and handed her best friend a ladle. "You can dish up the chili. Mary Kathleen knows where the soup tureen is."

"Abstinence isn't good for you." Berta called the warning back over her shoulder as she headed for the pantry. "You'll get zits."

"Zits," Chrys mumbled to herself, "are the least of my worries."

Chapter Four

The snow was slackening, falling fitfully. Eric dropped the heavy, ruby-colored curtain back into place and turned away from the windows. He paused in front of the fireplace. The grate was cold and empty. He couldn't ever remember seeing a fire glowing in its depths. Yet he felt too much of a stranger to start one.

Lord, a stranger in my own house. Being cooped up was really starting to get to him.

Today was only Sunday. The funeral wouldn't be until tomorrow, and after that, who knew how long it would take to clear up his father's estate. He hoped Jerome had things in order. Maybe then he wouldn't have to stay. Maybe then he could go home.

Running his hand through his hair, Eric turned back to the window. The snow had stopped.

Unable to stay inside any longer, Eric only paused long enough to retrieve his jacket from the front coat closet, before escaping from the confining house. Grabbing up the nearest shovel and feeling far less moody now that he had a specific goal in mind, he filled his lungs with the crisp, clean air and began to clear the long drive.

It took longer than he expected and the exercise left him breathing a little more quickly than usual. Yet it felt good knowing that he could move about freely with no twinge of pain in his lower back.

It had taken time to heal his body after the mine explosion on his last overseas job. Carelessness, a deliberate accident or an act of sabotage, he'd never known, and neither the local government nor the company he'd worked for had ever said. And at the time, he hadn't cared; he'd needed to turn all his concentration, all his effort, into the act of surviving, of making it through each day, of learning to walk again.

What he needed to do now was to use that same determination to heal his mind. He needed to see and accept the changes that had taken place during the eight years he'd been gone. And most of all, he needed to replace the old memories with new.

Ramming his gloved hands deep in the pockets of his sheepskin jacket, Eric started down the street. At first, he explored the part of town where he'd grown up. The streets were still lined with tall, thick trees and flanked by large lawns that guarded the privacy of the stately homes.

Turning toward the downtown area, he noticed long-established businesses had disappeared without a trace and others had taken on new faces. New stores—those were the ones that interested him the most, for they reflected more than just a change in proprietorship—gave the city a new tone, a new vibrancy. Platteville, at long last, was coming into its own and heading for a future filled with hopes and dreams.

Pleased to have found what he considered an improvement, Eric wandered down one side of Main Street, stopping now and again to poke through one of the stores. When he reached the *Shopping News* office, he crossed the street and explored the Mining Museum and eventually struck up a conversation with the curator. The two of them, delighted to have found a kindred spirit, soon found themselves embroiled in a discussion of old lead mining techniques, which lasted until the curator's secretary came in to remind him of the time.

Deciding to grab a quick sandwich back at the college, Eric headed toward campus. Then in no particular hurry to get back to his father's house, but no longer dreading it either, he paused to watch the maintenance crew finish clearing the snow from the Student Union's sunken patio.

"Hi!"

The high-pitched voice startled Eric and he looked down into a pair of clear blue eyes and a face filled with elfin charm.

"You're Momma's friend. Aren't you?"

A slow smile spread across Eric's face as he recognized the child. He wasn't sure Chrys would really care to call him a friend, but he definitely didn't want to be considered an enemy. "You're Mary Kathleen."

The child preened, pleased that he had remembered her.

"Mary Kathleen! Come away from there now."

The child turned and waved at the harried-looking woman with short blond hair who beckoned her from the far side of the snowy lawn, but she didn't leave Eric's side.

"Who's that?"

"Mrs. Corey. She watches a whole bunch of us while Momma does her shopping." Mary Kathleen shrugged, clearly determined to stay where she was.

"Is she your baby-sitter?"

"Naw." Mary Kathleen shook her head. "She's Cindi's mom. That's Cindi—" she pointed "—the one with the purple coat."

Eric hid a slight smile behind his gloved hand and a discreet cough. "Cindi's mom" wasn't much of an explanation, but it seemed that it was enough for Mary Kathleen. "Don't you think you'd better go and tell Cindi's mom that you know me? She probably thinks I'm a stranger, and I'm sure both she and your mother have warned you not to talk to strangers."

"Okay." Taking her own sweet time, Mary Kathleen skipped away, kicking up big puffs of snow as she went.

No longer bothering to hide his laughter, Eric watched the brief conference that took place, then to his surprise, Mary Kathleen gave a delighted whoop and started back to him at a dead run.

"Mrs. Corey said I could stay with you until Momma comes and picks us all up. We're supposed to be learning to skate today. Do you like watching the skaters? I do." Mary Kathleen hopped excitedly from foot to foot, her brown curls bobbing and her blue eyes dancing with childish glee.

"I want to be the best skater in the whole world. Momma bought me a pair of skates for my birthday but she hasn't had time to teach me yet. Can you skate? I try but I keep falling down."

Eric gave up waiting for the tiny tornado to run out of steam. He was pretty sure Chrys wouldn't be pleased to find him in charge of her daughter, but the child, imp that she was, was far too charming to resist.

Dropping to one knee, he nudged his Stetson back with one long forefinger. "Slow down, Mary Kathleen. I can't even begin to follow that list of questions. But yes, I can skate. And everyone falls down at first."

A wide grin spread across Mary Kathleen's lightly freckled face. "Did you ever teach anyone how to skate? I bet you could teach me. I learn real quick. Momma says I'm a good learner."

"You know—" Eric smiled at the half-forgotten memory of an ice-covered pond and the quick hugs and warm kisses that had been a part of the learning process "—I taught your mother how to skate a long time ago."

"Did you? Did you really?"

"Sure did." Eric's smile deepened, his eyes dark and glowing under the child's intent regard. Her short curly hair and warm blue eyes reminded him very much that she was Chrys's daughter. He reached out and laid his hand on the child's head. She was a beautiful little girl. Alive and free. All that a child should be. If things had been different between Chrys and himself, she could have been his.

Once again, Eric smiled at his thoughts. He would like to have had a little girl like her. She was a delight. "How old are you, Mary Kathleen?"

"Seven," she answered promptly and proudly. "And I'm in second grade."

"That old?" He chuckled, remembering how important being grown-up seemed at that age.

Knowing that she was being teased, Mary Kathleen chuckled, then began to tug at Eric's sleeve, pulling him along behind her. "There's a place inside that rents skates. You can teach me how to skate today and we can surprise Momma when she comes to get me."

I'll bet, Eric thought dryly, as he pictured Chrys's probable response. But he followed the excited little girl down the steps anyway. In fact, in his own way, he was just as excited as the child was. He hadn't had much experience with young children and was looking forward to spending the afternoon with Mary Kathleen. That, and the fact that she was Chrys's child, made this chance opportunity doubly special.

Renting a pair of skates for himself, he laced them quickly and tightly before checking Mary Kathleen's. She had missed several of the tiny hooks and the bow on one shoe was so long that its tail dangled only an inch from the blade.

"First lesson in skating," he began, tapping Mary Kathleen's nose cheerfully and bending to redo the lacings. "You can't miss any of the hooks and you need to tuck the bows inside the tops of your shoes. That way you won't trip over the strings. Okay?"

"Okay." Mary Kathleen nodded vigorously, extending her other foot.

Eric repeated the process. "Is that too tight?"

"No." The child pulled on her mittens and stood up, feet braced wide apart. She took three wobbly steps before toppling over into an ungainly heap. Giggling, she got to her knees, then bottom first, managed to regain her feet.

"Did Momma fall down as much as I do?" she asked cheekily, holding out her hands, expecting to be picked up.

"Just about." He swung her up, and when she wrapped her arms tightly around his neck he laughed as well, remembering just how tightly Chrys had clung the first time he had taken her out on the ice.

But the tight hug also brought a lump to his throat, reminding him that there was something very appealing, something solid and right, about holding such a trusting child in his arms. And he understood, then and there, all the fears that came with trying to safeguard a child's carefree innocence.

"You know—" he sounded gruff and a little strained "—you shouldn't go around talking to strangers."

"I know." Mary Kathleen pulled a comical face, then grinned. "But even Momma says I'm better than I used to be."

"Humph! I'll bet."

"No, really." The little girl giggled. "I am. I knew I knew you and I knew Momma knew you, too. So you were okay. Right?"

Eric laughed. "I guess." Setting the child back down, he steadied her on her feet and they began to skate.

In between falling down and skating forward in jerks and halts, they talked. Pets, friends, schools, favorite foods. Anything and everything that came to mind. Eric was amazed at the ease and confidence of the child, and he couldn't have been any more proud of her if she had been his own.

It was a little less than an hour later when Mary Kathleen made her third completely unassisted circuit of the rink. Delighted with her success she immediately demanded to be shown how to skate backward. Laughing down at her, Eric pushed his collar up, pulled his Stetson down and turned the child so that her back was to him. "Okay, poppet, hold on to your hat."

When Chrys arrived a few minutes later, she stopped in surprise. Her eyes narrowed and her lips pursed thoughtfully. Studying the mismatched pair carefully, she had to admit that she wasn't all that surprised to see her daughter with Eric.

But Eric with Mary Kathleen? That posed a number of interesting questions, and Chrys wasn't sure she was up to looking for the answers. Not when they involved Eric McLean.

"Your friend is really good with children, Chrys."

"My friend?" Acknowledging Ann with an absent smile, Chrys's mind was still busy wondering what Eric was doing there, and more important, why he'd decided to spend the afternoon with her daughter.

"You mean you don't know him?" Ann's round face took on a look of alarm and her voice rose. "Mary Kathleen said he was a friend. I assumed—"

"Relax, Ann, I know him." Chrys leaned over the guardrail and watched her daughter and the man below make another lazy circuit of the rink. "I just didn't expect to see him here."

"Whew! For a minute you had me worried." Ann pretended to wipe her brow, then smiled. "To be honest, I don't think he expected to be commandeered by Mary Kathleen, but he's been awfully good about it. He's a born teacher, and although she's been too possessive to let him out of her sight I can tell he's good with kids."

Again Chrys nodded absently.

So Mary Kathleen had engineered this little escapade, hmm? Well, as much as she loved her daughter, completely, mindlessly, unquestioningly—but drat the child anyway!—if she had to crave a father figure at this time in her life, why on earth did she have to pick Eric McLean as her prime candidate?

Chrys's frown deepened as an uneasy answer came to mind. Could Mary Kathleen have sensed something between them? Lord, she hoped not. Besides, she added hastily, there wasn't anything between them. Not anything at all.

Chrys sighed and her shoulders slumped. Now she was even trying to lie to herself. *Old habits die hard,* a tiny voice in the back of her head whispered mockingly.

As much as she hated admitting it, there still was something between her and Eric. She wasn't certain just what or how much, and she certainly didn't like acknowledging any part of it. But what choice did she have? If she didn't face up to it now . . . if she didn't learn to deal with it now . . . it could only get worse.

"Chrys?" Ann's hand on her shoulder brought her back with a start. "Are you okay?"

"I'm fine, Ann. Just thinking about other things, I guess."

Ann looked from Chrys's frowning face to the man and child below. "Do I sense a romance in the bud?" Ann's grin was as sunny as her blond curls and as bubbly as her bright personality. As the happily married mother of three, she was always willing to dabble in a little matchmaking when the opportunity presented itself.

"No." Chrys frowned, hoping that her tone wasn't any sharper than the situation warranted. She didn't need any more of her friends playing Cupid. Berta was bad enough. "All you're dealing with here is a distracted librarian."

"Distracted, I'd believe. But I think we're talking about a woman here, not a librarian." Ann kept grinning even as her brown eyes took on a darkly speculative glint.

Chrys, in Ann's opinion, had an annoyingly bad habit of turning potential mates into good, but decidedly platonic, friends. Mark Henshaw was a perfect case in point.

Mary Kathleen's newest find, however, didn't look the type to settle for anything as mundane as friendship. Shooting a sly glance in Eric and Mary Kathleen's direction, Ann sorted through the possibilities her mind began to plot. "He's awfully good-looking."

The hint was hardly subtle, and Chrys, inured to the intricacies of her friend's thoughts and intentions, hid a grimace behind her gloves. First Mark and his big mouth had dumped Eric in her lap yesterday. Then Berta had spent half the night telling her that she was crazy to pass up a prime catch. And now this! Eric McLean hadn't even been in town two full days yet, and she was beginning to feel like some sort of sacrificial lamb.

Why were all of her friends so willing to offer her up? And why, of all people, had they chosen Eric?

Chrys frowned. Whatever the reason, the one thing she didn't need was Ann Corey at her matchmaking best. Not only that, but she had to do something that would let everyone—Eric and Mary Kathleen included—know that she wasn't about to succumb to a memory from the past.

"Don't you agree, Chrys?" Ann nudged her in the ribs.

Chrys hadn't been paying attention, but she knew better than to mumble any kind of absentminded assent. With Ann, she could end up agreeing to just about anything. "Agree about what?"

Ann's mouth widened into a knowing smile. "That he's awfully good-looking."

"Of course he is. It runs in the family."

"Oh." Ann grimaced and her voice was ripe with disappointment. "Mary Kathleen didn't tell me he was a relative."

Chrys contemplated letting Ann's mistaken conclusion stand, but there were too many people, Ann's husband, Ed, being one of them, who would be only too glad to set it right. And then she'd be in worse trouble than she was now. "No, Ann," she corrected dryly. "Not my relative, Talbot McLean's."

"I didn't realize Talbot had a son," Ann added. "Have you known him long?"

"Mmm." Chrys's reply was a careful study in neutrality. "Ten years, off and on."

Ann grinned at the guarded quality of Chrys's voice. It boded well for her plans. "He's not a local. Not dressed like he just walked in off the range."

"No. Eric's living in New Mexico now."

"Ah, the land of enchantment," Ann supplied dreamily. "Ed and I have always wanted to take a vacation there. Is he married?"

This time Chrys wasn't caught off guard. After another quick debate with her conscience, she decided that in this case a lie was acceptable. "I don't know." Her shrug was carefully noncommittal. "I never thought to ask."

Ann's voice adopted the same tone. "How long will he be in town?"

Chrys didn't trust her friend's studied nonchalance any more than Ann trusted hers. "I don't know. At least until after his father's funeral."

"I see."

Chrys turned and gave her friend a wry look. "Look, if you're so curious, why don't you ask him this afternoon?"

Ann's face changed from contemplation to appalled understanding. "You're going to ask a gorgeous hunk like that back for the hot chocolate ceremony?"

"Sure, why not?"

"Why not? *Why not?*" Sounding thoroughly outraged, Ann sent a pitying look in Chrys's direction. "Chrys, eligible females do not issue hot chocolate invitations to eligible males. Not when fifteen overexcited, highly curious and downright rambunctious children come with the invitation. Don't you have any sense?"

Chrys forced a smile. "You're the one with the eligibility clause, not me. Besides, you can be sure that if I don't invite him back, Mary Kathleen will."

"I'm glad to see one of you has some sense," she added, then chuckled. "Smitten, is she?"

"Down for the count," Chrys agreed easily, hoping that Ann wouldn't realize that she wasn't anywhere near as complacent as she tried to act.

"Well," Ann conceded as she rubbed her mittened hands together, "I can't say as I can fault her taste. He is gorgeous."

"Careful, Ann. Ed'll—"

"Ed!" Ann took a quick peek at her watch. "Oh, my gosh! I was supposed to call Ed twenty minutes ago!" Ann's words trailed off as she ran for the nearest pay phone.

Laughing at her friend's mad dash, Chrys turned back to watch Eric and Mary Kathleen make circle after circle on the crowded rink. And, in spite of her own inner concerns, she had to admire what she saw. Tall and lean, Eric was undeniably exotic in his Western jacket and Stetson.

A slow, somewhat reluctant smile etched itself across Chrys's face. Mary Kathleen seemed to have a sudden taste for the exotic. She was also—drat the charming little piece of baggage—on her best behavior.

Maternal pride deepened into loving exasperation. No matter what the experts said, no child could ooze that much charm and innocent guile unless she was up to something. And what man, especially one who appeared to like children, could resist that particular combination?

Chrys could almost find it in her heart to feel sorry for Eric McLean. He didn't know it, but he was definitely being set up.

At just about the same time Chrys decided that she'd have to sit down and have a heart-to-heart with her one and only, Mary Kathleen looked up and saw her mother. Grinning happily, she began to shout and wave.

Eric, surprised by the unexpected outburst, looked up to see Chrys standing at the rail. Losing his concentration, he slipped, and when his skates tangled with Mary Kathleen's they both tumbled down onto the ice.

He heard the child's delighted laughter as she teased him about falling down. He heard her say that from now on, she'd have to be the teacher and he'd have to be the student. He heard a host of other noises as well: fellow skaters, students on their way to the library, cars driving through the wet snow and even the slow beat of the flag slapping in the wind. But the only thing he really noticed as he picked himself up off the ice was that Chrys seemed to be smiling at him as well as Mary Kathleen.

"Momma." The child flew forward breathlessly, fairly dancing on the blades of her skates as she began to show off her newly acquired skills. "Momma, did you see me skate?

"I can go backward and forward. I can even make a pira—piro—I can go round in a circle and stay in one place. Eric taught me how.

"And he calls me poppet—" her giggle was high and free "—'cause he said I'd fit in his pocket. Did he call you poppet, too? When he taught you how to skate?"

Chrys looked down into her child's eager face. The scamp. She knew she was pushing it. "No, he didn't call me poppet. I wasn't a pesky little girl like you."

"What did he call you?" Mary Kathleen wasn't about to be swayed from her eyelash-batting best.

"Chryssie. With a lot of exasperation. Just like when *I* say 'Mary Kathleen, didn't I tell you—' "

"But I didn't talk to a stranger." Mary Kathleen defended herself with an impudent grin. "I met him in our house. You said he was a friend. Berta thought he was neat and besides, he's Tally's little boy."

"Go change your skates!" Chrys waved the child off before she could see her start to grin. "And no more strangers! Even ones you think you know."

Mary Kathleen giggled and ran off, not the least bit abashed.

"Tally?"

"Mmm." Chrys was still watching her daughter with a rueful gleam in her eye, oblivious of the questioning male voice. Part of her was delighted that Mary Kathleen's world was so open and free. Another part of her, the more prudent part, wondered if she was ever going to convince her daughter that not everyone was lovable and loving.

"Does she mean my father?"

"What?" Chrys turned and frowned. "Oh!" Her features lightened as she realized what Eric was asking. "Yes, she does."

"I didn't know you knew him that well." Eric pushed his Stetson back, frowning.

"I don't." Her smile was wry and her shoulders rose and fell in a helpless gesture as Eric sat down and began to unlace his rented skates. "But Mary Kathleen's never been one to let a little thing like that hold her back."

Eric wasn't sure if he wanted to grin or keep on frowning. He was even less sure why it mattered. "I can't imagine my father letting anyone call him Tally."

Chrys chuckled softly. "I can't imagine anyone but Mary Kathleen trying. The girl's got no sense of rank."

"Rank?" Eric's face took on a quick look of exasperation. Surely, after all these years, Chrys wasn't still worried that she wouldn't fit in. "Even Platteville's not that feudal, Chrys. It never was."

"Of course not." Her reply was just as exasperated as his. "Give me some credit, Eric. All I meant was that the very proud and proper state senator, Talbot McLean, should have been addressed with a little more respect than a cocker spaniel pup."

Eric's features remained tense for a moment, but then, as the memories of his father's stern and serious demeanor took hold, he broke down and laughed. "God! I would love to have seen the old man's face the first time she called him that."

"I only have Mary Kathleen's word for it, you understand. But 'Tally' was your father's choice." Her eyes sparkled with shared laughter and light. "I didn't dare ask what other names he turned down."

Eric nodded. "Yes, I can see that she's a charmer. It would be hard to deny her anything."

"And guess who knows it."

"Oh, but she's not the least bit spoiled," Eric protested on the child's behalf. "In fact, she's absolutely engaging."

"And they say that only love is blind. You have to know," Chrys cautioned him seriously, "that all this charm comes with a flip side as well. My darling daughter is definitely used to having her own way."

A warm smile broke across his lean cheeks. "And you wouldn't change her a bit."

"Well—" Chrys's eyes sparkled with as much mischief and self-assurance as her daughter's "—only on alternate Tuesdays and Thursdays."

Eric laughed and moved off toward the rental counter. "Would you and Mary Kathleen like to go someplace and get something hot to drink after I return these skates?"

Chrys shook her head. "We have to be getting back to the house." Then, remembering that she'd planned to nip Ann's matchmaking in the bud, Chrys asked Eric if he would like to join them for a cup of hot chocolate.

Eric's surprise registered briefly on his face. He'd expected Chrys to be a little distant, maybe even a little cold when she found him playing courtier to her daughter. What he hadn't expected, what he'd never even dreamed of, was a warm and friendly invitation back to her house.

And then, as if unable to resist, he reached out and touched Chrys's cheek gently. "I'd like that very much indeed."

Chapter Five

"I'm afraid you don't know what you've let yourself in for," Chrys warned Eric when he returned from paying for his borrowed skates. "Hot chocolate at my place isn't as simple as it might sound."

"I don't mind."

Until Eric touched her face, Chrys hadn't given his thoughts and feelings much consideration. Now, having to admit that her primary reason in inviting him back to her house was to use the situation to put Ann's matchmaking on hold, Chrys was beginning to feel more than a little guilty. "I don't know. You may change your mind when you see what's involved. Just remember, if you want to back out, it's okay with me.

"And don't say that you weren't warned," she cautioned as she turned around and pulled off one glove. Then, placing two fingers between her lips, she let loose with a loud whistle, shrill and sharp enough to split the brisk winter air.

For a moment the entire rink was silent. No sound was heard. The next second, pandemonium broke loose as fifteen excited little children, ranging from five to nine years in age, gathered round: talking, shoving, giggling and pushing all at the same time.

Eric studied the scraggly line with a cautious eye. Then, with one side of his mouth quirked up in a wry smile, he laughed at himself for being such a fool. Chrys wasn't inviting him back for a tête-à-tête, not with this number of built-in chaperons.

"I take it this is an open invitation?"

"More like a semiregular tradition," she offered apologetically. "But you can back out if you want to. It's a bit daunting to the uninitiated."

"I think I'll tough it out." The look he sent her way was the kind often reserved for mild-mannered lunatics. "But I see what you mean about snap decisions."

The children giggled and pushed some more as Chrys began a quick head count.

"Are you sure you've got them all?"

Chrys grinned, relieved to find that Eric wasn't upset after all. "I'm sure. Are you?"

Eric knew a challenge when he heard one. Conceding the point with a tip of his hat, he grinned back. "Whatever."

Chrys, ignoring the irrational flutter in the region of her heart, smiled back before turning toward the eager young faces. "Okay, you kids. You know the rules, the first two of you who get to Mary Kathleen's house can pick sides for the snowball fight, and afterward, when you come in for hot chocolate..."

She caught each child's eye, frowned fiercely and wagged her finger with a telling gesture that didn't scare the children one bit. "The first one of you who gets slush on my clean linoleum, I'll—"

"Hang us up by our toes," they chorused and took off like a shot.

Eric chuckled. "Now there goes a cowed lot."

The grin Chrys leveled at Eric was every bit as impudent as the children's had been. "Don't be such a pessimist, Eric. They fear my every word and tremble in their boots at the very sound of my voice."

"Yeah. Just about as much as they fear me." Ann puffed as she came to a halt at Chrys's side. "Ed said that he'll meet us at your place in about an hour and a half," she told Chrys. Then she turned to Eric. "Hi, I'm Ann Corey."

"Ann is Ed Corey's wife." Chrys introduced the two of them. "I don't know if you remember him, but he was a freshman the same year I was."

Eric frowned, trying to picture the man Chrys referred to, but although the name was familiar, he couldn't quite conjure up a face to go with it. "I'm sorry. I don't think I do. Do the two of you—" he nodded to the racing children "—do this often?"

"Every third Sunday." Chrys nodded.

"Don't listen to a word she says," Ann admonished playfully as they started following the children at a more leisurely pace. "What Chrys really means is that I watch them all by myself while she does her weekly grocery shopping."

"And who feeds them?" Chrys flashed back, laughing. "That's certainly a lot more work than watching them one hour out of four. Don't you agree, Eric?"

"I don't know if I want to get in the middle of this." Eric chuckled and decided that remaining neutral might have its advantages. "At least not until I can figure out what's going on."

Both Ann and Chrys laughed, but it was Ann who filled him in. "A bunch of us were at a PTA meeting last year, complaining that we never have any time to ourselves with little kids and that, worse yet, good baby-sitters were hard to come by."

"I can imagine," Eric said with a grimace. "Especially if you're trying to do it fifteen at a time."

"One or fifteen, it's the same amount of work." Ann cinched her coat tightly against the cool air. "I ought to know. Three of them are mine. Anyway, eight of us got together, paired off and agreed to take turns watching each other's kids. That way, we all get three Sunday afternoons a month to ourselves."

Eric turned to Chrys. "So today was your day off?"

"No." Chrys laughed when his brow drew together in an uncomprehending frown. "When it's our turn Ann takes them all for the first hour while I do my weekly shopping. Then after she's worn an edge in their excess energy, we all go over to my place and put up our feet for the next two hours while the kids wreck my lawn. After that Ann usually takes off early and I get the kids—minus hers—for the next hour on my own. It's kind of complicated, but it all works out in the end."

"Is it worth it?" Eric sounded a bit skeptical.

Ann sighed with soulful envy and sent Chrys a speaking look. "Obviously the man doesn't have any children of his own. Otherwise he wouldn't ask." Then, looking up at Eric, she asked, "Are you married?"

"I should have warned you about Ann," Chrys interrupted wryly. "She's insatiably nosy and never curbs her tongue."

"Not at all, not at all." Ann dismissed the charge with a wave of her hand. "I only want to know how long you'll be in town. Where you live now. What you do for a living. Oh—" she grinned irrepressibly "—and whether or not you have any spare change lying around that you're just dying to contribute to a worthy cause."

She grinned, batted her eyes in a parody of Mary Kathleen's earlier behavior and added artlessly, "I'm in charge of fund-raising for several different charities. You can have your pick. Let's see, there's the Heart Fund, the Cancer Society, the League of—"

Chrys laughed at her friend's antics and took Eric's left arm, leaving Ann to grasp his right as they continued down the wide sidewalk, three abreast. "Whatever else anyone might say about Ann, they can't accuse her of being subtle. If I were you, I'd nail your wallet shut or you won't have a penny left by the end of the day."

IT WAS A QUARTER TO SIX and Chrys's linoleum was a disaster. A mountain of paper cups littered the kitchen table and nearly every wastebasket in the house was definitely in need of emptying. But Chrys didn't mind.

The children, for the most part, were content to stay in the basement playing grossly overrated music. Their parents, who had originally stopped by to pick up their offspring, were equally content to crowd into her living room and play catch-up with Eric's past.

Chrys grinned to herself. It hadn't come as any real surprise to find that most of the children's parents had known Eric in high school and college. Nor had she been particularly concerned when they had looked on his presence as an opportunity for an impromptu pizza party and class reunion.

In fact, things couldn't have been better. Ann, after a brief conference with Berta, had given in gracefully, and Berta, thank heavens, seemed content to hold her peace.

When the doorbell rang again, Chrys excused herself to answer it. Then, after directing the latest arrivals into the front room and making sure that everyone had cold drinks, she excused herself and began to set the kitchen to rights.

"Hey, Eric! Great to see you again," Pete Mellenkamp boomed forth as he strode across the room. "I couldn't believe it when Henry called to say you were in town. Where've you been all this time?"

"New Mexico," Eric said for the third—or was it the fourth?—time. He couldn't remember.

"What are you doing there?"

"I've been teaching history for the past couple of years. They've got a great school system and I really enjoy the climate." He grinned, knowing that he was beginning to sound like a broken record.

"Hell, yes." Pete thumped his fist against the padded arm of the couch. "Almost anything would beat Wisconsin this time of year. Say, my wife's got some family down in Santa Fe. Are you anywhere near there?"

"No. I'm a lot farther south and west. Closer to Silver City."

"Where's that?" one of the women asked. Eric couldn't remember whose wife she was.

"Just south of the Gila National Forest." He was beginning to wonder if the questions would ever stop. But he didn't really mind. In fact, it was kind of pleasant to find not only that he hadn't been forgotten, but that all of these old friends were more interested in him as himself than as the son of Talbot McLean.

"That's pretty close to Mexico, isn't it?"

"It's not far from the border." He laughed. "You can make it in a couple of hours most of the time."

"Say," Henry Grossen interrupted. "Where'd you disappear to when you left here anyway? I was in charge of our last high school reunion," he continued loudly, totally unaware that he might be walking on touchy ground, "and I did everything short of sending out the National Guard but I couldn't find hide nor hair of you."

Eric shrugged. He didn't like talking about that part of his past, but it couldn't be ignored. "I was in the Peace Corps for a while. Then later I joined up with Langtry and worked in Central America for a couple of years after that."

"Langtry?" Ed Corey inquired. "I've heard of them."

Pete leaned forward, an intense frown on his face. "Say, wasn't that the big mining corporation that went belly-up a few years back?"

"Yeah," Henry answered. "I heard one of their overseas projects literally blew up in their faces. Lot of men got hurt." Turning to Eric, he asked the obvious, "You in on that?"

"Yeah." For a moment, Eric couldn't smile through the grim reminder. He'd been doing pretty well up until then. "I was there."

"What happened?" Henry, oblivious as always, persisted.

"Officially, it was listed as an accident."

"Humph!" Henry snorted. "Sounds like bureaucratic double talk to me."

Eric forced himself to chuckle lightly. "Yeah, it does at that. Anyway, by the time the dust finally settled I'd decided that a change of career was in order and I was back in school and working on my master's in history."

Pete, who was a bit more sensitive to the nuances, took control of the conversation and steered it in other directions. "If you ask me, teaching in a high school can be just as dangerous. Did any of you read about that kid in Milwaukee who pinned his guidance counselor to the PA system?"

Chrys, who'd been catching bits and pieces of their conversation as she cleaned, tuned out the rest of Pete's story and found herself concentrating on what she'd learned about Eric. He'd mentioned the Peace Corps earlier, but hadn't said a word about working overseas after that. Funny, she wouldn't have thought that he'd have wanted to go back. Not after being so disillusioned in the first place.

"Ah, well," she mumbled to herself as she dumped a handful of paper cups into the nearest trash bag, "it just goes to show you how much you don't know about him."

"Chrys?"

Startled at the sound of Eric's voice right behind her, Chrys jumped.

"Sorry, I didn't mean to scare you."

Hand on heart, she laughed. "You didn't scare me. I just didn't hear you come in. How are the drinks holding out?"

"Fine."

She frowned at the tight reply, then noticed the expression of pain that was etched between his brows. "Does your head hurt?"

"Some." One hand rubbed at the persistent ache in the small of his back. "Do you have some aspirin?"

"Sure." She turned and led him up the stairs to the bathroom. "Did you strain your back skating with Mary Kathleen?"

"No. My back is fine."

Still watching his face, she handed him a small bottle with a childproof cap and then, when he couldn't seem to manage it, she took it back and opened it for him. "If your back is fine, why are you always rubbing it?"

"Am I?" Eric looked surprised as he took the bottle from her hand. "I didn't realize..." His voice trailed off.

"I've seen you do it several times." Her blue eyes narrowed thoughtfully. "Whenever anyone mentions Talbot or your job overseas. What happened down there?"

Eric didn't pretend to misunderstand. "I was there when one of Langtry's mines blew up." His words were flat and unadorned as he shook a couple of tablets into his palm and swallowed them without water. "As to what happened, they don't really know."

"Or won't say." Chrys's brow drew together in a frown. She'd heard about the accident. It had been in the news for weeks, and while she couldn't recall all of the details, there was one thing that she was certain of: there had been few, pitifully few, survivors. "But I didn't mean what happened to Langtry's mines. I wanted to know what happened to you."

"Me?" Eric shrugged. "I made it out."

"Out?" Chrys's breath caught in her throat. "I thought you would have had a desk job. I thought you would have been safe."

Unconsciously, Eric's hand sought the small of his back once again. "I was inside when it happened. A lot of us were." His eyes closed and he remembered. Remembered and wished that he hadn't.

"If you want my personal opinion, I think it was sabotage rather than carelessness, which is what the local *policía* claimed, or an explosion of an underground pocket of gas, which is what Langtry's claimed. But as to who or what was really behind it, I couldn't say. By the time I was shipped back to the States, just about every political faction in the country was lining up to take the credit.

"Anyway," he continued gruffly, "after it was all over, I just didn't have the courage or the desire to go back. I changed jobs and I'm glad I did. I like teaching back here in the States a lot better than I ever liked working overseas."

Chrys frowned, trying hard to understand Eric's past. "Why did you stay away so long? Especially if you didn't like it?"

"Who knows?" Eric shrugged. "Pigheadedness. A youthful determination not to let the bad guys win." He shrugged again, and this time grimaced with pain. "Trouble was, there were just too many bad guys. I couldn't make a difference no matter how hard I tried."

Chrys eyed his tall frame thoughtfully, taking in the many signs of stress. His shoulders were tensed, his brow furrowed and his hand rubbed persistently at the small of his back. "Maybe you ought to lie down for a bit and give those aspirins a chance to work."

Eric shook his head, then winced at the sharp pain that stabbed at him from behind his eyes.

"You always were too stubborn for your own good." She softened the accusation with a smile, and touched his face lightly. "I feel bad about this. I knew they'd come over, and I knew they'd be asking you all sorts of questions about what you'd been up to. I just didn't know that they would be as hard to answer as questions about Talbot."

Catching her hand in his, Eric held it against his cheek. "It's okay. It was a long time ago. It all was."

Chrys felt the muscles in her stomach clench at the husky tone of his voice. When he began to pull her forward, slowly, deliberately, Chrys swallowed the tight lump that rose in her throat. But it didn't go away. Instead, it hung behind her heart, making her pulse race and her words hoarse. "Eric, I—"

"Chrys, I—"

A little boy came flying through the bathroom door at the speed of light, and the door banged loudly making Eric wince once again. As the child shifted impatiently from foot to foot, Eric managed to grin, albeit faintly.

"Upstairs is off-limits, Stevie." Chrys's response was perfunctory; her gaze was still tangled with Eric's.

"I know, Mrs. Morrissey. But there's a line downstairs and I can't wait," the little boy wailed.

"All right." Chrys finally managed to drag her eyes away from Eric's face and told herself to be grateful for small favors. All she needed was for Ann or Berta to have witnessed this little scene, and there would be no convincing them that she and Eric weren't romantically suited.

Pulling her hand away from Eric's grasp, she ushered him down the hall, and opened the door to a book-lined study. "Stop playing macho martyr and rest for a bit. Everyone is having such a good time playing catch-up, they won't even know you're gone."

When Eric tried to catch her hand again, she pretended not to notice. "Go on. I'll be back in a bit and check on you. No one's likely to bother you in here, except maybe Hezekiah."

Eric attempted a halfhearted smile. "Hezekiah?"

"The cat. Be grateful the guinea pig is caged. Now get some rest."

When she closed the door behind her, Eric sighed and shut his eyes. It was dark, but not so dark that he couldn't see the colored lights that played across the back of his eyelids.

The colors were reassuring. In the mine, beneath the tons of earth that had trapped him and his friends, he hadn't been able to see anything, not even colors in his mind.

Bound by the darkness and unable to move, his only touch with reality had been the steady drip of water, the ragged moans of his companions and the heart-stopping sound of falling stones. Eventually, everything, the rumble of falling rocks, the coughing cries of friends and even the pernicious beat of the water had stopped. Only the darkness and his own breath had remained to tell him that he was still alive.

As the hours had melted into days, he'd been confident and afraid by turns. He'd begged and pleaded. He'd even learned to pray. Then, finally, he'd given up all hope of being found by one of the rescue teams.

But he hadn't given up altogether. Instead, he'd called on a part of himself that he hadn't even known existed. The survivor. And that part of him had come alive. He'd set about trying to dig himself free.

He hadn't managed to dig more than a few feet into the rubble, passing out from pain time after time. But someone on the other side had heard and helped. And when he'd heard them calling to him, he hadn't thought of his friends, he'd thought of Chryssie, and with her in his mind, he'd fought even harder to make it out.

Tossing his arm up over his head, Eric sighed and let the bitter memories fade away. It was a long time ago and an event long past changing.

Half an hour or so later, Chrys slipped quietly back into the room. "Eric? Are you feeling any better?"

Eric smiled faintly as she touched his brow. She'd always had a soft heart and a soothing hand for anyone who hurt. Maybe that was why he'd thought of her all those years ago. "What does the name Morrissey mean?"

Surprised by the apparent non sequitur, Chrys straightened up. "I don't know. Why?"

"A couple of years ago I read something that said the name Gallagher meant an eager helper. I remember thinking that it suited you."

Rather flustered by his admission that he'd thought of her after they'd broken up, Chrys's answer was sharper than warranted. "I'm not a Gallagher anymore."

"I didn't mean it as a bad thing. Just that you're still a helping person. Look at this mess you've let yourself in for today."

"These people are my friends, too. There's no reason why I shouldn't invite them over."

Eric groaned. "Lord, Chrys. I didn't mean to imply that they weren't your friends or that you shouldn't invite them over. It's just that..."

Eric's voice trailed off. How could he explain that she was helping him come to terms with his past by letting his first meeting with old friends take place on neutral ground?

Running one hand through his coppery hair, he shrugged. "I haven't talked to any of these people in eight years. If you want to know the truth, I dreaded meeting them at the funeral tomorrow."

She was too touchy where he was concerned and she knew it. But it was hard not to be. He'd only been in town two days and she was already being drawn back into his charm.

"Why?" Her voice softened and she touched his shoulder in silent apology. "Were you afraid they'd judge you by your father's standards?"

"No. Not really." Eric's brows drew together as he sought the right words. "I just didn't know who they'd expect me to be." He shrugged. "I can't play the grieving son. And there's no way I can manage the joyful heir."

Her fingers tightened soothingly over his arm. "Don't play anybody, Eric. Just be yourself. It's all you've ever needed to be."

"You know, I envy you that the most." His words were soft, almost wistful, as his tanned hand covered her smaller, paler one.

"What?"

"The ability to be yourself."

"I had a good teacher."

She tugged at her fingers, but Eric didn't let them go easily. He knew whom she meant and he was glad that she'd found someone special. Still, he wished he could have been the one to have grown with her. "Where did you say you met your husband, Chrys?"

"Madison." One brow rose repressively. She didn't want to talk to Eric about Ken, though she couldn't really say why. Maybe it was nothing more than a misplaced sense of guilt.

She'd loved Eric—or at least, she'd thought she had. But when they broke up, she'd hated being lonely and alone. She'd been ready for love, waiting for it all of her life.

Eric hadn't been the one, but he'd shown her the way and she hadn't wasted any time in finding someone responsible and grown-up to take his place. And then, after a while, she'd begun to question just how much of what she'd felt had been love for Eric and how much had been love for the sake of being in love.

It was oddly unsettling to be faced with that same unresolved question after all these years.

"Was he a student?" Eric interrupted her reverie.

"Hmm?" Chrys dragged her mind back to his question. "No. Ken was on the faculty."

"Faculty?"

"Yes. Faculty. I had a work-study job at the Memorial Library and he was putting some books on reserve. One thing led to another and we started dating.

"You know," she chided softly, smoothing a nonexistent wrinkle from her skirt, "for someone who needed peace and quiet to get rid of a headache, you ask a lot of questions."

Eric ignored the warning in her voice. "Does it hurt you to talk about him?"

"No."

Ken had never been jealous of Eric, she'd made sure that he'd never had cause. So why did she have the uncomfortable feeling that Eric might be jealous of Ken? He hadn't wanted her then. Surely he didn't want her now. Not really. Not in any ways that counted.

"Then why don't you?" he persisted.

"Why should I? He's always in my heart. I don't have to parade his memory around like a talisman to ward off evil spells."

Eric shifted uncomfortably, wondering if she saw him as something to be warded off. Yet how could it be any other way?

Turning toward the window that overlooked the side yard, he could see that some of the children were back outside playing in spite of the early sunset. He smiled as Mary Kathleen took aim and fired a badly packed snowball at a friend's back. "She doesn't look much like her father, does she?"

"No, she takes after me." Chrys's eyes narrowed into an uncomfortable frown. "Why all these questions about Ken?"

"I don't know." He shrugged and turned his back on the window and the dreams that could have been his. "I guess everybody asking me where I'd been and what I'd been doing got me to thinking about—'' He swallowed back ''us,'' knowing that she didn't want to hear it, and substituted, ''the past.''

Chrys's voice wasn't unkind, but it was firm. As much for her own sake as for his. ''Ken taught me a lot of things, Eric. One of the most important was not to look back.''

Chapter Six

Chrys sank down onto the overstuffed couch, kicked off her shoes, propped her feet up on the glass-topped coffee table and sighed, long, low and heartfelt. She could hear the wind beginning to pick up outside as it whipped around the pines and rattled the panes in the old-fashioned windows, but she was too tired to care. Tomorrow would be time enough to think about having to clear the sidewalks and drive.

She sighed again. Equally long, equally low and equally heartfelt. Tomorrow would definitely come too soon.

Berta, who'd been watching the ritual with an interested eye, leaned forward to pour another cup of coffee and nudged it in her friend's direction. "I know Mondays are the pits, but you really sound like you're wiped out."

Not bothering to open her eyes, Chrys let her head fall back against the sofa. "Sound like. Look like. I even feel like it, too. I thought Mary Kathleen would never get off to sleep."

"Did the funeral upset her?"

"Mary Kathleen?" Chrys pulled a face that could only be described as wry. "You've gotta be kidding." She sat up and let her voice rise to imitate her daughter's piercing tones. "'How come he's wearing makeup, Momma?'"

Berta's rich laughter echoed around the living room. "I've often wondered that myself."

Chrys grimaced. "Next time you can take her," she threatened.

"Just be glad it wasn't a closed casket." Berta chortled. "Couldn't you just have seen her demanding proof that good old Tally was really inside the coffin?"

"Don't give her any ideas, Berta. She comes up with enough on her own." Chrys eyed the cup of cooling coffee consideringly. Finally, she decided that it might just be worth the effort to lean forward and pick it up.

Berta eased off her own shoes and propped her feet on the coffee table, too. "I take it you were worried for nothing, then?"

"No, not for nothing. But for all the wrong reasons." Chrys sobered. "She was full of questions tonight."

"Anything you couldn't handle?"

"Mortality was kind of tough, but I think I squeaked through."

"Ken?" Berta's voice was now dark with sympathy. The reminder of all she'd lost couldn't have been easy for Chrys, even if she had lost her husband nearly four years ago.

"Not really," Chrys replied, surprising her friend. "Mary Kathleen seems to accept that Ken died because he was sick. She also knows that not all sick people die."

"So what's the problem?"

"Old people die."

"Old?" Berta's dark face knit itself into a puzzled frown. "What's that got to do—" Suddenly it dawned on Berta and she began to laugh.

Chrys blew a stray lock of brown hair out of her eyes. "Some help you are," she huffed, pretending to be miffed.

"Old. I love it! You must be all of—what is it now?—twenty-seven, twenty-eight?"

Chrys wrinkled her nose, trying not to grin. She really was too tired to grin. "My only child is worried about being left an orphan and you laugh. What kind of friend are you anyway?"

When Berta didn't stop laughing, Chrys added baitingly, "I told her you were thirty-six."

"You didn't!" Berta gasped back another laugh. "What did she say to that?"

"Ancient, was the first word that came to mind." Chrys started to chuckle as well. Maybe she wasn't all that tired after all. Berta's laughter was always infectious. "You think it's funny now, but you won't when you realize that she's got you pegged right up there with her Grampa Gallagher and Methuselah."

"Am I supposed to thank you for this?" Berta tried to sound aggrieved, but she wasn't very successful. She was laughing too hard. "You know that child will have it spread all over the neighborhood before noon tomorrow."

"No need to thank me." Chrys waved her hand in a lazy circle, grinning because she knew Berta didn't really care. "I knew you'd sacrifice me under similar circumstances."

"Thanks a lot," Berta answered wryly, then abruptly switched back to the funeral. "By the way, how was Eric holding up?"

"Fine." Chrys took a sip of coffee and changed the subject on her own. "Didn't you have to give a final tonight?"

"I gave two today. World Lit." Berta grimaced. "I love correcting essays. They take forever. And freshman composition tonight. Say," she added, neatly switching the subject back again, "what's with you and Eric McLean?"

"Nothing," Chrys answered quickly.

"And pigs fly," Berta responded just as quickly.

An annoyed frown clouded Chrys's normally pleasant features. "I've known him for years."

"Ann Corey might swallow that, but I don't."

"Well, I have."

"Then how come we've never heard of him before this weekend?"

Chrys tried to force her face into a carefree smile. It didn't quite work. "You don't know everyone that I know."

"Chrys, who are you trying to fool? I've been your best friend and next-door neighbor since you and Ken moved in here. I practically live here. And Ann has your chatterbox of a daughter over at her place almost as often as I do. Believe me, if you'd mentioned him before this, we'd have heard of him."

"Been comparing notes?" Chrys asked sweetly, but there was a tartness underlying her words.

"Why not?" Berta asked with studied nonchalance. "You're just old friends, right?"

Chrys got up and walked across the room. Turning her back on her friend, she picked up the brass fireplace poker and began to stir the dying embers with a series of sharp jabs. "Why are you so interested in my past?"

Berta frowned at Chrys's gruff tone. "And I could ask why you're so touchy."

"Because it's my past." Chrys shot her a defiant look.

"You know," the other woman continued, ignoring Chrys's stiff back and militant look, "all you have to do is say: 'Berta, mind your own business.'"

"Mind your own— Aw, Berta." Chrys's shoulders slumped. Berta was a good friend, perhaps her best friend, and she wouldn't ask just for the sake of prying.

Sending an apologetic glance over her shoulder, Chrys sighed. "Don't mind me, Berta. I just like being a grouch."

"Maybe you've been keeping too much inside."

"I don't know." Chrys gave the fire another couple of halfhearted jabs, then dropped the poker. "Maybe I have."

"I take it you two were serious?"

"You mean there's a choice at eighteen?" The mirror over the fireplace picked up Chrys's reflection as she stood and pressed both hands against her heart and sighed rapturously. "It was like a fairy tale come true. My first big romance."

"And you never quite got over him."

Chrys turned around and flicked her long hair back over one shoulder. "Don't be ridiculous. I've seen him exactly three times since he's been back. Saturday at his father's house. Sunday at the Union. And today at the funeral."

"And on two of those three occasions, you invited him back here."

"Only once. He invited himself the first time."

Berta wasn't buying any of it. "Don't try to fool me with that line of malarkey, Chrys. You certainly don't treat him like he was just another old friend."

"Sorry," Chrys snapped. "I guess I'm not up on the proper etiquette for meeting and greeting old flames."

"Touchy. Touchy." Berta watched Chrys from under lowered lashes, her brown eyes dark with sympathy and understanding. She didn't want to hurt her friend, but she could sense how desperately Chrys needed to talk—even if she wasn't willing to admit it. "If he dumped you—"

"He didn't dump me," Chrys interrupted. "We dumped each other."

"Well, don't tell me that either one of you got over it easily. You both act as if a rug's been pulled out from under your feet whenever you run into each other."

"Don't make me laugh." Chrys didn't sound as if she had laughter in mind.

Berta folded her arms across her chest and pursed her lips obstinately. "Come on, Chrys. Are you telling me that he doesn't get to you? That you sponsored that impromptu 'welcome the returning prodigal' party yesterday just to show him how much you didn't care?"

"Don't be ridiculous, I didn't—"

"You did!" Berta sat up suddenly as it all fell into place. "You let him come here to show Ann and me and all your other friends just how much he *didn't* mean to you. There's no reason you would have done that if you didn't care."

"I did not. I do not." She folded her arms stubbornly. "You don't know what you're talking about, Berta."

"Aw, come on, Chrys. This is me you're talking to. I feel closer to you than I do to anyone else in this town. And I know you as well as I know myself. I can read between the lines."

Plopping down at the far end of the couch, Chrys pulled her knees to her chest and wrapped her arms defensively around her legs. "He told me he was glad to have a chance to run into old friends before the funeral. He thought it would be less trying."

"When did he tell you that?" Berta asked astutely. "Before or after everybody showed up?"

Chrys scowled at Berta's persistence and her blue eyes darkened with annoyance. Throwing caution to the wind, she went on the defensive. "You're as bad as Ann, trying to play Cupid."

"Not Cupid," Berta corrected. "The devil's advocate. Lord, Chrys, I'm not blind. And I'm certainly not stupid. I've seen you with him and you sure as heck don't act like it's all over and forgotten."

"Well, it is."

"Keep telling yourself that. Maybe you'll start to believe it if you hear it often enough."

When Chrys looked as if she was about to protest, Berta waved her down. "Go ahead and lie to me, sweetie, but don't lie to yourself. You'll only end up hurting worse. I can tell you that from experience and you know it, 'cause you're the one who helped me get over Sam Cauldwell."

"I'm not lying to myself. I'm not lying to— Oh, hell." Chrys gave up. "Maybe I am."

Berta reached out and patted the younger woman's arm. "Don't sound so disgusted, Chrys. It happens to us all. There's nothing shameful about being human."

Chrys exhaled raggedly, then half grinned. "That advice sounds kind of familiar."

Berta reached out and patted Chrys's arm again. "It ought to. It's what you told me last year when Sam and I split up for good. You were right about me. Now I'm right about you."

"God, Berta, he's got me so mixed up." Chrys leaned forward to rest her chin on her knees, sighing wistfully. "I thought I stopped lying to myself years ago. Then he shows up in town and it's like I've forgotten everything I've learned in the past eight years."

"That's some time to carry a torch."

"I haven't been carrying a torch for eight years, Berta." Chrys flared up again. "Leaving Eric and finding Ken Morrissey was the best thing that ever happened to me. I loved him with all my heart and all my soul."

"I'm sure you did," Berta agreed solemnly. "But that doesn't mean that Eric McLean couldn't have left a lasting impression."

"He did that all right."

Berta chuckled at Chrys's dry tone. "So, what was he like?"

Chrys grimaced, knowing Berta would have trouble accepting her answer. Sometimes she had trouble accepting it herself. "All bluster and bluff."

"Now there's a nice combination."

One corner of Chrys's mouth tilted upward. "Don't be facetious. It was the pits and you know it. But I was eighteen. What did I know?"

Chrys hesitated, uncertain of how much she wanted to share with her friend. She'd put her past behind her with Ken's help, and she'd meant it yesterday when she'd told Eric she'd learned not to look back.

But Berta had been there herself, and she understood Chrys's hesitation. "I know you don't want to admit it, but whatever was between you and Eric McLean isn't over by a long shot. I just thought a sympathetic ear might help."

Chrys hesitated for a few seconds more, then admitted that Berta was right. Straightening up, she smiled, albeit wryly. "What would I do without you, Berta?"

"Probably lie awake all night remembering all this stuff anyway."

Chrys acknowledged Berta's words with a grimace of disgust. "Probably."

One dark brow rose questioningly. "So?" Berta rubbed her palms together as though anticipating the answer. "Let's hear the gory details."

Chrys laughed as her friend had hoped she would. "Give me a break, Berta. As relationships go, it was rated strictly PG."

Sobering, she continued. "I'd been on campus a couple of weeks and I'd seen him, mmm—" her hand waggled in the air "—maybe three or four times." Suddenly she grinned. "He liked to swagger back then, so he was kind of hard to miss."

"What better way to impress the impressionable?"

"Even so." Chrys acknowledged the accuracy of her friend's words with a nod. "But at eighteen, you can forgive a lot of stupid behavior when it comes from someone who's handsome and paying attention to you."

Her eyes half closed with the onslaught of memories. "He was two years ahead of me in school. A junior. A college man. And I was a freshman. Barely out of high school, wet behind the ears and young and impressionable. Definitely impressionable."

"You've got Amos Gallagher to blame for that."

"Dad's all right in his own way. He just doesn't know how to—" Berta snorted rudely and Chrys stopped trying to defend the indefensible. Maybe if her father had cared more, or if he'd known how to make her feel a part of his life, she wouldn't have been so eager to rush headlong into love.

Chrys laughed softly at her youthful eagerness to experience the best in life. "Sometimes I think it wouldn't have mattered if Eric had looked like a toad. The truth of the matter was, I was just plain ready to fall in love."

"So," Berta prompted, when the silence threatened to lengthen as Chrys became immersed in her bittersweet memories. "What happened with your toad prince?"

"He came on all macho and male while I tried to pretend that it was nothing new or exciting." Chrys grinned as if to say that she wasn't really all that affected, but her cheeks flushed and her eyes sparkled as she told Berta of their first meeting.

"I was in the Gold Room, down in the basement of the Student Union. It was the 'in' place to study. They still had that slightly suggestive sculpture of a nude—purple marble, I think—and all of us who wanted to think of ourselves as sexually liberated and adult liked to hang out down there.

"But our sophistication—or at least mine—wasn't very deep. The first time Eric came over to talk to me, my face got hot, my palms got sweaty and my heart started beating a mile a minute. And," Chrys continued, poking fun at her youthful self, "if you could have heard the breathless wonder of my sweet, young voice, you'd have never had to ask what happened next."

"Got to you the first time, did he?"

"Hook, line and sinker." Chrys sighed and fluttered her lashes, à la Mary Kathleen. "You've seen him now, Berta. Imagine him then. King of the campus. He was the handsomest thing I'd ever seen."

"Pretty hot stuff, I'd guess."

"Don't guess. Know." Chrys shook her head at her own foolishness. "He was twenty and cocksure of himself. I was barely eighteen and I'd never even been on a date. Take my word for it, the frog prince would have looked good to me."

"From first date straight to bed, hmm?" Berta's face showed both sympathy and understanding.

"No. Not at all. Eric wasn't looking for a girlfriend. He was looking for someone vulnerable, someone as insecure as he was. I think he thought it would make him feel better about himself.

"We went to Steve's—the pizza parlor down on Fourth Street—and I was in seventh heaven envisioning all sorts of romantic dreams. As much as I was looking forward to our date, I also couldn't wait to be back on our way home. I got goose bumps just thinking about whether he would try to kiss me and whether I should let him.

"Then—" she paused and lifted both shoulders in a hopeless gesture of futility "—before any of that could happen, we ran into a bunch of his fraternity brothers and their dates. I was the only one who wasn't pledged to a sorority. My clothes were dowdy and old-fashioned, and I was really starting to feel out of place when the talk turned to politics. I hadn't even realized that Eric was Talbot McLean's son and heir.

"Anyway, to make a long story short, Eric didn't help me a bit. Once we were seated he was too busy showing everybody else what a nice guy he was for setting up a pity date for me. And I was furious. With him for treating me like a nonentity and with myself for letting it happen."

"You fell in love with this?" Berta was definitely skeptical.

"Of course not. That was just the reason why he asked me out. It was also why I told him to drop dead after our first date."

"Ah. This is getting interesting. He comes on like a total jerk, you tell him to get lost and then you end up going with him for—what?—two years."

Chrys chuckled. "That's about the size of it."

"What did you see in him?"

"Myself," Chrys answered honestly. "Someone who was lonely. Someone who was afraid and trying not to let anyone else guess just how bad it was. Later that night, when he dropped me off at my dorm I told him that I knew it too, that he might be able to fool all the others, but that he wasn't fooling me."

Chrys shook her head at the memories. "You can't imagine how brave I was. I even went so far as to tell him that if he ever decided that he wanted to be liked for who *he* was as opposed to who his father was, he could look me up sometime. But until he grew up, I didn't want to see him again."

"I bet that went over well."

"It wasn't what he wanted to hear." Picking up the coffee service, Chrys headed into the kitchen. "He avoided me for a while after that."

"Not an easy thing to do on a campus this small." Berta trailed Chrys into the kitchen.

"No, but he got quite good at it." Chrys laughed, turning on the taps. "I'll bet he can still remember my class schedule better than his own."

"Ah-ha." Berta reached for a dish towel. "So that's why you've been playing—or maybe I should say *trying* to play it so cool. He still gets to you, doesn't he?"

"Yes," Chrys admitted with a sigh. "He still gets to me."

Berta gave Chrys a quick hug. "How did the two of you get back together again? So far, from what you've told me he was like, I wouldn't think he'd be worth the trouble. Let alone have the courage to apologize."

"I didn't think so either. Not at first. But I was starved for attention and he did apologize. Very nicely. Very, very nicely." Her voice faded away as she remembered how Eric had let down his guard and taken the first step.

"Don't leave me hanging on the seat of my chair. Spit it out!"

Chrys chuckled at the reminder. "I was just trying to figure out why he bothered. He could have had any girl on campus."

"Sounds to me like you were an easy target."

"Actually, I wasn't. We were too much alike for either of us to get away with playing games. Both of our mothers had died while we were young. Our fathers were busy and impersonal men. Mine preferred his farm; his preferred his political cronies. Eric had always felt shut out and alone. More than anything, he wanted his father to love and respect him. I wanted the same thing.

"It took time. A lot of time. But after we got around the first scuffle or two, we formed a truce and eventually became friends. From there, it was an easy step to go on to confidants, and after a while we ended up lovers. Because we could accept each other for who and what we were. No more. No less."

Berta reached out, touching Chrys's arm gently. "You really cared for him, didn't you?"

"Yeah, I did." She took a deep breath and released it slowly. "Sometimes I'm scared to death that I still do. Oh, Berta." She turned and faced her friend. "I don't want to like him. I don't even want to know him."

"I don't know that you can do much about that. He's here now."

"No, I guess not." She sighed again, not sure of what she felt. "Best I can do is be glad he's going away soon."

"You don't think he'll stay?"

"There's nothing for him here."

Berta shrugged. "There's his father's house."

"He hated that place almost as much as he hated his father."

"What about you?"

"Me? Oh, no. Not me. No way."

"That's a lot of protesting."

"I got burned once. I'm not going to let myself get burned again."

Chrys settled back on the living room's overstuffed couch. "We both had pretty heavy class loads. I was on a scholarship and determined to get through school just as fast as I could. Eric was trying to carry two majors. The one he wanted and the one his father wanted for him. But in spite of that we spent all our free time together. We even got a little place of our own as soon as I was able to move off campus. A little two-room cabin just a couple of blocks down from the Mining Museum.

"Can you believe it?" she asked. "I thought we got the cabin to have some privacy, not to hide away. And there I sat, making dreams."

Berta grimaced sympathetically. "Playing house does make breaking up rougher, doesn't it?"

"It also puts ideas into your head." Chrys sighed softly, sadly. "I think that's what made it hurt the worst for both of us. I started wanting more than Eric had to give. I stopped being able to accept him for himself and started wanting him to be what *I* wanted him to be.

"I thought of our place as the ultimate in romance. I started pretending that we were a family, that Talbot and my father didn't exist. Pretty soon I wanted to carry the fantasy over into reality. I wanted to get married, to start a family of my own, to have a home. A real home. Not just a pretend one.

"I knew Eric was unhappy with his father's demands and pretty soon it started making me angry that he wouldn't stand up for himself. He expected me to stand up for myself when it came to my father.

"One day I got so mad I told him I wanted him to march up to Talbot and tell him that he hated the idea of following in his father's footsteps. That he didn't want to be a lawyer and that he didn't want to go into politics and that nothing, nothing at all, was going to make him cave in.

"I wanted him to let Talbot know that he'd found someone to love him the way he should be loved. And that what Talbot felt and what Talbot wanted wasn't important anymore.

"I wanted— Oh, I don't know, Berta." Her hands waved helplessly through the air. "I wanted so many things back then. And I wanted them all right now. With none of the waiting and none of the growing up that we all have to do."

Chrys looked up and all the confusion that she'd felt eight years ago was plain to read on her face. "He helped me grow up, Berta. Yet at the same time, he refused to grow up with me. I—"

She shook her head in a helpless gesture and her long brown hair tumbled around her face, half hiding her expression. "Maybe if he'd talked to me, explained how he felt or reasoned with me, but . . ." She shook her head more forcefully this time. "He just couldn't do it. And I didn't know how to help him. I was too wrapped up in my own hurts.

"I just couldn't handle the fact that there was a part of him that could never be shared with me. I shared everything with him. And it made me furious when he tried to hide what we felt for each other." The words sounded lost and a little forlorn.

"Who was he hiding from?" Berta frowned, her face etched in concentration.

"I don't know. Himself I guess. At the time I thought it was Talbot." Chrys shrugged. "I guess it's always easier to blame your failings on someone else."

"You hadn't met Talbot?" Berta's deep voice rose in surprise.

Chrys's brow rose in painful irony. "Are you kidding? Our relationship was the best-kept secret on campus. I don't think more than a half a dozen people even suspected that we knew each other.

"Do you know," she continued softly, forgetting that there was no way Berta could have known, "I accused him of being ashamed of me, of knowing that his father wouldn't approve of us. I even accused him of using our relationship as a way of getting back at Talbot. That was when he told me that his father didn't even know about us and that if he had anything to say about it, Talbot never would."

Berta nodded sympathetically. "And you took that to mean he'd been toying with you all along."

"Wouldn't you?" Chrys defended herself. "He denied it. But I didn't believe him. And I knew—just as Eric did—that Talbot wouldn't have approved of our liaison if he had known about it.

"My family wasn't politically powerful. We never had a penny to spare after taxes. And I didn't even have the vaguest idea of how to behave and dress like a politician's wife. There was absolutely nothing to recommend me as Eric's wife."

"What about love?"

Chrys laughed, but it wasn't a humorous sound. "Neither one of us were naive enough to believe that our parents would understand that.

"In the end, I decided that I was Eric's act of rebellion. But that he wasn't brave enough to face his father with even that much."

Chrys closed her eyes against the bitter memories. "I got really angry and the issues got all clouded and confused. I ended up telling Eric that he had to choose between the two of us—between Talbot and me—when what I should have done was stand by him instead. But I was hurt and bitter and feeling utterly betrayed."

"And Eric chose Talbot?"

"I wish it had been that simple." Chrys buried her face in her knees. She hated this memory worst of all. It had the power to make everything that had been beautiful and pure, ugly and sordid.

Yet no longer able to keep the memory at bay, Chrys let the past wash over her. They were alone in the cabin, schoolbooks spread across the kitchen table, dinner half-cooked and the sheets still warm and rumpled on their bed. One minute they'd been in love and loving; the next, they'd been at each other's throats.

"Can't you let it go, Chryssie?" he'd asked in angry exasperation.

"No," she'd shot back and pulled on a robe. "We can't go on like this. I won't stay hidden away. Either you love me or you don't."

"You don't understand, Chryssie. You don't know what he's like. You don't know what he'll do."

"Dammit, Eric. He can't be that much of an ogre. Stand up to him. Tell him what *you* want. Tell him—"

"I can't."

"Can't?" she'd mocked scathingly. "Or won't?"

Eric had firmed his jaw and started gathering up his belongings. "Can't. Won't. It doesn't make any difference. You wouldn't understand anyway."

"Oh, I understand all right." The heat of righteous anger was building inside her and fueling her every move. "I've had it up to here—" her hand slashed the air over her head "—with you. You never had any intention of making a life with me. I was just convenient.

"Well I won't be convenient anymore. There's still time for me to transfer to Madison."

"Chryssie, that's not true."

"If it isn't, then stay with me. Be the person I need you to be," she'd pleaded.

"I can't." He'd sounded anguished, but she'd closed her mind to that part of him. Instead, she only saw that he would never change and that if she was to survive with herself intact, she'd have to make it on her own.

Blinking back the scalding tears, she'd told him, clearly, calmly and directly, that if he left her now, she wouldn't have him back. And then—

"He offered to give me money, Berta. Money to make a fresh start."

Berta's hand was light and warm as it rested against Chrys's arm. "Maybe he didn't mean it that way."

"I know he didn't, but that's the way it felt!" Chrys looked away. "God, I hated him for that more than for anything else. It made me feel like a prostitute when I'd been having dreams about being his wife."

"Did you ever see him after you broke up?"

"No. I was too angry and humiliated to stay around. I had my credits transferred to Madison and left just as soon as I could. I never heard from him—or of him again—until now."

Berta's eyes softened. "Did Ken know? About Eric, I mean?"

Chrys nodded and some of the strain eased away. "We didn't have any secrets from each other. I told him as soon as I knew he was serious about me. I couldn't have faced another dead-end relationship."

She smiled softly, reminiscently. "Ken seemed to understand. He proposed about a month after we first met and I never regretted loving him for one minute."

"And he didn't mind coming back here to Platteville?" Berta asked.

"To be honest, Ken almost didn't apply for the university position because he thought it might hurt *me* to come back. But I could tell he would have given his eyeteeth to get this job and I couldn't let him give it up just to save me my pride."

Chrys smiled, and Berta recognized it as her "thinking of Ken" smile. "It took some fancy talking on my part. In the end, I managed to convince him that this was where we both belonged and I've never regretted it either. He loved everything about this campus."

"You didn't know Eric had moved away?"

Wrinkling her nose, Chrys admitted that his absence had come as a pleasant surprise.

"And you think that in spite of the fact that you and Eric were together for nearly two years, Talbot never knew about it?"

Chrys shrugged. "I never met Talbot when Eric and I were together. And the only time Ken and I ever ran into him was at some of the university functions. Even then, we never really sat down and talked. I doubt he knew I'd done my freshman and sophomore years here."

"But surely he must have suspected something," Berta persisted.

"I don't know why you'd say that. Eric was always good at keeping secrets."

"I don't know either. Just a feeling that Talbot would have wanted to keep track of his son's extracurricular activities."

Once again, Chrys shrugged. "Maybe he did, but I don't see that it matters now."

Berta frowned, her expression one of deep puzzlement. "I got the impression from Mary Kathleen that you knew Talbot rather well."

Chrys's smile softened, taking on an air of amused indulgence, just as it always did when she thought of her only child. "Talbot was Mary Kathleen's doing, not mine."

"How so?"

"You know Mary Kathleen." She laughed. "He was another one of her finds. First I heard about it was when she announced that her 'newest' and 'bestest' friend in the whole wide world was named Tally, and that no, Momma, he wasn't a puppy."

When Berta tilted her head to one side curiously, Chrys laughed again. "Do you remember last year, or maybe it was the year before last, when everyone was out with the flu just before spring break? Everybody I knew was sick as a dog, including the sitter, so I had to bring Mary Kathleen in to work with me one afternoon."

Berta nodded.

"Well, Talbot came in and needed me to find something for some special project he was working on at the time. I went off to get it and left Mary Kathleen sitting at my desk quietly destroying her favorite coloring book. By the time I got back, she was all curled up in Tally's lap, having a story read to her."

"That sounds like Mary Kathleen."

"Doesn't it just?" Chrys laughed.

"After that, every time Talbot came by he asked about Mary Kathleen, and once or twice he even brought her a little present." Chrys's shoulders rose and fell expressively. "I figured he was lonely."

Berta reached out and laid her dark hand on Chrys's pale one. "You've got a soft heart, Chrys."

Chrys grimaced. "Just so long as it's not a soft head. Taking pity on a lonely old man is one thing. Taking pity on his son is something else altogether. And I'm not getting caught up in that bind. Not ever again."

It was a good thing that Chrys was too distracted to notice the complacent quality of Berta's quickly hidden grin.

IT WAS LATE and he was tired. The funeral had ended hours ago but there was still a lot of work to be done. Work that he didn't want to do.

Hesitating just inside his father's private sitting room, Eric ran one hand through his thick hair. Yesterday Chrys had warned him against looking back. Tonight her warning made sense.

A slight smile twisted around Eric's lips as he remembered the firm certainty of her voice. She'd made it sound so simple and easy to do. But there was no way he could follow her advice. Not when everyone he met today had started their conversation with "Do you remember?"

Oh, he understood why they asked. It was a way of reassuring themselves that they would be remembered in turn. But that knowledge didn't make their questions any easier to field. Not when his memories were so different from theirs.

Moving restlessly just inside the doorway, Eric stuffed his hands deep in the pockets of his trousers and rocked back and forth on his heels. He'd come back to Wisconsin in search of answers. What he'd found had been more questions.

Questions and a kind of unpleasant honesty that forced him to admit that he'd regretted the need for his estrangement from his father.

He'd thought about returning, especially after the Langtry mine had collapsed around his head. But he'd been too afraid. Afraid of his father, and worse, afraid of himself. His independence had been too new, too fragile and too untried to trust to his father's rough handling.

Once, his father's approval had meant everything to him. He'd thought that he'd grown away from that. Yet even now he feared that the need for approval might still be there, might still be too strong.

For as much as he hated to admit it, he wanted to find something, *anything*, that would prove that some spark of love between the two of them had remained.

Eric took a deep breath and released it slowly. His hand reached out, searching for the light switch. Whatever he found or didn't find wasn't going to be nearly as important as the answer itself.

He was stronger now. More confident in his own worth. More self-assured. Eric grinned at the litany.

"Stop stalling, McLean," he admonished softly, "and get it over with." His fingers found the switch, and the harsh overhead light sprang on in response.

Nothing much had changed. The room was as he remembered it. The furnishings stark and almost Spartan in appearance. The chairs, with the notable exception of his father's, were straightbacked, wooden and again, if his memory served him, as uncomfortable as hell.

Yet, in spite of its barren state, there was a vitality about the room, as if the essence of Talbot still lingered in the shadows.

Eric didn't have to close his eyes to see his father towering over his massive desk. And in his mind, even with his eyes open, he could actually hear Talbot's stern voice as the old man thumped the desk's polished surface with the flat of his hand in order to emphasize his point.

Caught by the memories, Eric's eyes closed and his mind dumped him in the middle of one of their last fights.

"Eric!" The voice was rough and gravelly, hoarse with impatience. "Get in here!"

"If it's about this summer, I'm not in the mood."

"I don't remember asking for your opinion, boy." Talbot jerked his head in the direction of the room. "Come in here and sit down. I don't want all the help bending their ears."

Eric's reply had been as sullen as the gesture that accompanied it had been rude. "What do you want now?"

Talbot eyed his son contemptuously. "If you're going into politics, boy, you'd best learn to curb that temper."

"Politics was your idea, not mine."

"As long as you're going to school on my money—"

"Pay the piper." The words burned in his mouth, hot and bitter with the taste of bile. "Dance the tune."

Talbot's eyes narrowed until Eric shifted uncomfortably, feeling both defiant and cowed. In the end though, he settled down on one of the hard, wooden chairs, sullenly waiting for his father's latest edict. What choice did he have?

"I've made arrangements for you to work on Ned Hawthorne's campaign committee this summer."

Eric turned his head and stared out one of the tall, narrow windows that lined the room. It was bad enough that the old man was bulldozing him into a career that he didn't particularly like or want, but did he have to try and run every minute of his life as well?

"Can't you let me off that damned leash of yours for the space of one summer? I've done everything else your way. Isn't it about time you—"

"Don't be a fool, boy." There wasn't even a hint of love or concern in Talbot's voice. Only autocratic demand. "This is important for your future. You need to get yourself known in the right circles. Hawthorne's a winner. It'll—"

Somewhere in the empty old house, a door slammed loudly and the unexpected sound brought Eric back to the present with a start. He sighed and rubbed one work-roughened hand across his face. Lord, but those memories were clear.

Had it really been eight whole years? Sometimes it was hard for him to remember that he'd been gone that long. Eric tilted his head to one side and rubbed absently at the back of his neck. Sometimes it was even harder to remember that Talbot wasn't waiting around a corner, ready to take him to task.

Lord, they had fought. Morning, noon and night. And yet their last fight, like so many of their arguments, had been trivial in the extreme.

"Mr. McLean?" The cook's thick brogue broke into Eric's musings. "I just wanted to be giving you my condolences before I left for the day."

"Thank you, Janet." He'd give anything never to hear another well-meant eulogy. "I'd like to thank you for the buffet today. It was delicious."

"Why thank you, lad." The woman's face creased into a giant smile. "Is there anything I can be getting you before I go?"

"No, not a thing." Eric wished the woman would leave, but he understood that she was worried about her job and that she had stayed behind, hoping to hear something good. But what could he tell her? He hadn't seen a copy of the will yet. He didn't know what, if any, provisions his father had made.

"Well..." Janet hesitated for a few seconds more, then nodded briskly. "I'll be seeing you tomorrow then, lad."

"Yes." His lips formed a slight smile of sympathy. "Jerome will be coming by early tomorrow morning. I should have some answers for you and the rest of the staff about your jobs later in the day."

"Now then." She smiled in a motherly fashion and patted his arm. "You're a kind lad to care."

They chatted for a few minutes more, and by the time she turned and left him on his own, Eric was feeling less tied to the past, but still wary.

Jerome had already indicated that aside from a few political and personal bequests, Talbot had intended to leave the bulk of his estate to his only son. And Eric, the only son in question, couldn't help but wonder why.

He gave a soft snort of laughter at his own misgivings. He knew other people who would have felt grateful or even that it was their right as blood heir to come into the bulk of Talbot's estate. But he didn't feel any of those things.

Instead, he felt cheated and ill-used. All he'd ever wanted was his father's love and respect. All he'd gotten were tangibles: a fat bank book and a white elephant of a house that he had no intention of keeping.

What could the old man have had in mind? Surely he must have known that the magnanimous gesture would be neither appreciated nor wanted.

"Ah, well. It could have been for spite."

Suddenly, unexpectedly, Eric found himself laughing out loud. Spite. It would be just like the old man to try to have the final word.

Eric's laughter drifted away into a deep, soul-cleansing chuckle. Well, for all of Talbot's intentions he hadn't taken into consideration the changes that had occurred within his prodigal, and far from repentant, son.

If there were too many restrictions, he would walk away, leaving the estate to whomever else might be willing to play Talbot's petty games.

And if he was given an open hand . . .

This time, Eric's gaze moved around the room with an unholy gleam in his eyes. There were things that could be done with a house of this size. A teen center. A shelter house. Perhaps even a group home. The possibilities were endless.

And nothing, Eric admitted with another wicked laugh, would have pleased his father less.

Still chuckling under his breath, he moved briskly around the dark room, opening curtains and switching on more lights. It was time, long past time, to admit once and for all that there was nothing he ever could have done to earn his father's love and respect. It was also time to admit that even if he had managed, neither love nor respect was half as important as his own feelings of self-worth.

Taking a seat behind his father's massive desk, Eric closed his eyes once again, and this time there was no sense of Talbot, no onslaught of memories. Only a feeling of peace and serenity, a feeling of having arrived, of being whole.

Chrys had been wrong. Looking back was just what he needed to do. For now, in the space of this one evening, he'd learned all he needed to know about himself and his father. And Talbot couldn't hurt him anymore. No one could.

Truly at peace with himself, Eric felt all the tension that had held him prisoner since Joe Beniki's call fade away.

He would do what was necessary to help settle his father's estate, and then, afterward...

Afterward, he would go home. Where he belonged. To a life that he'd created, to a world that he knew.

Rolling up his sleeves, Eric began to sort through his father's private files. Many were political in nature. Those he set aside for Mark Henshaw to take to Chrys at the library. Several pertained to household and business matters. He glanced at them briefly and put them back in their original folders. Either he or Jerome would go through them again at a later date, making sure that all accounts were brought up to date before the house was closed. The last pile, and surely the smallest, held letters that seemed to be more personal.

As he continued to sort through the folders, Eric found himself thinking that it was a shame that a man as important and influential as his father had had so few personal friends. Eric had been only fifteen when his mother died, but he did remember that it had taken Spencer several days to deal with her personal papers. Still, Talbot had never been one to turn to others for comfort and support.

Half an hour later, Eric flipped open the last folder. Other than a single letter, open but seemingly unread, the file was empty.

Pulling the single, crisp sheet out, he scanned it quickly. Then again, more slowly, with a growing furrow inching across his brow.

What was Talbot doing with a copy of Chrys's marriage certificate?

Could his father have known about their relationship all those years ago?

No, he shook his head stubbornly, that didn't make any sense. If Talbot had known about Chrys, he would have done something about it then.

Eric frowned down at the open folder. There was nothing else inside and no markings on the file. Absolutely nothing that could give him any clue to his father's thoughts or intentions.

So? The question came again. What was his father doing with Chrys's marriage certificate? And what had he hoped to gain by holding on to it?

Chapter Seven

"Hurry up, Mary Kathleen. Or you're going to be late for school." Rinsing the last of the breakfast dishes, Chrys wiped her hands.

"How come I have to go to school and you don't?" Mary Kathleen tumbled down the stairs, dressed but obviously reluctant to be on her way.

"Because I worked late two nights last week and all day Saturday besides. And I'm not taking the whole day off, only this morning."

Mary Kathleen's pout was an accusation by itself. "You didn't go to the library on Saturday."

Chrys eyed the clock, then her daughter. Actually there was still plenty of time before Mary Kathleen's friends came by.

"Remember I told you Talbot left a whole bunch of his papers and books to the Area Research Center?" When Mary Kathleen nodded, Chrys continued. "Well, that's my department. So I had to go over to Talbot's to see whether it was books or papers or journals or other kinds of records. I also had to see how much there was, so I could make plans to shelve it and start making an inventory."

"What's that?"

Giving one of her daughter's curly brown locks a playful tug, Chrys laughed. "Okay, I'll give you the long explanation. But when your friends come by, off you go whether we're done or not."

"Okay." Mary Kathleen giggled, suddenly all sunny and smiles.

"An inventory," Chrys began, "is a list. Jerome needs one to show everybody what Talbot gave to the archives, and I need one, a different one, so that people coming to the library will be able to use Talbot's collection."

"Did you make the list on Saturday?"

Chrys laughed. "I started it. But I didn't finish it. And it'll probably take me weeks to get it done. But I won't have to go back over to Talbot's after today."

"Why not?"

"Mark Henshaw is going to have all of Talbot's papers brought over to the archives later on this afternoon. They'll be waiting for me after lunch. Then I get to sit down and start measuring, labeling and describing every type of record he sends."

Mary Kathleen grimaced. "Do you have to do all that?"

"That's only the start." Chrys added cheerfully, "After I finish this part I have to go back through everything and decide which things are useful, which things might be useful in the future, which things will be useful for a while but not forever and which things to get rid of. Then I have to decide where to put everything—"

"I don't want to be a librarian when I grow up," Mary Kathleen interrupted with a groan. "It's too much work."

"It isn't work if you like it, and you've kept me talking long enough. Your friends will be by any minute." Chrys gave her daughter's bottom a loving swat. "Now scoot!"

"Aw, Mom."

"Aw, Mom, yourself." Chrys pulled Mary Kathleen's hat down around her ears. "If you don't get going I won't have enough time to finish my shopping before I have to be over to Talbot's. And then you-know-who won't get any you-know-whats for Christmas."

Pushing her hat back up, Mary Kathleen giggled. "Cindi's uncle's dog had puppies last week."

"I know." Chrys tugged the hat back down, then rolled up the brim. "You must have told me a thousand times."

"Can I—"

"No." Chrys held up a warning finger. "And don't sulk. I don't have time to train a puppy. You'll have to make do with what you've got."

"But I want another pet."

"You've got enough pets!"

"You can't hug a fish." Mary Kathleen pouted.

"But you can hug cats, guinea pigs and hamsters. And if you're not too fussy, you can even hug your turtle." Chrys placed her hands on either side of her daughter's face and tilted the child's head so that their eyes met. "Maybe someday, but not now. Okay?"

"Okay." Dragging the word out despondently, Mary Kathleen let herself out the front door and started slowly down the front steps.

When one of her classmates called out for her to hurry up, Mary Kathleen managed to put her disappointment aside and practically flew down the remaining steps. "Hey! Wait for me!"

Dropping the sheer curtain back in place, Chrys smiled. "So much for puppies."

Twenty minutes later, Chrys let herself out of the house and started downtown. Even though Christmas was right around the corner, she still had quite a bit of shopping to do, and this morning looked to be one of the few free times she would have and she was really looking forward to it—especially after last night.

She'd expected to lie awake all night, tossing and turning, reliving the memories over and over again. But she hadn't. Instead, the minute she lay down, she fell into a deep and, to the best of her knowledge, dreamless slumber. This morning she felt terrific, and not even Mary Kathleen's nagging for a puppy could get her down. She would simply have to find something else that the child would like as well.

She found a great gag gift for Berta in Kincaid's and a lovely locket for Mary Kathleen's gift from Santa in the jewelry store next door. But she still needed something special. Something that could take the place of a puppy.

She paused in front of the hardware store, studying its colorful display of bicycles and tricycles. Slowly, she began to smile. Laughing softly under her breath as she contemplated a shiny, red two-wheeler, Chrys decided that a bicycle was almost as high on Mary Kathleen's list of priorities as puppies were.

Mary Kathleen might have her heart set on something warm and furry, but she'd be more than willing to settle for transportation. Especially if said transportation came complete with training wheels, glittering handle grips and rainbow-colored streamers.

Ten minutes later Chrys tucked her checkbook back in her purse and left the hardware store with only a lingering glance down one of the jam-packed aisles. As much as she would have liked to spend more time browsing, there was no sense in pressing her luck and ending up late for her appointment. Not when it seemed that half the town and all the town fathers would be waiting to hear the contents of Talbot's will.

As Chrys walked up the long drive that led to the McLean mansion, she was surprised to note the difference Eric's presence had already made to his father's home. The grounds were as immaculate as ever, but the ragtag shovel line that edged the sidewalks and drive gave the whole place a more welcoming air.

The house, too, seemed to be more welcoming. Pine wreaths, topped with bright red bows, hung on each of the garage doors, and another, larger wreath hung slightly askew on the front door. From here, it looked as if all the drapes had been pulled back to let in the sun.

Just as Chrys raised her hand to ring the bell, Mark Henshaw opened the front door. Helping her off with her coat, he ushered her down the hall. "Better hurry, Chrys. Jerome's set up shop in the formal dining room and Dr. Waller's champing at the bit."

"Isn't he always?" Chrys's voice dropped low. "Am I late?"

"No," he whispered back and rolled his eyes in exasperation. "Everybody else was early. Time is money, you know," he quoted the university president perfectly.

Chrys swallowed back a giggle. "Shh. He'll hear you," she cautioned.

"Ah, Chrys." Jerome looked up as Chrys followed Mark into the room. "Right on time. Have a seat, my dear, and we'll get started."

Chrys nodded as several of the men rose to their feet. That Eric was one of them didn't surprise her. He'd always had beautiful manners once he'd gotten past his macho stage.

Chrys draped her coat over the back of the chair Eric held out for her and slid into place. "I hope I haven't kept you waiting," she murmured, wishing that she didn't feel so flustered about being the last to arrive.

"Not at all. Not at all." Jerome handed each member a thin manila file folder. "I don't know if she's told you or not, Eric, but Chrys is in charge of the university's Regional Archives."

"Hardly in charge," she corrected with an easy smile. Jerome had a way of making it sound as if she ran the archives single-handedly, and as flattering as his opinion was, it was hardly the whole truth.

Jerome's tongue clicked against the roof of his mouth. "Nonsense, Chrys. You've done wonders with your department, as I'm sure Dr. Waller will agree."

Peering over the top of his bifocals, Jerome continued. "Chrys has been instrumental in doubling the archives' holdings over the past few years. She's also been given the dubious task of collecting and cataloging all of your father's political papers."

Eric, still caught up in the unexpectedness of Chrys's smile, made an effort to drag his gaze away from her face. "Yes, I know."

Chrys's spine gave an involuntary shiver of response at the low, husky sound of Eric's voice. She took a quick breath and told her body to behave itself. She wasn't going to let a remembered timbre of voice upset her equilibrium. The past was just that—the past. Over and done with. And she'd be wise to remember it.

Jerome, unaware of the undercurrents, went back to the head of the table. "Well, now, Talbot's estate is rather an extensive one, so I suspect we'd better begin or we'll be here all day."

There was a good-natured groan from several of those present, and the university's president, Dr. Waller, voiced everyone's thoughts. "This is a terrible waste of time, Weaver, especially when a certified letter would do just as well."

"Don't blame me, George." Jerome adjusted his glasses. "It wasn't my idea. But you can see from the copies I've just handed out, it was something Talbot insisted on."

"My father always did like to run things his own way."

Surprised, Chrys looked at Eric out of the corner of her eye. His tone had been so even, so calm and unconcerned, that she found it hard to believe that he'd been speaking of his father.

Eric acknowledged her look of astonishment. "Coming to terms with yourself is a good thing, isn't it?" he whispered quickly as Jerome began to outline the steps that had been taken to probate Talbot's estate.

"Well," Jerome finished, "Talbot kept excellent records, so I think we should be able to clear everything away within the next few months. There's no problem, and of course," he added quickly, "no need for delay with bequests like the one you're handling for the university, Chrys. But I'm going to want to hold off for at least a short while before I release any funds for the larger grants and scholarships. Any questions?"

The housekeeper, who had been asked to sit in on the meeting as the staff's official representative, raised her hand and wanted to know if she should turn her accounts over to Mark, Jerome or Eric.

"Eric," he answered. "He'll be taking over the management of the house today."

Chrys hadn't thought that Eric would want to stay in Platteville any longer than he had to. Chancing another look in his direction, Chrys found, much to her chagrin, that he was looking back. When their eyes met, his shoulders rose and fell in a gentle arc.

"Well, then, let's begin."

Chrys barely heard Jerome's voice over the trip-hammer beat of her heart. Eric was staying, at least for a few more days. Why did she feel both pleased *and* frightened?

As Jerome finished reading the first page of his father's will, Eric found his thoughts drifting and the older man's words melted one into the other. The size of Talbot's estate never had been of much interest to him. Chrys, on the other hand, was.

He'd seen the look of startled surprise in her lovely blue eyes when she realized that he'd be staying on, but he hadn't been able to tell what else she was feeling. Once, her feelings had been easy for him to read. Her face had been like an open book.

But now, in some ways, she was more of a stranger to him than she'd ever been in the past. His eyes narrowed as he studied her profile. Like him, she had yet to open the file Jerome had given her. And while he couldn't fathom her thoughts, it was clear that her mind, like his, was on different things.

By the time Jerome had finished reading the next two pages, the legal pad in front of Chrys was covered with myriad pencil lines. A few minutes later the lines coalesced into something that looked suspiciously like a bicycle. Eric's left hand rose to cover a grin as she added training wheels to the sketch.

He liked her this way. Dreamy-eyed and a little distracted. He wanted to lean forward and fill his lungs with her lovely scent. She'd always smelled sweet, like summer rain. He wanted to close his eyes and remember. He wanted to reach out and touch her hand, her hair, her face. But he knew that he couldn't. Not with so many others present.

Edging just a little closer, he draped one arm casually on the back of her chair and continued to watch her draw, wishing that they could be alone. They needed to talk.

Chrys, oblivious of his thoughts, added streamers to the bike.

"Christmas?"

Chrys gave a guilty start at the sound of Eric's voice so close to her ear and quickly covered the designs with her hands. Then, with a sheepish smile for having been caught in the act, she nodded.

Instead of returning to her drawing, she placed the legal pad face down and laid her pencil aside. It wouldn't do to be caught doodling again. Not in such illustrious company.

She tried to pay attention but it wasn't easy. Jerome's voice, for all that he was well-spoken, was monotonous as he read clause after lengthy clause. Not to mention the fact that the subject matter was also exceedingly dry.

Once, in a fit of anger, she'd accused Eric of having more money than sense. Talbot, whether sensible or not, appeared to have had more money than he knew what to do with. As Jerome read on and on, it seemed as if he had left donations to nearly every organization in the county—and all with lengthy, involved and complicated strings attached.

Chrys frowned. And, as if listening to all this wasn't bad enough, there was always Eric. With his right arm draped across the back of her chair and his left hand resting on the polished surface of the dining room table only inches from her own, she was far more aware of his physical presence than she cared to be.

"Now, Chrys, this last bequest affects you."

Giving a guilty start at the sound of her own name, Chrys straightened in her chair and sent Jerome an apologetic smile for the wandering of her mind. Then, as the announcement registered, she said, "Me? I thought you already read the part where Talbot donated his papers to the archives."

"I didn't ask you here to represent the library, Chrys," Jerome explained. "Dr. Waller is doing that."

"You didn't?" She looked at him in blank surprise.

"No, I didn't."

Chrys looked around in confusion and found herself even more perplexed than ever as she became the object of scrutiny of several pairs of curious eyes. An unsettling frisson of unease ran up and down her spine and lodged itself uncomfortably in the pit of her stomach. If she wasn't here to represent the university, then why had Jerome asked her to come?

"Mary Kathleen," Jerome continued, "is a very lucky little girl."

"Mary Kathleen?" she asked. "Why would Talbot leave anything to my daughter?"

"I suspect—" Jerome looked through the top of his bifocals and grinned "—because he liked her."

"Well, I know he liked her." Chrys was still at a loss, although Jerome's words and the pleased reactions of the men and women around the table were finally beginning to sink in. "I'm sure it's very nice, but it's totally unnecessary."

Jerome's gaze slipped briefly from Chrys to Eric, then back again. "Well, I wouldn't worry about it, my dear. It was obviously something Talbot wanted to do and he could certainly afford the gesture."

Puzzled by something in Jerome's voice that defied definition, Eric sent the older man a sharp look, but Jerome's attention was focused on Chrys as she continued to protest the need for Talbot's generosity.

"Other than the fact that this was something he truly wanted to do, I can't tell you what Talbot had in mind, Chrys." Reaching inside one of his numerous folders, Jerome took out a sealed, legal-size envelope and handed it over to Chrys. "This might."

Chrys turned the envelope over and read her name and Mary Kathleen's in Talbot's bold hand. "I knew Talbot cared for Mary Kathleen. But I never expected anything like this."

"With today's inflation rate, I think you'll find that trust very handy when she goes to college. And I'm sure that Eric will make an admirable trustee."

While Eric had been both pleased and surprised to find that Mary Kathleen had meant so much to his father, the knowledge that he was to be the child's trustee—her sole trustee—came as a complete surprise. As Jerome read on, Eric found his surprise quickly turning to astonishment.

The bequest, like most of Talbot's bequests, was hardly as straightforward as it had originally appeared. Oh, it had all the obligatory phrasing about predeceasement or mental incompetency and it was certainly legal and binding, but the long and short of it was that should he, for any reason—any *personal* reason—refuse to administer the trust, the monies were to be turned over to the university's Political Science department and Mary Kathleen would receive only a token sum of five thousand dollars when she turned eighteen, not even enough for one year of college let alone four.

Although Eric managed to keep his expression from giving away his thoughts, he suddenly felt as if a cold, dark vise had settled around his heart. *Damn it, but the old man loved to manipulate!*

Everyone else in the room, including Jerome and Chrys, seemed to think that the trust meant that Talbot had cared for the child, but Eric, unfortunately, couldn't be persuaded to feel the same. In fact, all he could think was that the child, who had loved Talbot openly and honestly, was nothing more than a pawn in some obscure game the old man had wanted to play.

Eric's bitterness increased with the realization that if he refused to accept his father's managing hand, Mary Kathleen would be the loser. Oh, Chrys could try to contest the will on her daughter's behalf, but Talbot, by naming the university as the alternate recipient, had all but assured that the child would never see a penny of the trust unless things were done just so.

It was clear that Talbot hadn't just wanted to leave a sum of money to a lovely young child. For that, he could have named Chrys as the sole trustee. She was certainly capable of administering the trust.

As anger and resentment continued to build inside his stomach and chest, Eric found himself thinking that if Mary Kathleen had been his child he would have—

His child!

Eric's head jerked up at the thought. His eyes, wide and startled by his half-formed thoughts, sought first Chrys and then Jerome. Chrys was fumbling with her pencil, head down. Jerome was watching him. When their eyes locked, the older man's mouth twisted into a shape that was neither grimace nor smile. Both brows lifted owlishly and his head tilted—almost imperceptibly—to one side. Well? he seemed to ask.

Eric's hand rose to the breast pocket of his Western shirt in a gesture that was both acceptance and denial. At the sound of paper crackling beneath his fingers, his eyes widened further. He'd brought along the certificate he'd found last night. He'd been planning on giving it to Chrys.

Once again, Eric sought Jerome's eyes. Yet when they met over Chrys's head, he saw no answers in the other man's face. Only a single question that was the mirror image of his own.

Eric watched, almost objectively, as the hand he had placed on the back of Chrys's chair tightened into a punishing fist. Lord knew, he'd failed Chrys before. But could it be that he had failed her in this, too?

Closing his eyes, Eric bit back an angry groan. It couldn't have been easy for her, not if she'd been alone and pregnant with no one to turn to. Lord knew, Amos Gallagher wouldn't have lifted a hand to help. Had she tried to find him? Had she gone to Talbot only to be turned away?

Eric's eyes opened with a snap. Was that why she'd turned to Ken Morrissey? Because she'd been alone and afraid with no one else to turn to?

Leaning back in his chair, Eric looked at Chrys, seeking some kind of confirmation, but all he saw was a small, slender woman, who looked as confused as he felt. She was reading Talbot's letter.

"Eric?" Jerome's voice was empty of nuances. "I take it you're agreeable to managing the trust?"

"Of course." Eric nodded and somehow managed to force himself to act as if the rug hadn't just been pulled out from under his feet.

"Good." Jerome cleared his throat one final time and began to read Talbot's last bequest, the one that gave Eric absolute and total control over the remainder of his father's estate. There were no stipulations. No last bits of advice.

But Eric's thoughts were elsewhere. He didn't notice when Jerome stopped speaking, nor even when the other members of the little assembly got up and walked out of the room one by one until only Jerome remained. His thoughts, all of his thoughts, were centered on Chrys and her—their!—child.

Once she had begged him to make their relationship both public and permanent, but he'd refused, telling her that he wanted to protect her from Talbot. And the tragedy was that he'd really meant it.

Eric looked down at the will and felt the vise around his heart tighten. So much for sincerity.

He hadn't protected her at all. He'd only hurt her more.

Two days ago she had warned him not to look back. He'd thought she meant it as a general warning. Now he knew the real reason why. She was afraid of what he would find.

His shoulders sagged and his hand rose to rub at the tight knot in the back of his skull. Why hadn't she told him?

Jerome came over and laid his hand on Eric's shoulder. "You . . . uh . . ." He fumbled for words, cleared his throat again and then, unable to think of anything to say, settled into an uneasy silence.

Eric looked down at his copy of Talbot's will. Chrys hadn't told him, but Talbot had done his best to ensure that Eric would accept his responsibilities.

Accept them? Eric's breath caught in his throat as he felt his heart swell with a sense of pride and elation that he'd never known before.

Accept them, hell. He would welcome them! But he would do it with care and consideration for Chrys's feelings. No one would be able to accuse him of being a user. Not like his father had been.

Suddenly, angrily, Eric's fingers tightened around the legal sheaf, crumpling the papers beyond redemption.

Hadn't the old man held anyone or anything sacred? He swore softly, but with stunning vehemency.

"She's mine, isn't she?" he asked soberly.

Jerome didn't have any trouble following the younger man's train of thought. "I wondered. But I didn't know."

Eric's fingers were still tightened in a stranglehold around his father's will. How he wished it was Talbot's neck instead. Or maybe it would be better if it was his own neck. *He* was the one who'd let Chrys down.

"You suspected it." It was a statement, not a question.

"Yes," the other man agreed. "I suspected it."

"When?"

"Certainly when I read your father's will. Before that . . ." Jerome shrugged. "I'm not sure. Talbot always spoke of Mary Kathleen as if she were the grandchild he'd never had. I just never put it together."

"I know what you mean." Eric's laugh was without pleasure. Reaching into his breast pocket, he pulled out the copy of the marriage certificate he'd found last night and tossed it down. "I didn't put it together either."

Jerome picked it up, glanced over the names and dates, then looked back up at Eric. "I don't know if I should ask how or where or when first."

"I found this last night in some of Talbot's personal papers. I was going to ask Chrys if she knew why he had it." Eric bit back a bitter laugh. "Now I don't have to."

"Are you certain the child is yours?"

"As certain as I can be without asking Chrys."

Jerome took off his glasses and wiped the lenses. "Then you really don't know for sure."

Eric didn't even hear Jerome's comment. He was too caught up in his own thoughts. "If I'd known back then—God! I don't know, Jerome. I was so much in awe of Talbot. And as much as I resented him, I'd have given or done anything to make him proud of me.

"I took courses that I didn't want. I let him direct my life as if it was his own. I made friends with the right people. I wasn't Talbot's son. I was his pawn. And I was too afraid of losing his..." Eric's hands moved restlessly, searching for the right words. "I was too afraid of losing him to grow up."

His long fingers raked through his hair. "Chryssie was my only act of rebellion. But I loved her, Jerome. I really did. And I'd have done anything to keep her from harm.

"Can you believe it?" This time his bitter laugh rang around the room. "That's why we broke up. She wanted to get married and I wanted to keep her out of Talbot's reach."

He gave a disgusted sigh. "I couldn't do that if she was my wife. So I let her go. Hell! I practically shoved her out the door. And all the time she was carrying my child."

"Maybe the child's not yours, Eric."

Eric stood and rubbed the back of his neck with his hand. "What other explanation could there be? Look at the date on the marriage certificate. She married him just seven months after we broke up."

In spite of the seriousness of their conversation, Jerome laughed. "One doesn't necessarily lead to the other."

Eric glared. "Ken Morrissey was twenty years older than her. It says so right there. Look at their birth dates."

Although Jerome's face was still filled with humor, his words were decidedly dry. "I know what you're thinking, Eric, and you're wrong. Dead wrong."

Eric turned toward the high windows that overlooked the lawn. "Am I?" he asked bitterly. "Am I really?"

"Definitely." Jerome's answer was uncompromisingly firm. "You'd have known that if you'd ever seen them together. Don't delude yourself about that," he warned, though not without a bit of sympathy warming his words. "Ken loved Chrys just as much as Chrys loved Ken."

"I wish I could believe that." The sun glinted on Eric's hair, turning it to molten copper. "You know," he continued slowly, his heart twisting inside his chest, "yesterday I would have felt jealous to hear you say that, but today...

"God, I hope it's true." Lingering in the back of his mind was the fear that Talbot had somehow engineered Chrys's marriage. "I hope to hell my father never even heard of Ken Morrissey."

Turning around, Eric faced Jerome squarely. "I've seen how she's changed. I've seen how much faith she has in herself and I don't want—" Eric stopped himself short, took a breath and expelled it. "Whether Ken Morrissey loved her or not, it's obvious that she loved him. I wouldn't want *anything* to take that memory away from her."

Jerome recognized the anger that was building inside of his old friend's son and knew that it had to be defused. "Nothing should, as long as you stay calm. Let me check this out. Let me make sure of the facts."

"The facts seem pretty clear to me."

"What you're talking about isn't a fact," Jerome cautioned. "It's speculation."

"Why else would Talbot have her marriage certificate? Why else would he leave a trust to Mary Kathleen with such a bizarre stipulation?" Eric's voice rose with his frustration. "Can you give me one other sensible explanation?"

IT'S A HARLEQUIN HONEYMOON— A SWEETHEART OF A FREE OFFER!

HERE'S WHAT YOU GET:

1. **Four New Harlequin American Romance Novels—FREE!**
   Take a Harlequin Honeymoon with your four exciting romances—yours FREE from Harlequin Reader Service. Each of these hot-off-the-press novels brings you the passion and tenderness of today's greatest love stories...your free passports to bright new worlds of love and foreign adventure.

2. **A Lighted Makeup Mirror and Brush Kit—FREE!**
   This lighted makeup mirror and brush kit allows plenty of light for those quick touch-ups. It operates on two easy-to-replace batteries and bulbs (batteries not included). It holds everything you need for a perfect finished look yet is small enough to slip into your purse or pocket—4-⅛″ x 3″ closed.

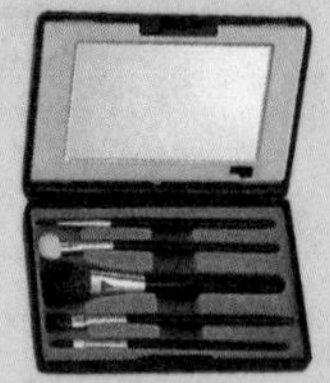

3. **An Exciting Mystery Bonus—FREE!**
   You'll be thrilled with this surprise gift. It will be the source of many compliments, as well as a useful and attractive addition to your home.

4. **Money-Saving Home Delivery!**
   Join Harlequin Reader Service and enjoy the convenience of previewing four new books every month delivered right to your home. Each book is yours for only $2.25—25¢ less per book than what you pay in stores. And there is no extra charge for postage and handling. Great savings plus total convenience add up to a sweetheart of a deal for you!

5. **Free Newsletter**
   It's *heart to heart*, the indispensable insider's look at our most popular writers, upcoming books, even recipes from your favorite authors.

6. **More Surprise Gifts**
   Because our home subscribers are our most valued readers, we'll be sending you additional free gifts from time to time—as a token of our appreciation.

START YOUR HARLEQUIN HONEYMOON TODAY—JUST COMPLETE, DETACH AND MAIL YOUR FREE-OFFER CARD

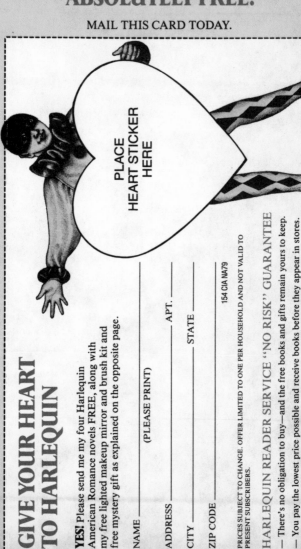

Jerome's reply was sobering. "A lot of things your father did never made sense to me. What about the child's birth certificate? Have you seen it?"

"No." Eric closed his eyes and took a deep breath. "But she told me that she was seven and that she was in the second grade." His eyes snapped open. "That makes her old enough to be my daughter."

"You *think* she's seven." Jerome persisted with a lawyer's ingrained need for caution. "It'll only take a few days to get the proof. Let it ride until then."

"Kids know how old they are." Eric picked up the crumpled will and flipped to the section concerning Mary Kathleen. "I've wasted too much time already."

"Damn! I can see why Talbot claimed that you used to drive him nuts with your single-mindedness."

Eric stopped, startled by Jerome's tone; then slowly, he began to laugh. "I never thought about how I must have appeared to him. Only about how he appeared to me."

"One of the follies of youth is self-indulgence," Jerome inserted with a dark glower. "What are you going to do?" he continued roughly. "Try and take the child away from her mother?"

Stunned, Eric blinked. "Take Mary Kathleen from Chrys? Are you crazy?"

"Well, if you go rushing over there, demanding your rights as the child's father, what can you expect her to think?"

Jerome's hands waved in exasperation. "If you're not careful you're going to hurt her worse than she's ever been hurt before."

"Chrys has got nothing to fear from me." His voice was firm.

"She has everything to fear from you." Jerome was just as determined. "Think about it. If you are the child's father, you could get equal custody. And with you living in New Mexico, she could lose half of her daughter's life. Winters here, summers there."

Not giving Eric time to interrupt, Jerome continued. "And if you're not the child's father and you rush around acting like you are or demanding rights that aren't yours to begin with, you'll only confuse and hurt the little girl. Is that what you want?"

"No. Of course not." Eric slumped back into a chair.

Eric wanted a lot of things, more each day. But none of them involved hurting Chrys or Mary Kathleen. But most of all . . . Most of all, he wanted it to be true. A child. His child. A chance to try again with the woman he'd always loved. A chance to build something for himself, and for them.

The slow, almost hopeful smile that eased some of the tension from the younger man's face told Jerome that Eric would allow himself to be swayed in this matter. Jerome's voice softened, taking on a persuasive quality. "Then take it easy. Don't rush into this blindly. Let me do some checking. Let me find a copy of Mary Kathleen's birth certificate. It shouldn't take more than a few days."

"And what do I do in the meantime?"

"You told me the other day that you were working on your dissertation. Is there any reason you can't work on it here?"

"Yes. No." Eric stopped, thought about it for a minute, then shrugged. "I could work on it here. At least for a while."

Jerome smiled when he realized that Eric was no longer protesting the need for caution. "Is it only the child you want?"

"No," Eric answered honestly. "It never was just the child."

"I didn't think so."

Jerome's eyes narrowed pensively. "You know, you can't write and study all the time. You're going to have to take some time off to eat and maybe even relax a little after a hard day at work. There's no reason you couldn't look up some old friends over the next couple of weeks and revisit some of your old haunts. After all, you haven't been back here in a long time."

Eric's lips lifted in a half smile and his eyes darkened at the images Jerome's words brought to mind. "Do you think Chrys can be wooed?"

"I think that will depend on you." Jerome grinned. "Talbot was always a very persuasive man. Surely you must have inherited something from him besides this house."

Eric grinned back. For once, the prospect of being Talbot McLean's son didn't sound like such a bad thing.

Chapter Eight

"How did I get myself talked into this?"

Standing in front of the bathroom mirror in nothing more than a full-length half-slip and a thin silk robe, Chrys frowned at her reflection.

Berta chuckled from her place in the doorway. "What's to talk into? The man's a hunk."

"Hunk or no, I should have had more sense." Chrys turned and waved the mascara wand at her friend. "And I would have too if you hadn't been so eager to offer your services as a baby-sitter."

"I love watching Mary Kathleen."

Berta's grin was wide and white. It reminded Chrys of a Cheshire cat. "You love meddling," she corrected, still waving the wand.

Berta's grin took a complacent turn and became rather smug as well. "That's because I do it so well."

Chrys ducked her head and began to gather up her makeup in order to hide the smile that tugged at the corners of her mouth. Berta always could make her laugh, even when she didn't want to.

"Now, Chrys," Berta continued to tease, "tell the truth. You really did want to go out with him. Otherwise you wouldn't have given in so easily."

"I thought I put up a pretty good fight."

Berta shook her head from side to side, in a gesture that connoted pity, sympathy and humor. "Chrys, even you must admit that a little polite side-shuffling and a 'I don't know if that's such a good idea, Eric' does not a firm negative make."

"Oh, all right!" Chrys spun around, her blue eyes bright and brimming with laughter. "I did want to go out with him."

Berta's brown eyes danced with laughter. "'Cause he's such a hunk, right?"

"No." Although Chrys was still smiling, there was something darker, something more serious hiding in her eyes. "And I wasn't curious either. So stop trying to play matchmaker. It's not what you think.

"He called up and said that he wanted to get together to discuss the trust Talbot left for Mary Kathleen. Well, that's fine with me. But I'm not skulking around and playing hide-and-seek for anyone. If we go anyplace or do anything, we do it in public. With an audience."

"Oooh." The single word rose and fell over several syllables. "Is this like getting back at him for all the times he didn't take you out?"

Guilty as charged, Chrys shrugged and turned back to the mirror, giving her makeup one final inspection. "It's more like cutting off my nose to spite my face. Not very commendable, is it?"

"Human," the tall, black woman corrected gently. "What's wrong with that?"

"What's wrong is that it isn't really fair to Eric."

Berta's dark brow rose at the note of concern in Chrys's voice. For someone who professed not to care, Chrys was doing an awful lot of worrying. "Eric's a big boy now. I suspect he can handle it."

"I don't know." Chrys, oblivious of her friend's thoughts, frowned on her way into the bedroom. "Sometimes I think he can; sometimes I'm afraid he can't. He was never mean or cruel, Berta. And I get angry at myself for wanting to get back some of my own."

"Sounds like you're the one who isn't all that certain."

"I wouldn't be surprised." Chrys slid out of her robe and quickly slipped into a thin miniblouse of blue silk and Banaras gold. Her fingers hesitated over the tiny hooks and her eyes darkened thoughtfully. "I keep telling myself that I don't care and then again..." Once more, she shrugged. "I can't explain it to myself, how can I explain it to you?"

"You don't have to explain it. I've been there, remember? One minute you know who you are and what you want, and then all of a sudden something happens to make you realize that everything isn't as cut and dried as you'd like."

"Yeah." Chrys laughed softly, but there was little humor in her tone. "Stupid, isn't it?"

Berta disagreed. "Not really. You were important to each other once. You know—" the older woman paused thoughtfully, as if she was debating the wisdom of her next words "—you told me about a lot of bad times last Monday night. But what I remember most is the look on your face when you talked about the good times."

The dark frown that hovered around Chrys's brow melted away as she smiled and her eyes grew soft and dreamy. "We did have more good times than bad," she added quietly.

"So," Berta urged, "admit that you've both changed and give yourselves a chance to find out if it's been for the better. What can it hurt?"

"I'm a coward." Chrys shook her head and tried to act offhand and nonchalant, but her fingers gave her away. They were trembling slightly as she smoothed the gold-trimmed fabric that ended just below her breasts and left her ribs bare. "I don't want to find out that I made the wrong choice back then."

"There isn't a chance in the world that you made the wrong decision eight years ago. Not when you loved Ken the way you did."

"I know that. It's just..."

"Chrys, don't go feeling guilty about the might-have-beens. All I'm saying is that what was the right decision then doesn't necessarily have to be the right decision now. Give yourself a chance."

"A chance to do what? Make an idiot of myself all over again?"

Berta wasn't fooled by Chrys's act. "Maybe you could be friends. Maybe more than friends. Maybe nothing. Take a chance. It can't hurt."

"Now there you're wrong." Chrys reached out for the yards of silk and gold that made up the rest of her dress. "It can hurt."

"And Eric McLean was the one who did all the hurting."

"No," Chrys acknowledged honestly, "he had help."

"At least you admit that much. You know that's a start." Berta reached out to stay Chrys's hand. "Hey. Didn't you promise to show Mary Kathleen how the sari went on?"

"Wha—? Oh, heavens, I can't believe I almost forgot. If you hadn't reminded me I'd be in Dutch for a month."

Chrys went to the top of the stairs and called for her daughter. A muffled reply floated up the stairwell.

It was a bit of a relief to know that her child's presence would curtail any further discussion of her feelings about this date. She wasn't ready yet to admit, even to herself, just exactly what she felt—or didn't feel—for Eric.

"Listen to that child, will you?" Berta's rich laughter floated across the room. "You'd think a hundred elephants were taking a slow march up your stairwell."

Chrys grinned, well aware of the meaning behind her daughter's determined stomp. "She's miffed and wants me to know it. I, on the other hand, am playing cool, levelheaded mother and trying to ignore it."

"And just what did you do to incur all this righteous wrath?" Berta asked.

"Nothing much," Chrys answered with a laugh. "I just told her she couldn't come out with us."

"She wanted to go to the restaurant with you?" Berta's eyes opened wide.

"No." Chrys's voice dropped lower as the slow, meaningful tread of her child's footsteps drew near. "She wanted Eric to change his dinner reservations. McDonald's was her first choice, but either Pizza Hut or Dairy Queen would have done in a pinch."

Berta laughed. "What was Eric's response to this?"

"He doesn't know about it yet. I declined on his behalf." Chrys's voice dropped lower still. "That's what put me in the doghouse."

Mary Kathleen hovered at the doorway until she had her mother's eye. "Did you call me, Momma?"

The words were sullen, but the watchful look on Mary Kathleen's pouting face told Chrys that the child was aware of the fine line she was treading. Deciding to ignore the petulance, Chrys nodded. "I'm ready to put on the sari. Do you want to watch?"

Mary Kathleen's whole body turned itself into a giant shrug. "I was watching cartoons."

Turning her back to pick up the length of rich cloth, Chrys sent Berta a broad wink. "Well, whatever you want, pussy willow. It doesn't matter to me either way."

Ignoring the child hovering in the doorway, she took one end of the silk and tucked it into the waistline of her half-slip. Her fingers moved nimbly as she continued to wrap the cloth until the thin, blue silk made a complete circuit of the floor-length half-slip.

As Chrys began to pleat the remaining fabric, Mary Kathleen dragged herself one reluctant step farther into the room. Berta and Chrys shared an amused wink over the little girl's head, when the child finally asked how much material went into one skirt.

"Seven yards."

"Twenty-one feet?" Berta's surprise wasn't feigned.

"Umm-hmm." Chrys nodded and continued folding the silk just in front of her left hip. "And most of it goes into this pleat right here."

"Why?" The child's lower lip was still stuck out, and she even managed a put-upon tremble. Yet despite her pose, Mary Kathleen's eyes were growing bright with interest.

Chrys's eyes met Berta's in the mirror and they both fought to keep from grinning. "To give the dress balance when I pull the material around me once again and drape the rest of it over my left shoulder."

Mary Kathleen reached out to touch the thick folds of blue silk that Chrys tucked into her waist. "It's pretty. All bright and shiny. Like gold."

"That's because it is gold. Or at least gold threads woven into blue silk."

"It is? Real gold?" Mary Kathleen forgot to pout as she leaned forward and touched a metallic design once again. "Where did you get it?"

"Your father bought it for me in Banaras, India, when he was over touring some industrial plants."

"Did you go with him?"

"Nope. I was busy taking care of you. You were too little to leave and your daddy was only gone for a week." Taking the remaining fabric, she circled it around her body once again and began to pleat the ends. Shaking the pleats down, she tossed the end of the cloth over her shoulder and turned. "Well? What do you think, ladies?"

Berta was impressed by the line and the design; Mary Kathleen was more practical. "Will it stay up without any pins?"

"It should, if I've done it right." She backed up, out of reach. "And if you don't tug on it."

"What if you haven't?" the child persisted.

Both Chrys and Berta laughed. "It'll stay up," Chrys answered.

Which, in Mary Kathleen's opinion, was no answer at all. "But—" The doorbell rang and the child whirled around and raced down the stairs, calling over her shoulder as she went, "I'll get it. I'll get it."

"Think she's over her miff?" Berta chuckled.

"No." Chrys took an assortment of thin gold bracelets out of her jewelry box. "But if I'm lucky, Eric won't give in when she demands that he invite her along."

"Ahh, now I know why she's so eager to answer the door."

"That was obvious from the start. Why else do you think she's been waiting around downstairs instead of getting under our feet up here?"

Chrys chuckled when Berta mumbled something about having to think like a child in order to outsmart one. "Feel like running some interference?"

"What are baby-sitters for?" Berta asked cheerfully and headed out the door. At the last second, she paused, watching as Chrys placed a thin gold-and-sapphire necklace around her throat. "Will you be long?"

"No." Chrys met Berta's eyes in the mirror one final time. Her grin was slow and just a touch wry. "I need to put on my earrings and then bolster my courage so I don't chicken out."

"Be still my heart," Berta intoned, then broke off with an abrupt laugh. "Listen to your daughter, will you? She's just asked Eric if he likes to eat at McDonald's. Ah, well, I'm off to effect a rescue. Something tells me you'd better hurry if you don't want to have to change into blue jeans and eat a Big Mac."

Chrys laughed too, but once she had the room to herself, she found that her comment about courage wasn't far off the mark. She hadn't been this nervous about a date in years. Was it just because of their past? Or was it the man himself?

But halfway down the stairwell, Chrys felt her world jump back into focus. Everything was normal. That is if you could call the scene below normal.

Berta—no help at all—had managed to curl her six-foot-plus frame up on the boot box and was smiling broadly. Eric, dressed to the nines in a three-piece suit, was down on one knee, an intent look on his face as he listened to Mary Kathleen's far from subtle plea for inclusion in tonight's excursion.

"Mary Kathleen," Chrys interrupted from her position on the landing. "I told you earlier. This subject is not open for debate."

Eric looked up, his eyes opening wide at the sight of Chrys as she stood framed in the back light of the bay window halfway up the stairs. The overhead light was soft yet emphasized all the glitter and gold of her dress and jewelry.

He felt as if all the wind had been knocked out of him. She was beautiful. More than that even. Regal. Foreign. Exotic. And sexy as hell, with her midriff partially bared.

Her long hair had been drawn to the top of her head in an intricate twist that seemed to defy explanation. And every time she moved, her body, from the bottom of her sandals to the tips of her long, dangling earrings, shimmered and sparkled with gold. Even her eyes, normally the color of the summer skies, seemed bluer than ever before.

"Do you like Momma's dress? It's got real gold in it."

"It's beautiful." Eric nodded, still on his knees. "But your mother," he added huskily, "is lovelier still." His eyes moved over her from head to toe. She'd always been pretty. At times, he'd found her beautiful. But never, not even in his wildest dreams, had she left him utterly speechless.

Chrys's breath caught at the caressing quality of Eric's voice and her left hand sought the support of the banister. Even after all these years he could still manage to make her feel as if she were young and blushing, a child trembling on the verge of womanhood. And tonight his appearance alone would have been enough to steal her breath away.

He'd left his boots and Stetson behind and he'd exchanged his jeans and sheepskin-lined jacket for an impeccably tailored suit. The fabric was wool and clung to his lean body lovingly. The color, neither blue nor gray but a soft blend of both, brought out the color in his eyes and enhanced the rugged, masculine texture of his sun-bronzed skin.

"Daddy bought it for her when he was in India," Mary Kathleen piped up.

Chrys closed her eyes in exasperation as a dark shadow of hurt crossed Eric's face.

"It's a lovely sari, Chrys." Slowly, he rose to his feet. Even more slowly, he held out a florist's box for Chrys to take. "You look beautiful. I didn't expect anything so perfect, so I'm afraid the flowers may have been a mistake."

Chrys came down the rest of the stairs and took the box from his hand. "Flowers are never a mistake, Eric."

"These are." He grinned, but the smile didn't reach his eyes. "They won't go with the sari. They're pretty, but they aren't elegant. Leave them here."

"No." Chrys opened the box and took out a large spray of miniature carnations. They were pure white tipped in blue, highly scented and both ruffly and frilled.

Eric was right. They definitely wouldn't go with her dress, but she'd seen the pain in his eyes and although it had been unintentional, she knew she'd hurt him badly by wearing the sari.

Taking off the jangle of gold bracelets on her right arm, Chrys turned to her daughter. "Mary Kathleen, would you run upstairs and put these in my jewelry box and then go into the sewing room and get me some of that white ribbon I used on your dolly's dress. I'll wear Eric's flowers on my wrist."

"Good idea, Chrys," Berta spoke up quickly and then, when neither Eric nor Chrys acknowledged her, she brushed past them, offering to help the child find just the right ribbon.

Alone with Eric, Chrys raised the tiny carnations to her nose, inhaling their spicy aroma. "I always liked carnations."

"I know." Eric's hand rose and his finger tapped one gold earring, setting it dancing next to her throat. "You don't have to spoil your elegant look for me.

"I bought these flowers for Chryssie. She was very young and very unsophisticated. I'd forgotten just how beautifully she'd grown up."

His fingers lingered over the jewels at her throat. This woman was no Chryssie. Suddenly, passionately, he wished he'd been there to see the changes.

"Eric." Chrys faltered over his name as he took the flowers from her hand and tossed them aside. "Eric," she began again, feeling strangely ill-at-ease. "I can change the dress. I've plenty of others."

"It's not the dress." He tried to hide his feelings behind a smile. "I like the woman who took Chryssie's place. She's very beautiful. Very elegant."

"Oh, Eric." How could she explain to him that his thoughts were all wrong? She hadn't worn the sari to remind her of Ken. She'd worn it for different reasons. Reasons that had to do with no one but him. The trouble was, the real reason was likely to be just as insulting as the wrong one.

"Eric." She stooped to gather the flowers he'd tossed aside. Holding them close, she rose. "Why did you bring them?"

"Why does any man bring a woman flowers?" He tried to smile again and failed.

"They could mean a lot of things." She paused, just as uncomfortable with his answer as he had been with her question. "Maybe you give everyone you take to a fancy restaurant a corsage."

This time his smile was a little more genuine. "Or maybe I just saw them and remembered how much you'd liked them and thought they might please you tonight."

"Or, maybe..." Chrys took a deep breath and decided that truth, no matter how painful, was the lesser evil. "Maybe they could mean that you know how important it is to me to have some visible proof that you're not ashamed to be seen with me."

Eric's jaw tightened at the old argument and the smile that had been hiding in his blue eyes died. "I've never been ashamed of you, Chrys. Never."

"I hope that's true." Chrys's fingers trembled as she touched the flowers first to her face, then to his. "I didn't wear this sari because Ken gave it to me. I wore it because it's the most flamboyant thing I own. I chose it, not to spite you, but because of you. I wanted everyone to know that Chryssie Gallagher was going out on a date with Eric McLean."

"You wanted... Oh, Chrys." His expression softened and his hand touched her cheek tenderly. "Have I hurt you that much?"

Chrys closed her eyes. She couldn't say yes. She couldn't say no. She wasn't sure how she felt. Or why. Except that all of a sudden she wasn't nearly as worried about the past as she was the future.

Eric, far more perceptive than he'd ever been in his youth, caught her hand in his and lifted it to his lips, flowers and all. "Would it help to know I've always thought carnations were gaudy and their scent too spicy and sweet?

"Believe me, Chrys. I want to be seen with you. And not just because you're such a beautiful woman."

Chrys's eyes blinked open in surprise. Her smile was slow in coming, but it grew, soft and warm, as she saw the understanding look on Eric's face. "I always did like carnations."

"And I always, *always* liked you."

Chapter Nine

The restaurant Eric chose was perfect. There was low music, a small, but not too crowded, dance floor and an extensive menu to choose from. Their table overlooked the snow-covered grounds, made bright by the pale light of the moon and the myriad pinpoints of white lights that were strung through the bare branches of numerous ornamental trees.

After the maître d' had ceremoniously lit a small candle on their table, he presented them with a menu handwritten in calligraphy and told them that both the waiter and the sommelier would be by shortly.

When the man bowed once more and took his leave, Eric looked up from the menu and grinned. "A sommelier? In Wisconsin?"

"A sommelier in Grant County." She laughed as well. "We're getting quite cultured. How about in New Mexico?"

"Oh, we're definitely big time. I live in Sorrento, which isn't even on a road map. Silver City, the nearest big town, has just about the same population as Platteville." He looked around, one brow lifted comically. "But nothing as fancy as this."

After the sommelier and waiter had both come and gone, Eric asked Chrys what she'd thought of his father's will.

"If you mean the trust, I don't know." She leaned forward, propping her chin in her palms and resting her elbows on the linen-covered table.

"Are you angry?"

"Angry?" She thought about it for a minute, then shook her head. "No, I'm not angry. More resigned than anything else." Her shoulders rose and fell in an apologetic shrug as she sat up and laid her hands flat on the table. "Your family has a disturbing tendency to offer mine money."

"Chrys—" Eric broke off, swallowed hard, then started over again. "I never meant it the way you took it."

"I know," she acknowledged softly, then shook her head. "We didn't come here to talk about that."

"Maybe we should." Eric reached out and traced the shape of her hand with one finger.

"No. It's in the past. Let's leave it there." Although Chrys's voice was firm, she didn't attempt to pull her hand away. "I read Talbot's letter and he seemed sincere, so I'll leave it at that."

"What did the letter say?"

"Nothing much. You can read it if you like. It was mainly a note to Mary Kathleen, telling her that since he didn't have any grandchildren of his own, he liked to think of her in that light."

"Have you shown it to her yet?"

"Yes. She was very pleased." Chrys felt her heartbeat quicken just a little as he laid the palm of his hand flat over the back of hers.

"Do you know what puzzles me the most about all of this?" she asked, trying to distract her own thoughts from the warmth of his touch.

"What's that?" Eric's thumb slipped under her palm and unconsciously began caressing the soft skin.

The last action was too much for Chrys's strained nerve endings. Gently, she pulled her hand away. "Two things," she continued quickly. "The first is why Talbot insisted that you administer the trust."

"I don't know, Chrys. I never did understand my father."

"Did you ever tell him anything about us?"

"No." Eric sat back. "Did you?"

"No." Chrys leaned back as well. "Do you know what really has me puzzled?" She didn't wait for him to ask. "I don't think Talbot saw any more of Mary Kathleen than her own grandfather did."

"You still keep in touch with your father?" Eric asked as the waiter placed their meals in front of them.

"Keeping in touch," she agreed, picking up her fork. "That's about the size of it. Mmm. The chicken marsala is delicious."

"This steak isn't bad either," Eric concurred. "Does your father still have his farm just outside of Benton?"

Chrys nodded. "Amos Gallagher and dairy farming are synonymous. I take Mary Kathleen down to see him about once a month, but he's never comfortable with us for more than a few minutes, and by the time we've finished lunch we're all looking forward to leaving."

"Why do you go then?"

"I don't know." Chrys shrugged. "I think Mary Kathleen ought to know her grandfather. And I guess because I worry about him. He's all alone."

She shrugged again. "After Ken died, it was easier for me to understand why he changed so much after my mother's death. I guess I keep hoping he'll stop being so cold and distant and change back into the warm and loving man I remember when I was six."

"Has he changed at all?"

"Not a bit." She smiled gently and shook her head. "And if you want a truly honest opinion, I doubt he ever will. Not after all these years. But I have and I'm learning to accept him the way he is."

"A semi-interesting stranger you share a genetic relationship with?"

Startled, Chrys put down her fork. "How did you know?"

"Going through Talbot's belongings helped me make that same conclusion about myself. I wish I'd had the courage to come back sooner. I might have even learned to like him, just for himself." He went on to say that he'd been going through some of the old family albums and that they'd been an enlightening experience.

"How so?"

"I'm surprised at all the good times I'd forgotten." Eric's thoughts drifted for a moment, lingering over some of the more memorable times. "Say," he continued more briskly, "I'm only going to keep a few of the pictures. Do you want the rest for the archives?"

"Maybe." Chrys sat forward eagerly. "It might help to round out the collection. Particularly if there are any of Talbot at political events or with other public figures."

"There're dozens of those. You can have them all."

Chrys nodded and laid her napkin on the table. "I don't know about all of them, but once I get a handle on Talbot's collection I'd like to take some of them. You might check to see if the Iconographic department at the State Historical Society in Madison would like some too."

"I'd forgotten about them. They're kind of a visual archives, aren't they?"

"Mmm-hmm. Anything to do with history in pictorial form. If you like, I can give you their number. You might want to talk to them before you go back home."

Laying his own napkin aside, Eric signaled the waiter to clear the table. Then, when Chrys turned down the offer of dessert, he asked her to dance.

She came into his arms easily, then gave a tiny start of surprise when his warm hand came to rest on her bare back. Looking up, she saw by his wide grin that Eric was aware of her thoughts.

"I think I like this sari a lot." His grin widened even more.

"You would," she answered dryly, then laughed and eventually began to relax in his arms.

She loved dancing and Eric was very good, holding her neither too tight nor too close. After a while, she closed her eyes and let the spicy scent of carnations and Eric's woodsy cologne drift around her head.

Eric tugged her a little closer when the music grew slower, dreamy and sweet, and Chrys found it very easy to forget about the past. She was enjoying herself immensely here in the present.

"Chrys." He said her name softly, barely whispering. "Would it bother you if I stayed around a bit?"

Her eyes blinked, overwhelmed by the serious expression on his face. For a moment, her breath was suspended in her throat; then instead of answering him, she asked him when his classes started again.

"I'm not teaching right now. I took this year off to finish up my Ph.D."

When she didn't answer right away, he turned and led her back to their table. The arrival of Jerome at the restaurant was a pleasant diversion, but a diversion nonetheless. It wasn't until Eric and Chrys were finally on their way back to her house that he continued his explanation. "I get back to Sorrento most weekends, but I've been spending most of my time in Albuquerque doing research for my thesis. I thought I could stay around here for a while since I don't have to be back any time soon."

Chrys pulled her coat closer, not quite sure what she felt. Part of her liked toying with the idea that he'd decided to stay because of her and what they'd once meant to each other. The other part of her was scared, for exactly the same reason.

"Don't you have to discuss your dissertation with your advisor?"

"My advisor knows what my dissertation is about and has already approved the outline. I don't have to see him again until I've completed my first draft."

"Your topic...you said you were writing about disputes concerning mines and...what? Land use?"

Eric grinned as he turned the car toward Chrys's house. "You've got a good memory. Specifically, I'm taking a historical look at the types of laws that have come into being as a direct result of mine operations."

Glad to have something other than her own nebulous feeling to talk about, Chrys seized the subject of his thesis gratefully. "Isn't that kind of a broad topic for a dissertation?"

"I've limited the perspective quite a bit by keeping my comparisons to laws that have come into being since the European colonization of this hemisphere. Also I've limited myself to four countries with large mining interests."

As Eric pulled into Chrys's drive, she asked him how many different types of mining operations were involved in his dissertation.

"Three," he answered. "Deep mines, open pit mines and placer or surface mines. And I know you're not any more interested in those at this moment than I am."

Then, before she could reply, he got out of the car and came around to help her out. In silence they walked side by side to the front door. It was only when Chrys reached for her keys that Eric spoke again.

"Is it too late for us, Chrys?" He took the keys from her hand and pocketed them. Then, laying his hands along the sides of her jaw, he lifted her face until her troubled eyes looked into his. "I'd give anything to be able to start over with you."

She looked down and away, unwilling to commit herself one way or the other. If they'd met as strangers, she'd have been both eager and willing to know him better. But they weren't meeting as strangers.

He waited for her answer, patient and undeterred.

"I like you, Eric. I like what you seem to have become." Chrys sighed softly, confused and uncertain. "But it isn't that simple. We've got too much excess baggage from the past to just start fresh."

"I'd like to try again, Chrys. It's very important to me." Eric lowered his head slowly, giving her every opportunity to turn away. She didn't meet his lips eagerly, neither did she resist.

As his lips brushed softly against hers, Chrys once again found herself surprised by the degree of tenderness and warmth he managed to put into a simple kiss. As his mouth moved persuasively over hers, she found it harder and harder to resist.

He tipped her face up, and she could feel the cold night air twining around her ankles and the warmth of his breath as it mingled with her own. She knew his hands were powerful and strong. She could feel muscle, sinew and bone beneath his suit coat. Physical changes. The new Eric.

Yet how far did those changes go? How different was he from the boy she had known? Had he grown mentally? Emotionally? Were they still too different? Or had they at last come to want the same things?

"Chrys," he whispered softly. "I won't hurt you. Not this time. Not ever again."

It was almost as if he had read her thoughts. Still confused, still uncertain, Chrys hesitated, then, just as quickly, capitulated.

Her hands were swift and sure as she lifted them to his neck. The fingers of her left hand caressed his nape while her right hand traced his jaw. "Don't lie to me about this," she pleaded softly, her lips a mere kiss away from his.

"I won't, Chrys. I won't."

She closed her eyes at his husky vow, knowing that for her it was already too late. It was more than want, more than need. *Oh, please,* she thought silently, *don't let me be falling in love again.*

For a moment, his kisses were enough. Warm and tender. Reassuring. Soothing. But when his hand remained on her face, when he made no attempt to take her into his arms, to deepen their embrace, Chrys found herself growing unaccountably impatient.

Desire, restless and unfocused, rose within her. Its presence was echoed by the almost silent moan that clutched at her throat. Her hand opened to trace his jaw;

her lips trembled and sought his. As her fingers tightened in his hair, her tongue probed his mouth delicately.

Eric groaned as her lips parted beneath his. When her tongue touched his, he felt his desire burst free of its tenuous restraint. His hands dropped, first to her shoulders and then to her back. When her fingers feathered across his shoulders, down to his chest and back up to hold his mouth over hers, it was all he could do to keep from crushing her slender body to his.

He'd dreamed of her like this. Open. Responsive. His. As she'd been in the past. As she was now. And as, God willing, she would always be. His forever.

Chrys's hand trembled as she stroked the nape of Eric's neck. His hair was as soft as the silk of her gown. His scent was strong and masculine, far more alluring than her own. But it was his mouth, warm and compelling, that called to her. Their kisses, hot and passionate as they had been, were no longer enough.

When his hand slipped beneath her coat, Chrys moaned softly. She knew it was near freezing out here on the porch. She knew his ungloved hand had to be just as cold, yet it burned like a brand when he touched her bare midriff. She shuddered slightly and buried her lips in the warmth of his neck between his coat and his chin. She didn't want him to stop.

Eric groaned deep and low as she nestled close, encouraging him. His arms tightened around her slender body and his mouth touched hers in passionate abandon and his hand sought for and found the softness of her breast.

"Chrys. Chrys." He whispered her name helplessly and pulled her closer still. "Chrys," he repeated achingly as he felt her begin to tremble. "Please believe me. I've never stopped caring for you. I've never stopped wanting you. I've never stopped loving you."

"Oh, Eric," she breathed, "I—"

"All right! All right! I'm coming. Jeeze! You don't have to keep ringing— Oh!"

The porch light flicked on and Berta grinned as the entwined couple sprang apart and blinked owlishly under the harsh glare of the yellow light. "Sorry," she tossed over her shoulder as she headed right back into the house. "If you don't want an audience, you shouldn't lean up against the doorbell."

She left the porch light burning in her wake.

"Damn!" Eric released Chrys slowly, reluctantly, watching her face as she backed away in embarrassment. "Chrys, I'm sorry. I—"

When he reached out to touch her arm, she jumped away as if scalded, then cursed herself for a fool. What on earth was she doing? Blowing hot and cold was hardly her style. Berta had taken her by surprise, that was all. She didn't have to make a federal case out of it.

She put her hands against her face and breathed deeply, then with a softly apologetic glance in his direction, she grinned and shrugged. "Damn is right. She could have turned off the light."

Eric felt as if a great weight had been lifted off his chest and grinned. It was a relief to know that Chrys wasn't going to try to deny what they had shared. "I was enjoying myself, but now I feel like a teenager who got caught trying to take liberties by his date's parents."

Chrys grinned back, equally relieved and piqued that Berta had left the light on. Kissing was one thing, but what they'd been leading up to— Well, she wasn't ready for that yet. No, not yet.

"Are you going to invite me in?"

The hesitation in her eyes was so brief that Eric almost missed it. He reached out and rubbed his thumb tenderly along her flushed cheek. "I want this to last, Chrys, and I know it won't if I push. If you ask me in I won't expect—or ask—for anything more than coffee."

She tilted her head to one side and smiled. "You know, I like you better now than I did in college."

Eric responded in kind. "I like me better, too."

Impulsively, Chrys leaned forward and kissed his lean cheek. "It's a nice improvement."

When they slipped through the front door, the foyer was empty. A loud whistling from the nether regions of the kitchen told them that Berta was busy making herself scarce. When Eric helped Chrys off with her coat, their eyes met, shied away, then met again.

"Do you recognize the tune?" he asked lowly.

"With Berta you're never too sure." Then in a raised voice Chrys called, "It's all right, Berta. You can come out now."

Berta stuck her head around the door and grinned. "I take it the evening was a success?"

"We had a wonderful time." Chrys nodded, certain that Berta's ear had been plastered to the doorway listening to every word. "Although Jerome almost didn't recognize Eric without his boots or Stetson."

"Jerome Weaver?" Berta asked. "It's nice that you met some people you knew."

Feeling herself start to blush at the accuracy of Berta's gentle gibe, Chrys turned and headed up the stairs. "I'd better check on Mary Kathleen."

"Well," Berta said, chuckling at Chrys's hasty retreat, "I think I'd better make myself scarce. If what was happening on the front porch was any indication, at least one of you is going to find me *persona non grata* if I stay."

Eric held her overcoat as she slipped into it. "Berta, could I ask you something before you go? Something about Chrys and—" He stumbled over the other man's name. "Chrys and Ken."

"If I can reserve the right not to answer." Berta stood back, her hand hesitating over the wooden buttons on her coat. "What was it you wanted to know?"

"Did you know them long?"

"From the day they moved in." Her head nodded toward the house next door. "I live right there."

Eric's eyes were clouded, thoughtful. "What was he like?"

Berta pursed her lips, then answered honestly. "Kind, generous. Never the kind to begrudge anyone anything."

Eric nodded. Chrys would have needed someone like that. He turned and moved away, then turned again. "What did he look like?"

"Look like?" Berta parroted, for once at a loss.

"Was he tall or short? Dark or light?"

Berta's brow puckered as she tried to figure out what he was getting at. "Dark hair, dark eyes. Not too tall, not too short. He was nice enough looking." She was even more puzzled when none of her speculation made sense. "Why do you ask?"

Eric didn't meet her eyes. "I just wondered if Mary Kathleen took after his side of the family."

"Anyone who's ever looked twice," she began slowly, thoughtfully, "knows that Mary Kathleen's the spitting image of her mother."

Eric closed his eyes briefly. Yes, Mary Kathleen was the spitting image of her mother. Not at all like the man Berta had described.

When he'd arrived at the house tonight and Mary Kathleen had answered the door, he'd looked deep into her face, searching for signs of himself. But it had been a waste of time. He'd never been any good at picking out features and similarities. All he'd seen was a face that made him think of how Chrys must have looked when she was a little girl. Except that Mary Kathleen's world was a lot safer and a lot more secure. What right did he have to take a chance on damaging that kind of security?

"What are you getting at?" Berta's voice was dark with suspicion and concern for her friend.

"Did Ken love her, Berta? The way she needed to be loved?"

Berta's eyes widened in surprise. "Yes," she answered hastily. "Yes, he did. Utterly and completely."

The relief Eric felt was overwhelming. Whatever the outcome of their relationship, old or new, at least Chrys had had that much.

"You know," Berta said, moving forward and giving Eric a very intent, scrutinizing look, "I think there's more going on here than either you or Chrys want to admit."

Eric shook his head, half denying Berta's unvoiced accusations.

The expression on Berta's face didn't change but it was clear what she was thinking. "If you'd asked me if Chrys loved Ken, I'd have put it down to male ego or even masculine pride. But to ask if Ken loved her—and be glad that he did..." Berta's eyes narrowed thoughtfully once again. "You've got it bad, haven't you?"

Eric's lips twisted into a half smile. "I guess maybe I have."

"Well, well." Berta was starting to smile. "There might just be some hope for you yet."

"You think so?"

"Maybe. Just maybe." At the sound of Chrys's footsteps on the top of the stairs Berta buttoned up her coat, pulled on her hat and turned her back on Eric. "Well, Momma, which was it? Asleep or awake?"

"Sound asleep." Chrys smiled, her eyes all soft and maternal. Then she noticed her friend's coat. "Oh, Berta, aren't you going to stay for coffee?"

"No. I don't think I will." Berta's eyes moved thoughtfully from Eric to Chrys and back again. "I think you two have a lot to discuss tonight and I'd just be in the way." She waggled her fingers in a wave and left.

Chrys was puzzled by her friend's uncharacteristic quick exit and her parting remark. "Now what did she mean by that?" she mused aloud.

Eric cleared his throat abruptly. "Mary Kathleen was so intent on staying awake, I half expected her to still be up."

"What—? Oh." Chrys smiled as she turned away from the back door. "The spirit was willing, but I suspect that the flesh was weak. Still, to give her her due, she'd set her clock to ring in another half hour."

Eric chuckled. "She's a determined little thing, isn't she?"

"I did try to warn you."

"So you did. Still, you have to admire her ingenuity."

"You mean her ability to get her own way," Chrys added pointedly.

"Ah." Eric had the grace to look ashamed. "I knew I made a tactical error the minute I made that offer to take her to McDonald's tomorrow."

"So you did." Chrys turned his own words back at him but smiled to soften the bite.

"Will it help if I promise not to do it again?"

"Actually it would probably be best if you simply canceled out."

"I don't want to do that, Chrys," he answered soberly. "Not unless you insist. There've been too many times in the past when I've let people down. But I'll let her know that I'm on to her now and that I won't let it happen again."

"And if I don't agree, I get to play the heavy, right?"

"No." His hand reached out and he caressed her cheek lightly, trying to tell her so many of the things that had to remain carefully hidden in his heart. "I'd never do anything to come between you and your daughter. If you don't want her to go, tell me and I'll take the blame. She'll never know you had anything to do with it."

"Kids are smarter than you think."

Eric smiled and let his hand fall to her shoulder. "What if we change it from a twosome to a threesome and spend the afternoon shopping at the mall in Dubuque? That way I'll still keep my word but it won't be quite what she had in mind. How's that?"

When Eric's fingers tightened over Chrys's shoulder she gave up trying to figure out the right and the wrong of it all and moved willingly into his embrace. "I'd like that very much."

He kissed her then, just as she had known he would. And his kiss was warm and compelling, just as she had known it would be. And then he let her go.

"Maybe you should go and get the coffee Berta started."

"Mmm," she agreed halfheartedly. "Maybe I should. Why don't you start a fire?"

"The fire's already been started."

Chrys grinned and broke away. "In the fireplace, Mr. McLean."

Eric chuckled as she disappeared into the kitchen.

"What were you and Berta discussing so intently?" Chrys called from the other room.

"Mary Kathleen," he called back, telling himself that this was one time being totally honest could only hurt. "What about you and Jerome? The two of you had your heads so close together when I went for our coats that I didn't think I'd ever get you apart."

"Business," she answered, coming back into the room with a tray. "I told him I thought some of your father's papers seemed to be missing. He was pretty upset."

Eric took the tray away from her and set it down on a nearby coffee table. "Anything special?"

It took her a minute to realize Eric was talking about his father's papers. "I don't know. It's kind of hard to tell what's there and what's not since I haven't completely appraised the collection yet."

Her shoulders lifted and fell in a brief, noncommittal gesture. "They'll probably turn out to be nothing of any real value or interest when we do find them."

Eric cleared his throat. "I've been cleaning out his desk and personal files the past couple of days and saw some stuff that may be what you're looking for. Did Mark bring them over yet?"

"Mmm-hmm." Chrys nodded. "That's what got me started looking for these other papers. There were some references that didn't make any sense."

Putting his arm around Chrys's waist, Eric pulled her down onto the couch. Her bare flesh was warm against the palm of his hand. "I'll keep my eyes open."

Grinning, Chrys straightened the sari over her shoulder. "Me too."

"Why," he asked the room at large, "do I have a feeling that we're not talking about the same thing?"

Looping her arms around his neck, Chrys sobered. "Maybe because we're not. Remember what you promised, Eric."

"I won't forget." His eyes and mouth smiled softly as his finger set one of her long earrings dancing. "Nice. And slow. And easy." He punctuated each sentence with a kiss.

Chapter Ten

Acquiring Mary Kathleen's birth certificate turned out to be more difficult than Jerome had expected, but Eric found that he didn't mind nearly as much as he'd thought he would. For, as much as he wanted to know whether the child was really his, Eric was finding other things even more important.

In fact, he enjoyed the week immensely. Going out with Chrys, shopping *en famille*, eating a quiet Sunday dinner, had shown him just how much he'd been missing. He hadn't realized how important—and how comforting—those kinds of activities could be. Especially when they involved spending time with Chrys.

At the end of his second full week in Platteville, Eric had established a routine for himself. He spent his mornings working on the rough draft of his dissertation. And his afternoons were divided equally between clearing up his father's estate and daydreaming about spending more time with Chrys.

Then fate stepped in and lent a hand, giving him a perfect excuse to look her up in the middle of the day.

A drawer in an out-of-the-way corner of the house revealed another cache of Talbot's political papers. That in itself wasn't so unusual. Eric had been finding papers tucked here and there ever since he'd started putting his father's house in order. What was nice, though, was that this particular collection of miscellany was large enough to warrant a special trip over to the archives.

After getting directions from a perky coed at the checkout desk, Eric made his way down the back stairs and into Chrys's domain. The main room was large and silent. The term had ended just the day before and all the students had left. In fact, the only person in sight was Chrys.

A slight smile played around the corners of Eric's mouth as he watched her work. Her head was down, so it was hard to see her expression, but he could imagine a tiny, concentrating frown. A jacket, in a dusky rose color, was draped across the back of her chair, and the cuffs of her silk blouse were rolled back revealing slender, fine-boned wrists.

And her hands...he'd always loved her hands. They were beautifully shaped with long, slender fingers and tapered nails. She'd had a way with her hands, a way to make a young man crazy with wanting. He could just imagine what she could do to a grown man.

Realizing that he was letting his thoughts carry him away, Eric tried to banish his erotic musings by clearing his throat. "Hi, Chrys."

Startled, Chrys dropped the papers in her hands and looked up.

"Sorry." His grin was charmingly lopsided. "I didn't mean to startle you."

Tossing her pen to one side, Chrys returned his look. "Well, I can't exactly deny that you did. Not when I jumped nearly a foot off my chair."

Lounging in the doorway to her office, Eric found himself hard-pressed not to rush into her office and gather

her up in his arms. For all that she was as neat and as precise as the proverbial pin, her cuffs turned back just so, she still managed to look soft and touchable. Eminently touchable.

Perhaps it was because her hair, in spite of its rather elegant twist, was slowly but surely beginning to slip—just a little—and a number of soft tendrils were clinging to her face and neck. Nothing would have pleased him more than to reach out and touch her just then.

He smiled, a gentle light warming his eyes. "You look like you could use a break," he said softly, enjoying the moment.

Defensively, Chrys's hand went to her head and a number of the clinging tendrils disappeared. "That bad, huh?"

"Hardly," he replied dryly. "I've never seen you look less than lovely whether you were in scruffy jeans or a thousand-dollar sari."

His words had been light and teasing, but the glimmer of indefensible truth in his eyes made Chrys flush and look down. She'd learned to accept compliments, but this one, coming from him, was enough to make her feel both flustered and thrilled. But then, Eric had always managed to make her feel that way.

She stumbled over an awkward thank-you and rushed on. "But I'm sure you didn't drop by just to tell me that. What can I do for you?"

Eric grinned. Straightening up, he held out a sheaf of papers. "Shall I paraphrase Kennedy? Ask not what you can do for—"

More at ease with this kind of teasing, Chrys held up her hand. "No quotes. Not today." Waving Eric into the chair across from her desk, she reached for the box of papers. "It looks like Talbot really started squirreling things away, didn't he?"

"Tell me about it," Eric agreed. "You'd never believe where I found these. I wonder if the old man—" He shrugged and shook his head ruefully. "Talbot, the man I remember, was so compulsively neat that it really feels kind of strange to find bits and pieces of his life scattered about."

"You think maybe he was a little senile toward the end?"

Eric stopped in surprise. He hadn't really thought that at all. "Was there something wrong with him?"

Chrys frowned. "Not that I know of."

"Jerome said he was with him just a day or two before he died and that he seemed just as sharp as ever."

"I know. Mark said the same thing. But it still seems kind of strange that he would— Oh, never mind. It's hardly important now. Was there something else?"

"Well, when I was going through these—" he nodded to the papers in her hand "—I noticed that several were about land disputes. Most of them were old and had been settled years ago. But there was one, or part of one, that seemed to be more recent. Something about a mine up in northern Wisconsin. Do you remember seeing anything about that?"

"No, I can't say that I do." Chrys shook her head. "I've only examined about half of your father's collection. But if there's anything like that in the half that's done, there'll be a file card on it in that box. Why don't you look in there while I glance over these and then if you don't find what you're looking for, we can take a look at the inventory sheets. They won't be as complete, but they'll give us a place to start."

"I'd appreciate it."

After Chrys had read through the papers and Eric came up empty in the files, they both tackled the remaining stacks of uncataloged materials. Half an hour later, Chrys sat back and sighed. "Something tells me this isn't going to be as simple as it looks."

"No kidding." Eric sat back as well, rubbing at the ache in his lower back. "The man was a political pack rat."

Chrys grinned. "Now, now. Don't speak ill of the dead. Besides, archival librarians love pack rats."

"Strange people, archival librarians."

"Look who's talking." Then before he could come up with a reply, "Are you planning on using any of this for your dissertation?"

"I doubt it. Most of my research is already done."

"Then why this?"

"I don't know." Eric shrugged and managed to look both boyish and masculinely appealing at the same time. "Curiosity, mostly. I didn't know we had anything in common, then when I found this..." He shrugged again. "I guess I just wanted to see it for myself."

"Eric?" Chrys hesitated, then quickly, before she lost courage, blurted, "Can you think of any reason why someone might want to take some of your father's papers?"

Startled, he sat up. "No, can you?"

"No," she admitted reluctantly. "But it's becoming pretty clear that there are papers that are missing from the collection."

"These?"

"These and several more."

"Are you sure?"

"Positive." Her shoulders slumped in defeat. "But I don't have any proof. Just a hunch and what looks like the beginnings of a code."

"A code?"

"Yes. Turn that top sheet over. Do you see those letters in pencil in the bottom left-hand corner?" When he nodded, she continued. "I think your father used some kind of code to catalog or cross-reference his collection."

"Do you know how it works?"

"Not completely. But I'm getting bits and pieces. Trouble is, he doesn't use it on every record. Just certain ones."

She stood up and went around the desk. Leaning over Eric's shoulder, she pointed to the bottom line. "I'm pretty sure this number refers to the paper you're holding. The other numbers, the ones that go up from here, I'm not so sure about, but I think they refer to other papers on the same general topic."

"Have you looked for those numbers on other pages?"

"I have. And I've found a lot of them. Enough to make me think that I'm right. The problem is that I haven't found enough to draw any valid conclusion about the system. Besides, sometimes I run into a whole series of numbers that don't seem to exist anyplace else."

By now, Eric was frowning as well. "Do you have a couple that do work?"

"I think so." Chrys quickly sorted through some of the papers she'd already shelved and handed them over to Eric. "See?"

"Yeah." After a moment, he looked up. "Why can't we just put them in order and see what's missing."

"We can. If we can figure out the system. But I haven't been able to do that yet. The way your father was setting up his collection is totally different from what I'm doing for the archives."

Chrys continued. "Normally, I'd retain Talbot's system, but with all the records coming in helter-skelter, I can't figure out what the original order was. All I do know is that they don't appear to be chronological or filed by subject.

"And then, just when I do think I've got a handle on something I find that one of the lines has been penciled out or it's got a letter next to it, or something else really weird."

"Maybe he did that to indicate that something was thrown away?"

"I thought about that. But some of the ones that are crossed out are still a part of the overall collection."

"Have you talked to either Henshaw or Spencer about this?"

"Of course," she uttered on a tiny sigh that was both frustrated and amused. "And neither one of them has paid it any mind. I think Mark thought I was nuts and I'm sure Sam Spencer thought I was looking for something mysterious and intriguing to light up my life."

"That sounds like Spencer," Eric replied absently. "Listen, Chrys. This seems like a pretty elaborate system. Wouldn't Talbot have kept a record of it someplace?"

"If he'd meant for someone else to use it, yes. But not if it was meant just for his own use. And since neither Mark nor Sam knew about it . . ." Her shoulders rose and fell, signaling her frustration. "Personal notation systems just aren't the kind of thing you keep a separate file for. They either mean something to you or they don't."

"Like photographs in an album?"

"Exactly."

"Chrys," Eric began slowly, "the papers that are missing, can you tell what they were about or when they were written?"

"Not for sure. There are gaps throughout the whole collection. And like I said, whatever order your father used, it wasn't chronological."

"Can you take any kind of an educated guess?" he persisted.

Caught by something in his voice and in his eyes, Chrys frowned. "I don't know. I— Do you have an idea?"

"Maybe." He fingered through one of the piles again. "Tell me what you think. I don't care if you're right or wrong at this point. I'm just looking for a starting place."

"If you want an off-the-wall, no-facts-available guess, I'd have to say that the biggest gaps seem to be during the past two or three years. But I don't know that that's unreasonable. Your father was getting older. He was less involved."

"Older maybe," Eric agreed. "But less involved I'll never believe. One thing about the old man that never could have changed: if there was a pie around, he'd simply have to have his fingers in it."

Chrys thought about it for a minute, then agreed. Whatever else Talbot McLean had or hadn't been, he'd never been one to sit quietly on the sidelines. "I don't even know where to begin."

"I think I might." There was a rising enthusiasm in Eric's deep voice. "There's an album at the house."

"A photograph album?" she echoed.

"Yeah."

Puzzled, Chrys sat back down at her desk. "How could that help us?"

Eric shrugged, but his eyes were alight with the possibilities. "I don't know for sure that it can. But it might be a place to start. If we could figure out where he was and who he was with, we might also be able to figure out what he was doing. And maybe, just maybe, the two match up."

"I'd recognize most of the people if they were influential." Chrys leaned forward, her own enthusiasm for the project growing. "After all, that's part of my job. But the places would be harder. Still, I doubt Talbot sneezed but what the local paper knew of it. And what they don't know I'd be willing to bet Mark or Jerome do.

"You know," she said with enthusiasm, "if we all put our heads together, we might just be able to come up with something."

"Chrys..." Eric hesitated, not perfectly sure if his reasons for wanting to keep this between the two of them were valid.

Arrested by the dark look on his face, Chrys faltered. "Oh, Eric, I can't believe—"

"I can't either. But who else had access to Talbot's papers?"

"Mark. Jerome. But why would either of them—"

"I don't know that either of them would. But if—and it's a big if—if it was one of them..."

"All right," she agreed reluctantly. "But I'm sure you're wrong."

"And I hope you're right."

"So. Where do we begin?"

"Let's concentrate on finding all references to this piece." Eric tapped one of the papers he'd brought with him that morning.

"The mine in northern Wisconsin?"

"Yeah." He nodded. "You can start checking out your code system and see what you can come up with. Meanwhile, I'm going to start making a few calls."

Surprised, Chrys tilted her head to one side. "Who would you call?"

"I've made some contacts with my thesis work that might just help."

"Here in Wisconsin?"

"No. But I don't live too far from Santa Rita—it's a big open-pit copper mine. There's a man down there who could help. I'll give him a call later."

"But would he know anything about a copper mine in Wisconsin?"

"Wait till you see his grapevine," Eric warned. "He's got it beautifully trained."

Chrys laughed, then cautioned him that trying to find out if the missing papers were real or imagined could take a lot of time.

"I've got time." Eric came around to her side of the desk. He touched her face gently, his fingers light against her cheek. "I told you last week that I'd be staying for a while."

"Eric . . ." Chrys started, then, not knowing what else to say, fell silent.

"Don't be angry with me." His finger felt callused against the smooth skin of her jaw. "I just want to give us both a chance to see if there's anything left to build on."

Fighting to keep her eyes from closing and her body from succumbing to his touch, Chrys stiffened her spine. "I'm not angry."

"Scared?" he asked with tender concern.

That brought her eyes up, flashing with defiance and pride. "Wouldn't you be?"

He leaned forward, brushing his lips against her cheek. "I'm way past scared. I'm verging on petrified." His hand slipped to her shoulder and began doing wonderful things to her nervous system.

Chrys shot him a dark look in spite of her body's desire to respond. "For someone who's supposedly petrified, you seem to be making all the moves."

Eric eased his weight onto the corner of her desk. "I said petrified," he said with a grin. "Not dead."

Tilting her head to one side, Chrys studied him with a contemplative air. "Why," she began suspiciously, "do I have a feeling that there's something more to this than you're telling me?"

Feeling guilty about his questions concerning Mary Kathleen, Eric stiffened. "What do you mean?"

"If I knew what I meant, I wouldn't need to ask. Now would I?"

He almost asked her then. But as he hesitated, the minute was lost. If the child was his, she would still be his in a few days' time. If she wasn't his, then he needed time. He needed to make Chrys care for him and want him as he wanted her. And more, he held back because of his own fears. He knew if he asked her now, she would misunderstand and think that Mary Kathleen was all that he wanted.

Chrys straightened as well. "There is something else, isn't there?"

"Like what?" *Damn, but she was always too perceptive.*

"I don't know. That's why I'm asking you."

When Chrys's brow furrowed in suspicion, Eric forced a light, teasing tone to his voice. "Maybe you've got the guilty conscience."

"Me?" Chrys's eyes widened in surprise. "Not a chance. What about yours?"

"I'm as innocent as a newborn babe."

"This isn't a game, Eric." Getting up, she paced to the other side of the room. "We're talking about my life. You hurt me once. I don't want to be hurt again." She wheeled, her chin lifting, her eyes dark with determination. "And there's so much more to consider this time around."

"Mary Kathleen?"

"I won't have her hurt," she warned, still standing defiantly on the other side of the small office.

Eric stood up and moved away from the desk. "I wouldn't do anything to hurt either of you, Chrys."

"I'm already taking more chances than I feel comfortable with." Her hands trembled as she straightened a stack of books that had no need of straightening.

He was so close that she could feel his breath on the back of her neck. "Are you telling me that you want me to leave?"

Her fingers fumbled and she nearly tipped the whole pile over. "I don't have the right to do that."

"Dammit, Chrys." Eric took her in his arms and turned her around. "You have every right."

His eyes were dark and sincere. So sincere that Chrys's heart skipped a beat and thumped erratically in her chest.

"Chrys," he continued honestly, "you're the only reason I'm here instead of back in New Mexico. You have to know that."

"What about your father's papers?"

"All right. I'm curious. I'll admit it. But I could leave those in a minute if I had to." His hand rose to touch her, first her cheek, then her brow. "You, I'm not so sure I could ever leave."

Though she remained stubbornly silent, Eric persisted. "I'm not going to let your fears chase me away. Not if that's all that they are. Just fears."

Chrys refused to speak.

"Dammit, Chrys," he pleaded impatiently. "If you don't care for me at all then send me away, but if there's a chance then let me take it." He drew a ragged breath then continued, his words tight and clipped. "I've changed. But I'm sick to death of saying it. Can't you see the changes? Can't you believe in them?"

"I can see them." Chrys turned her head, her eyes unfocused on the books by her side. Her voice shook. "I'm just not sure I can trust them."

"Why not?" His hand, large and strong, was as gentle as a light summer rain as it brushed against her hair. "Give me one reason, Chrys, one good reason for not believing what you've seen of me. Help me understand what still stands between us."

"I don't know if I can trust my own judgment to be objective," she confessed softly. "You see, I want to believe in those changes almost as much as you want me to believe in them."

She moved forward, into his waiting arms. "The truth is, I want us to have another chance, too."

CHRISTMAS DAY dawned bright and clear. The air was crisp and invigorating, but not so cold that it hurt to breathe. Although he'd never fully reacclimatized himself to the north, his steps were more sure. And fortunately, there were few icy patches between his house and Chrys's to test his newfound skills.

Taking the front steps two at a time, Eric smiled with pleasure. Chrys had invited him over for Christmas dinner—without any prompting from her friends or any hinting from him. He considered it a major coup.

Pushing his Stetson to the back of his head, he rang the doorbell. She'd told him to dress casually, that gifts were unnecessary and that if he wanted he could bring a friend.

Well, he'd dressed casually: boots, jeans and a thick flannel shirt. He'd made up his own mind about the gifts: two tiny packages tucked snugly away in the sheepskin lining of his jacket. One for Chrys and one for Berta. And he'd brought a friend: Max.

"Hi," he said softly when Chrys opened the door. Stepping forward, he lowered his lips to hers. She was soft and warm, smelling of spice. "I brought a friend."

Flustered, Chrys backed away, overly conscious of her audience of two. No, make that three. A terrier, head tipped, ears cocked, tongue lolling, had nudged his way forward to join Mary Kathleen's giggles and Berta's snicker.

"I didn't know you had a dog," Chrys observed.

"I don't." Eric smiled, just as pleased as punch, knowing that he'd come up with the perfect solution to one of Chrys's problems. "You do."

"Me?"

Before Chrys could utter another sound, Mary Kathleen's delighted shriek split the air and she flung her arms first around Eric's waist in an excited babble of thanks and then around the dog's neck.

Equally as excited as his new friend, the dog began to bark. Loud and sharp.

Mary Kathleen laughed in delight; Berta groaned at the sound of impending doom; and Chrys stiffened in anger. Eric said, "Quiet, Max," and all sound ceased.

The tail, what little there was of it, of course, still wagged.

"Sit."

Down went the tail, but Max still managed his best doggie grin. He knew love when he saw it and the kid clinging to his neck was all his.

Never a particularly slow child, Mary Kathleen decided that both she and the dog would be happier—and safer—outside. "I'll take him out where we can play, Momma. Come on, Max. Let's go."

Eric still hadn't caught on. Grinning down at the delighted little girl, he said, "You say 'heel' when you want him to follow you."

"Heel, Max." Mary Kathleen made for the door. Berta choked back a muffled laugh and quickly disappeared into the kitchen. Strangled sounds could still be heard from behind the door. Chrys still hadn't moved. That was when Eric first caught the first inkling of unease.

"Chrys?" he asked hesitantly, "is something wrong?"

"Wrong?" Furious, Chrys turned on her heel and walked away. "Don't you dare ask me what's wrong." Then, eyes narrowed, hands clenched into tight fists, she whirled back. "Obviously I've seen Mary Kathleen's present. What did you bring me?"

Eric was too stunned by her anger to do anything other than hand the gift over.

Refusing to touch the gaily wrapped package, Chrys glared at it as if it were something loathsome. She recognized the wrap. She'd bought Mary Kathleen's jewelry at the same shop. "Earrings? A pendant? What?" she asked angrily.

"A brooch."

She turned and faced the Christmas tree, her arms wrapped tight around her waist. "Dammit, Eric."

"Chrys, what did I do wrong?" he asked, reaching for her.

She shrugged off his hand and whirled, her words scathing. "You can't buy me, Eric McLean. Not me and not my daughter."

Eric started to protest, then stopped, knowing she wouldn't believe him. "Chrys, I'm sorry."

As angry as she was, it didn't stop her from noticing that he seemed utterly sincere and that made her angrier still. "A seven-year-old kid tells you she wants a puppy and you just run right out and buy her one."

"I didn't think there was any reason why I shouldn't."

"Any reason why you shouldn't—" Seething, Chrys fought to control her temper as she stormed around the living room.

"Well I didn't," he added defiantly.

"You should have," she shot right back.

"What do you want me to do? Take the dog back?"

"Don't be ridiculous!" she snapped. "The one thing you can't do is take back a dog." Then, still caught up in her righteous fury, she raged, "I thought we had this out once before."

Eric groaned, only now aware of the similarities. "You're talking about McDonald's."

Chrys didn't bother to reply. Instead, she turned, picked up the fireplace poker and gave a burning log a tremendous poke, wishing all the time that it was Eric instead.

"Chrys, I don't think it's the same."

"It's not the same." She swore softly and replaced the poker before she was further tempted to do him bodily harm. "This is far worse."

"Why?"

"Why? *Why?*" Chrys spun around, her fists braced stiffly on her hips. How on earth did he manage to sound so innocent when he was as guilty as sin? "Don't you dare pretend that you don't understand."

"I'm not pretending anything." His own temper started to rise along with his voice. "I *don't* understand."

They glared at each other, neither one backing down until Eric finally sighed and ran one hand around the back of his neck. "I thought you objected to a puppy," he began reasonably.

"Damn right I did."

"So I bought her a dog."

One hand arched upward in an "oh, now I see it all" gesture, but she didn't say a word. She was angry, far too angry for words.

"Look." He ran his hand over his hair again. "I'll admit I made a mistake."

"That's all you do."

More hurt by her cutting words than he wanted to admit, Eric turned away. "Yes, I know. But I still don't understand why."

"You do not give children live pets without their parents' consent."

"Dammit, Chrys, we're not talking about that dog and you know it. Mary Kathleen has pets up the wazoo."

"Fish. Turtles. Hamsters."

"And a guinea pig and a cat. Chrys, this place could get funding as a zoo."

He drew a long, ragged breath. "It's not as if she's irresponsible. She takes care of them all. You've told me that a hundred times. You even told me that you liked the fact that she had all these pets. That it was a way of teaching her responsibility."

"And you also heard me say no to a puppy."

"Yes, I've heard you tell her no to a puppy. But I've also heard you tell her that you didn't want one because you wouldn't have time to train it. I didn't think you objected to the animal. I thought you objected to the time it would take to train it. So I got a dog. A trained dog. He won't give you any problems and he will give you protection."

"Protection from what, for heaven's sakes? This is Platteville, not Chicago or Los Angeles." She glared. "And the only thing I seem to need protection from is you."

"Chrys."

"How much did you spend on that dog?"

"Chrys." He understood now. And wished he didn't.

"How much on the brooch?"

Sighing, Eric backed away. "I never had a chance, did I? You never even tried to accept—" Unable to go on, Eric turned away.

Chrys nearly cried when he walked away. She did cry when she heard him tell both Mary Kathleen and Berta that something had come up unexpectedly and that he was going to go away for a few days and that, no, as much as he wanted to, he couldn't stay for dinner today.

The minute the front door shut behind him, she wanted to call him back. But she didn't. She knew it was better that way.

Chapter Eleven

"He's really neat, Momma."

"Yes, I know." Chrys didn't have to ask whom Mary Kathleen was talking about. In fact, she hadn't talked about anything but Max all day long.

Mary Kathleen kicked off her slippers and climbed into bed. "He likes me, too."

"I'm not surprised." Chrys tucked the covers up around her daughter's chin and tapped the tip of her nose teasingly. "You're a very nice little girl—most of the time. But not," she added with motherly wisdom, "when you're trying to put off your bedtime."

Momentarily distracted, Mary Kathleen giggled and snuggled down under the thick quilts, giving her mother an artless smile. "Eric said he'd been to obedience school."

Chrys returned the child's guileless smile with one of her own. It was a very forthright "you're-not-fooling-me-for-a-minute-young-lady" kind of smile. "Mmm. I've been thinking a lot about obedience training recently."

"Aw, Mom."

"Aw, Mary Kathleen."

The child giggled and returned to the subject at hand. "Blue likes Max."

"That doesn't surprise me. That guinea pig is too indolent to dislike anyone who isn't a threat to his lettuce patch."

"What's in—indo—"

"Indolent. Lazy. And you're still stalling."

Mary Kathleen grinned, unrepentant and unabashed, as she continued her bid for more time. "Hezekiah's not indolent."

"Mmm." Chrys spared the gray-and-white tabby at the far end of the bed a sympathetic look. She knew just how he felt. Suspicious. Ruffled. Put out. Ticked off. Any of those words would do. "I don't think Hezekiah shares your enthusiasm for Max," she added dryly.

"He will." Mary Kathleen was a born optimist and, as was any healthy young child, a bit of an opportunist as well. "You'll like Max, too, Momma. Once you get to know him."

Yet in spite of the fact that she knew her daughter was trying to manipulate her, Chrys was concerned, truly concerned, about the troubled look in Mary Kathleen's eyes.

She knew what Mary Kathleen wanted her to say—that the dog had been a wonderful present—but Chrys wasn't ready to relent. Not when she still had reservations about Eric's intent in giving them the terrier.

"Don't you think so?" Mary Kathleen persisted.

"I suspect Max and I will get along just fine...if you keep him off your bed at night."

Chrys looked down at the terrier, who was curled into a tight ball, his bright eyes watching her every move, his expression just as guileless as the child's. As much as she hated to admit it, Eric's choice had been flawless. The dog and her daughter would make an unbeatable pair.

She told her daughter as much.

Mary Kathleen giggled; then, in an abrupt change of subject, she hunched herself up on one elbow. "Is Eric really going away?"

Chrys sighed under her breath and fought to keep her expression noncommittal. She had no one but herself to blame for bringing him up. Besides, she'd have had to be blind not to know that that question was coming sooner or later. "That's what Eric said this morning. Remember?"

"Yeah, but—" Mary Kathleen darted an apprehensive glance at her mother, then plunged on. "I didn't think he'd really go. Not after you got over being mad at him."

Leaning back against the bedpost, Chrys tucked her knees under her chin, wrapped her arms around her legs and gave her daughter a long, appraising look. Mary Kathleen was growing and with it, she was becoming surprisingly perceptive. Just like her father.

Mary Kathleen looked up at her mother. "Are you real mad at him?"

All this perception was a bit disconcerting to have to deal with at this age. "No." Chrys smiled wryly. "I think I've gotten over the worst of it now."

The child perked up. "Then he can stay?"

"That's not our decision to make, pussy willow. Besides, you already know that Eric lives in New Mexico. Whether he goes back this week or next, sooner or later he *will* go back."

"Can't he stay in Tally's house?"

As angry as she'd been, part of Chrys sympathized with her daughter's question. Reaching out, she brushed a lock of hair away from Mary Kathleen's brow. "He could, if he wanted to. But he won't."

"Why not?" the child persisted.

Chrys's smile was very solemn. "I know you liked Talbot, but he and Eric were never close. Not like you and I are."

A dark frown settled across Mary Kathleen's face. "Kind of like you and Grampa Amos?"

"Just like me and Grampa Amos." Chrys nodded. The child was even quicker than she'd thought. "I love your grampa and Eric loved his daddy, but that didn't mean that either one of them was easy to live with."

Mary Kathleen thought about that for a while, then settled back under the covers. "I don't like going to visit Grampa Amos very much. He's kind of grouchy all the time and stares at me a lot. It makes me feel kind of weird."

"Well," Chrys pulled the covers up once again and tucked them snug, "I think that's how Eric feels about staying in his father's house even though Talbot isn't there anymore.

"Now," she said as she leaned over, her voice firm as she kissed her daughter's soft cheek, "I suspect you'd best stop worrying about what Eric's going to do and get some sleep."

"Momma?" The hesitant tone of Mary Kathleen's voice stopped Chrys at the door. "Can I keep Max?"

Chrys turned, her blue eyes warm with love and understanding. That question had been very hard for her daughter. "I thought you weren't going to ask, that way I couldn't say no."

Mary Kathleen looked guilty as charged, then grinned sheepishly back at her mother. "I didn't ask about Pete but you made me give him back anyway."

Chrys shuddered. "Pete was a snake. If I were you," she added repressively, "I'd stop while I was ahead and settle for the dog. Now go to sleep."

Mary Kathleen ducked under the covers. "Night, Momma."

"Good night. I love you."

Chrys closed the door softly. After a moment—as she'd half expected—she heard Mary Kathleen snap her fingers quietly. There was a brief click of doggie nails on the wooden floor and then an abrupt, warning hiss from Hezekiah before the room once again settled into its own form of peace.

Folding her arms across her chest, Chrys sighed, knowing that she was going to let her daughter get away with having the dog on the bed in spite of what she'd said earlier.

Heading downstairs, she felt unaccountably alone and lost. She'd learned to live without Eric once and she'd learned to live without Ken. Ken couldn't come back, but Eric had.

Chrys sighed. She hadn't wanted to admit it, not even to herself, but she'd had hopes, high hopes, that there might have been something to build on. Something other than memories.

In the past, she'd been able to conjure up Ken's face. She'd been able to remember all the good times they'd shared. And now...

And now, conjuring up Ken didn't seem to work. Eric, for all of his sins and all of his faults, was far too near. And far too real.

ALTHOUGH ERIC HAD TOLD Chrys he was going back to New Mexico, he hadn't been able to just pick up and leave. There were too many loose ends for that. And then, when he was finally in a position to go, he found himself wanting to make one more attempt at setting the record straight.

But Chrys was proving elusive. There hadn't been a car in her garage or a light in her home for more than a week. Berta was nowhere to be found either, and Mark, when questioned, only knew that since the university was practically dead over Christmas break, Chrys had taken a few days off to visit a relative somewhere "up north."

As the days progressed with no sign of Chrys, Eric worried that remaining in Platteville would only prove to be a waste of time. Especially when Chrys seemed to be unwilling—or unable—to separate the past from the present.

Yet, he had his moments of hope as well. He knew she was attracted to him. He'd felt it every time he'd taken her into his arms. And he'd even begun to suspect that deep down, beneath all the protective shielding, she'd begun to care for him as he cared for her.

The chance that she might listen to him, given enough time and space, was a slim one. But it was one he wanted to take. Even if it meant getting hurt. Even if it meant failing. Eric knew that he would have to try—at least once more.

Yet as the days passed, his resolve weakened. He'd just about decided to give up, when an unexpected call gave him another reason for staying in town.

"Eric." A burst of static broke across the phone line with an annoying buzz, then abruptly disappeared, leaving the speaker's next words echoing hollowly across the miles. "I'm glad I caught you in."

Eric didn't recognize the speaker. "Who is this?"

"Joe. Joe Beniki. Listen, I haven't got but a minute to make this call. I'm going to be back in Wisconsin early next week. Let's get together. What do you say?"

"I'd like that, Joe," Eric answered absently. "But I've been thinking about going home in a few days."

"To what?" the other man asked. "The only thing you've got waiting back there for you is a pile of junk mail and your dissertation."

Eric sat up, a warning bell going off in his head. Until last month, he hadn't heard from Joe since their fraternity days, and now, twice within one month.

"I don't recall mentioning my dissertation to you."

In spite of the thinness of the wire, Joe's voice grew stronger and a bit amused as he recognized the suspicion in Eric's answer. "You didn't tell me a lot of things, but I know them just the same."

"Like how to find me when no one else did?" Eric's tone was cautious, a bit reserved. No one else had known anything about him since he'd left Platteville—not even the state he'd lived in since his return to the U.S. Suddenly, it struck him rather strange that Joe, a man he hadn't known all that well, was the one person who had managed to keep track.

"That and more." Beniki chuckled, amused by Eric's telltale caution.

"What's going on, Joe?"

"Nothing much. I ran into your father a while back and you came up in the conversation."

"Are you telling me Talbot kept track of me all these years?" Eric's voice rose in surprise.

"Well," the other man hedged, "not exactly."

"I didn't think so." Eric leaned forward, holding the phone's mouthpiece close. His curiosity was well and truly piqued. "So, Joe, how did you know where to find me?"

"I'll tell you all about it when I see you next week. Okay?"

"If I'm still here."

There was a brief pause, and what sounded suspiciously like a muffled curse. "Did you ever hear of a place called Indian River?"

"The copper mine?"

"Sounds like you've been doing your homework." Joe's satisfaction was apparent in his tone of voice. "Hang on a sec."

There was a muffled pause, as if Joe had put his hand over the receiver and begun to confer with someone else. Eric frowned, wondering what was going on. And what, if anything, Joe could tell him about the papers that seemed to be missing from his father's collection.

"Listen, Eric." Joe's voice came clear across the line once again. "I've got to go. They're calling my flight."

"Where are you?" he asked quickly.

"Right now? New York. Tomorrow, I'll be on my way to D.C. But come next week Wednesday I'll be at your place, drinking your father's best booze and spilling my guts out—if you're still there." Then, before Eric could form a reply either for or against, the connection was severed.

Eric dropped the receiver back in place and frowned absently. How much did Joe really know about the Indian River project? And why all the mystery?

The next day, when Eric met with Jerome, he considered asking the older man what, if anything, he knew about Joe Beniki or Indian River, but in the end he held back. Few people had had access to Talbot's papers right after the old man's death. Jerome was one of them. Eric couldn't be too sure Jerome had nothing to do with their disappearance.

Over lunch, the two men covered a variety of topics, hopping from one subject to another at will, until Jerome asked Eric how much longer he would be able to stay in Platteville.

Eric grimaced, knowing that his answer depended on Chrys. "I'm not sure. I've taken a leave of absence until next fall, so I suppose I could stay until then if I had to, but I'm getting anxious to go back home."

"Well, personally, I hope you stay. It's been nice having you around." Jerome took another swallow of his drink. "Talbot would have been proud of the way you turned out."

"Thanks, Jerome." Eric let the older man's comment about his father slide. This trip back had helped him get over a large portion of his resentment, but he'd never feel at home here.

"An old friend called and, frankly, he's got me fairly curious about what he's been up to lately, so I suspect I'll be here a bit longer. But one way or the other I think I'm going to have to cut my ties with Platteville."

"I thought maybe things were better this time around." As a closet romantic, Jerome had hoped that things had been progressing well between Eric and Chrys.

Although it was more of a reflex action than any reflection of pleasure, Eric managed to grin. "I guess some things just aren't meant to be. Still, I didn't drag you off to lunch to discuss that.

"I'd like to have you talk to the city council for me and see if they've got some use for my father's house. You can tell them that I'll remodel the building and put starting funds in a trust for any kind of social-aid program they want to set up. Anything, that is, as long as it's useful and doesn't turn out to be a shrine to Talbot's memory."

Jerome studied the bottom of his glass thoughtfully. "That's a very generous offer. Are you sure you want to do that?"

Eric shrugged. "I've got no use for that place and it's too large to be anything but a white elephant for anyone else."

"The city'd probably give you zoning clearances to turn it into apartments or condos if you'd ask. You could make quite a bundle on it if you did."

"I'm not looking to make money off my father, Jerome. I just want out."

"I see." The older man nodded thoughtfully. He'd respected and admired Talbot for years. But even he had to admit that his friend had failed when it came to his son.

"I guess you and Talbot were just too much alike and too different to ever get along. But I'd hoped you'd be able to put that all in the past."

"I think I have, to a certain extent, Jerome. But I'll never be comfortable here. And it doesn't look like there's anything here for me." Eric hesitated, then looked up, meeting the other man's eyes questioningly. "Not unless you've heard something?"

"Not a word." Jerome shook his head and frowned. "I really should have by now."

"What's the problem?" Eric leaned forward, resting both arms on the table.

"It's beginning to look like the birth records just don't exist." When Eric started to interrupt, Jerome held up his hand warningly. "Oh, it's not possible. Not in this day and age. The record's there. The trick is just figuring out where."

"Maybe Talbot—"

"No." Jerome shook his head at Eric's willingness to paint his father black. "Even Talbot couldn't have arranged anything like you're talking about."

"I don't know...."

"Come on, Eric, be reasonable. Whatever other flaws your father might have had, cover-ups just weren't his thing. Talbot was never anything but scrupulously honest. Besides, what would have been the point?"

Eric, who'd seen his father as anything but scrupulously honest, stared at the older man in surprise. He really meant it. Jerome Weaver truly believed that his father had been above reproach in that respect.

Reaching over, Jerome patted Eric's arm encouragingly. "When I didn't have any luck in Wisconsin, I started checking around in the neighboring states. But it's harder to get records there. I don't have the same..."

"Strings to pull?" Eric's smile took the sting out of his words.

"Contacts," Jerome corrected, also grinning. "But I will find it and when I do, I'll let you know."

CHRYS OPENED THE DOOR reluctantly. She knew who was calling on her. She'd known Eric was still in town almost as soon as she'd returned. "I thought you were leaving, Eric."

Eric thought of several replies to her abrupt statement, but knew that she wouldn't want to hear any of them. He shrugged and tried to act as if his palms weren't sweating and his heart wasn't beating double time. "I changed my plans."

"I know. The Platteville grapevine is quite effective," she answered stiffly, not wanting to meet his eyes. She was afraid of what he might see in her own.

"You've been gone."

"We spent a few days with some relatives up north."

"I heard." Eric attempted a smile. It fell short. He cleared his throat and went on. "An old fraternity buddy called a couple of days ago. I think he might know something about those papers we've been looking for."

Chrys looked down and away, making no attempt to ask him in or speak. He hadn't needed to come over here to tell her that. A phone call to her office or house would have done just as well.

She'd suspected that his reason for coming by had to do with their fight on Christmas Day. And that was something that she didn't want to discuss.

"Aren't you going to invite me in?"

"I don't think so." Chrys squared her shoulders and stepped back. "It's late and we really don't have anything to say to each other." When Eric reached out his hand as if to touch her, she jerked her head back and away. "Don't."

His hand dropped slowly back to his side. "Am I that much of a threat to you?" he asked sadly.

Chrys took a deep breath and released it in a tight and angry sigh. She'd gotten over being angry with him—at least a little. But each day she'd grown angrier and angrier with herself.

"Look, just say whatever it was you came to say and leave. I don't have the time or the energy to play games with you tonight."

Ignoring the angry confusion in her eyes, Eric stepped inside the foyer and closed the front door behind him. "Chrys, tell me what's wrong."

"Nothing's wrong. It's just been a long and trying day. You're making it even more trying by not going away when I ask you to."

"Are you still angry about the dog?"

Chrys turned her back to him, hiding her face from his probing eyes. Anger didn't come into it. Hurt. Disillusionment. Disappointment. Those emotions were only the beginnings of what she was feeling.

She'd thought he understood her fears. She'd thought he really cared about her and about her feelings. She'd thought—no, she'd hoped that they might have had a second chance.

She was tired of being alone and lonely, but she wanted someone who could help her face each day. She wanted someone to love. Someone she could share her life with. Not someone who would try to buy her affection.

"I didn't do it to hurt you, Chrys." Eric put his arms around her and turned her to face him.

"I know this has always been a sore point for us in the past, but I wasn't trying to buy you or even impress you. I just wanted to give you both something you would enjoy. I picked the brooch for you because I thought it would look nice on the dress you were wearing at the library the other day. And," he confessed, "because I didn't know what else you might like."

"What made you think I'd like jewelry?"

"Most women do." When she started to interrupt, he laughed, but there was little humor in the sound. "I thought it would be a safe bet."

"Bad choice," she said darkly, turning away.

"So I found out." He reached out and caught her arm, keeping her near. "Next time I'll know enough to stick to flowers. You seemed to like them well enough."

Chrys looked up, meeting Eric's gaze for the first time, her eyes wide with surprise. Next time? Was he really thinking there would be a next time?

When she saw and recognized the dark look in his eyes for what it was—desire—Chrys turned abruptly away. She didn't want him to look at her like that. Not tonight. Not when she was feeling more vulnerable and alone than she'd ever felt before. She shouldn't have let Mary Kathleen stay up north.

Realizing where her thoughts were leading, Chrys panicked and sought to cling to the remnants of her anger. "What about the dog?"

"The dog?" Eric echoed, lifting his hand to her shoulder.

"The dog. You know. Max, the expensive, purebred terrier." She shook his hand off.

"You didn't need to buy Mary Kathleen a dog because you couldn't think of anything else she might like. Anyone who spent more than ten minutes in a mall with my daughter would have had complete access to her entire Christmas list. In fact," she continued tightly, wanting only for him to go away, "it was about the most unsafe thing you could find to give her."

"Honest, Chrys—"

"Honest?" she scoffed. "Don't make me laugh."

"Chrys—"

She wheeled, her hands balled into tight fists. "Why can't you be honest and admit what you did?"

"You want honesty?" he ground out in a tight gritty voice. "All right, I'll give you honesty. Total honesty. But I don't think it's going to be what you want to hear."

Chrys glared, her eyes bright with defiance. "Did you ever stop to think that honesty might just be the one thing I *could* accept from you?"

"That's rich, coming from you."

Chrys stiffened, then turned and walked to the bottom of the stairs. If this was all he had to say, she didn't need to wait around and hear it.

"I'm sorry." Eric took off his Stetson and fingered the brim. "I didn't mean it to come out the way it did."

"Just what did you mean?" she asked with icy control.

Eric sighed and tossed the hat down on the padded seat of the boot box. "Only that I don't think you've been any more honest with me than I've been with you."

Chrys paled briefly, then crossed her arms defensively across her breasts. "This is just another trick to sidetrack me, isn't it?"

"No," he sighed. "No tricks."

"Well then?" She didn't change her stance.

In spite of the challenge in her eyes, Eric shrugged out of his coat and hung it on the nearby coatrack. "I wasn't trying to buy you with that pin. But I can't *honestly*—" he emphasized the word, giving it extra meaning "—say that my intentions were as altruistic with Mary Kathleen."

He turned, meeting Chrys's hostile gaze directly, and ignored her pointed remark that she hadn't asked him to make himself at home. "I was honest when I said that I didn't think your objection was to the dog, only to having to train a puppy. I wasn't honest in leaving it at that."

While Chrys stood formally by the newel post, Eric moved restlessly around the foyer. "And yes, I *honestly* knew that if I got her the dog, she'd . . ."

He paused, looking for the right words to explain his actions and what they'd meant without condemning himself completely in Chrys's eyes.

"You didn't need to buy an expensive, obedience-trained dog just to gain Mary Kathleen's affection." Chrys glowered. "At her age, a Cabbage Patch Doll would have accomplished the same thing for a whole lot less."

Trying to make a joke out of it, Eric attempted a dismal grin. "Aside from the fact that they're basically pretty ugly, they're not nearly as warm and affectionate as the dog."

Chrys was not amused. "Why, Eric? I mean she's a nice enough kid and I'll admit that the two of you really seem to click, but why would you want to try and buy my child's affection?"

Eric's hand clenched so tight that his knuckles shone white. "I did it because she's my daughter and you'd have let me go back to New Mexico without ever telling me. That's why."

"Your *what*?"

"Chrys." Eric took a step forward but stopped when Chrys backed up. Slowly, as though he feared that she would slap his arm aside, he held out his hand in a tentative gesture of truce. "Don't you think we've played enough games? Isn't it time we sat down and talked about this?"

"You've got to be kidding." She didn't sound angry. Just stunned.

"It's all right, Chrys. I'm glad it's so." He forced himself to smile reassuringly in spite of the turmoil in his mind. She wasn't reacting the way he'd expected. She wasn't defensive. She wasn't defiant.

Wide-eyed, Chrys looked up. Surely he didn't think—

One look at his face told her that he did. Moving away from the newel post, Chrys walked toward the center of the room, her voice as confused as her thoughts. "Why on earth would you think she was yours?"

"Chrys, don't," he pleaded softly, hurt that she would try to deny it.

"Why?" And when he didn't answer, she became insistent. "Why? What would make you think such a thing?"

"Because of the trust. Because of the way my father insisted that I take the responsibility for it. And because Mary Kathleen's seven years old."

More confused than ever, Chrys stopped where she was. "What do either of those things have to do with anything else?"

"Talbot obviously knew something I didn't when he made me her guardian."

Her eyes widened as she began to get a glimmering of how his mind had worked through his jumbled facts. "Eric—"

Eric wasn't ready for any easy denials. "And you married Morrissey right after we broke up. I know because I saw a copy of your marriage certificate. Talbot had it."

"Eric—" Chrys tried again.

"And," he finished quickly, "I want her to be."

"Well, at least one of your reasons holds water." Chrys's reply was acerbic enough to catch his attention. "Eric, I'm sorry if it's what you wanted. But she's not yours. She's mine. Mine and Ken's."

"Talbot had a copy of your wedding certificate." Eric was sure of his facts.

"I can't help what Talbot had. Or even what he thought." Chrys took a tentative step forward. "It's true. Ken and I were married shortly after you and I broke up." She touched the back of his hand hesitantly, strangely unwilling to cause him more pain now that she had the perfect weapon. "But Mary Kathleen isn't yours."

"Then why can't Jerome find a copy of her birth certificate anywhere?"

"Maybe because he's not looking in the right places. Ken and I were living in Georgia when she was born."

"Are you sure?"

"Of course I'm sure." Chrys was both touched and exasperated by his question. She touched his hand again, pressing it warmly with her own. "Believe me, Eric, if she had been yours I would have found a way to let you know."

Eric didn't say anything, but his shoulders seemed to slump.

"I'm sorry."

"Me too." He turned toward the door, defeated, ready to leave. There was nothing here for him. The child wasn't his and Chrys wasn't any closer to loving him than she'd ever been. The one hope he'd had, the one hope he'd been able to cling to, was gone. It was surprising how much that hurt.

"Eric," she called softly. "Why didn't you just ask me?"

"I don't know." He turned and shrugged. "A lot of reasons, I guess. None of them make much sense right now."

"Were you afraid I'd lie?"

"Maybe. I don't know," he repeated helplessly. "Maybe I was just more afraid to know the truth. I really wanted her to be mine. Ours."

He moved back into the room, until he was only a step away from Chrys. His hand rose and rested warmly on her neck. "I've let you down in so many ways. So many times. I'm sorry, Chrys. Truly sorry."

Chrys swallowed the hard lump that had lodged itself in her throat. "Is that— Is that what this taking me out and asking about your father's papers has all been about?"

"No," he whispered once, then once again, more urgently. "No. No. It was never that."

Wordlessly, Chrys dropped her defenses and walked into his arms, feeling as if, at last, she was on the verge of coming home.

"How could you think such a stupid thing?" The words, hoarse and aching with love, were lost in her hair as he closed his arms around her. He wasn't sure that he could ever let her go.

"It isn't hard when you're as insecure as I've been," she answered hoarsely, her arms looping around his neck.

"Chryssie Gallagher might have been insecure. Lord knows I gave her reason." His lips moved to trace a line of kisses along her jaw and his hands held her tight. "But Chrys Morrissey's got no reason at all."

Chrys sighed, her eyes certain in some ways, uncertain in others. "Doesn't she?" she asked tentatively.

"I love you, Chrys." Yet even as he said the words, Eric knew that they weren't enough. In the past, and for him, the words had always been easy. Too easy. And they'd both known it. But in bed, making love together, he'd never lied to her. Not once.

Stooping, Eric lifted Chrys into his arms and headed up the stairs. The time for words was past. Long past. It was time to show her what she meant to him.

Chapter Twelve

"Eric," Chrys whispered uncertainly as he shouldered the bedroom door aside.

"Chrys," he murmured in a low, soothing voice. "Words aren't going to change how we feel."

Four short steps, and he had crossed the room. At the side of her bed, he lowered her legs to the floor and steadied her. When she gained her balance, his hands closed gently around her throat. He held her face up to his. *Trust me,* his eyes begged silently. *Trust me to care for you. Trust me to love you.*

Chrys shivered under the open heat of his eyes. The urge to give in was great, perhaps too great. She hesitated, trying to muster the strength to say no.

Eric lowered his head. Their lips brushed, met and brushed again. He tempted her over and over. His lips were soft and warm. Always asking, never demanding. And in the end, Chrys wasn't sure if she could remember her name, let alone what she'd been going to say.

Right or wrong, she needed him now. Tonight. As much, maybe more, than he needed her.

Sensing Chrys's acquiescence, Eric's heart began to pound. His mouth sought hers again and again. Lips parted, they kissed. And as each kiss broke, he tempted her more with the tip of his tongue until she moaned softly and reached up to hold his mouth to hers.

Their tongues touched. A game. Touch. Retreat. Touch again. Passion built, growing and swelling with each moist caress.

Eric filled himself with the taste of her mouth. Soft. Slightly parted. Moist beneath his. He breathed deep, filling his lungs with her sweet scent. She was as warm as a winter's fire and as welcoming as a summer's breeze. She cleansed his soul. She brought him hope. She made him whole.

His hands lingered, reluctant to leave her face. Her skin was softer, smoother than he'd remembered. Yet leave they must, for he was anxious to have her naked in his arms.

Slowly, ever so slowly, he lowered his hands to the neckline of her blouse. The fabric was crisp and cool, yet faintly warmed by the heat of her skin. His fingers curled in anticipation—and fear that she would change her mind.

One by one, he undid the tiny pearl buttons. When they were all released, he slid his hand beneath the cloth and traced tiny, enticing whorls against her skin, edging the blouse away. And through it all, his mouth never once left hers.

Chrys closed her eyes and shivered once again as Eric slipped the blouse off her shoulders. Step by deliberate step, he was seducing her. She knew what was happening. Yet she was powerless to resist. Deep down inside, she wasn't even sure she wanted to try.

Chrys closed her eyes and was swamped by his clean, masculine scent. No, she didn't want to resist. Not tonight. Not now. Not when his hands were warm and strong and gentle as they rested against her burning flesh.

There had been too many nights when she'd been cold. Too many nights when she'd been weak. Too many nights when she'd been alone. And lately, too many nights when she'd lain awake remembering his touch.

"Look at me, Chrys," he pleaded softly, his fingers feather-light as they rose to trace the line of her jaw tenderly. "Look at me and see what's in my heart."

She trembled, her lashes lowered against the erotic power of his deep, husky voice. She didn't want to look at him. She was afraid, not of him but of recognizing reality. She didn't want anything to intrude. If she kept her eyes closed, she could tell herself that it was all a dream. Unreal. Unthreatening. A once in a lifetime aberration.

For a moment, the weight of his hands lay heavy on her shoulders and Chrys felt a rising sense of panic. It was almost as if he sensed her thoughts, as if he contemplated defeat. Then, slowly, gently, tenderly—oh, so tenderly—his thumbs came to rest on her collarbones. His fingers traced tiny circles along her shoulder blades and he used the rhythmic motion to draw her near.

"I won't hurt you." His soft whisper moistly coaxed her lips further apart. "I only want to show you how much I care," he whispered again.

Mesmerized by his low words and his gentle hands, her eyes opened slowly. And when she saw the look of love on his face, it stole the last of her senses away.

Drawn by the tenderness in his eyes and the sweetness of his words, Chrys's hands rose to Eric's face. His skin was warm beneath her fingertips. His jaw was firm and the beginnings of his beard the merest bristle against her palms. She touched his lips wonderingly with her thumbs and told herself that allowing herself to be seduced would solve nothing. Nothing at all.

Nor would refusing him. Eyes wide, her emotions clear to see, she met and faced the truth. Denying him would be the same as denying herself.

Eric's breath caught in his throat. Knowing that she would accept him, his hands rose to the buttons of his own shirt. He didn't ask her to help him remove his clothes. He knew she wouldn't. Nor did he ask her if she was having second thoughts. He knew that she was. But he hoped—and prayed—that his love would be enough. That by the evening's end, they would have shared more than just their bodies. Their future relied upon it.

Caught up in the spell of his gentle lovemaking, Chrys gave a soft murmur of approval when the panels of his shirt parted to reveal a well-muscled chest. Although her fingers didn't move from his cheeks, she was compelled by a rising tide of desire that she could not and would not name to lean forward and place a lingering kiss in the hollow at the base of his throat. She wanted to tell him what she felt, but the words wouldn't come.

Eric groaned softly and the shirt fell unheeded to the floor. His hands rose and trembled as he brushed a stray lock of her hair back from her face. Slowly, reverently, his hands lowered and pushed the straps of her brassiere down off her shoulders.

Chrys trembled beneath his hands and his fingers fumbled, as clumsy as a young boy's, over the tiny hooks and eyes. His whole being shook with desire when he drew th smooth fabric down and away from her silken skin. Sh was so beautiful. So soft.

A sharp, deep breath, meant to give him strength, fille his nostrils with her scent and Eric trembled even mor One hand, tentative for all its strength, rose to cup h breast tenderly. The other clasped her waist tightly. H pulled her close, so close that his growing desire was blatant against the soft line of her stomach.

Eyes closed, his lips blindly sought and found the gentle slope of her breast.

Chrys gave a tiny gasp of surprise at the unexpected warmth of his mouth and the contrasting coldness of his tongue as he ran it across her breast and swirled it around the puckered peak. "Oh, Eric."

Eric lifted his mouth away. All that he felt was plain to see in his eyes. When she whispered his name once again, he reached behind her to push the covers down to the foot of the bed. Slowly, carefully, silently, he eased her down onto the smooth, crisp sheets.

Reaching down, he slipped off her shoes and silently cursed his own tight boots. He was afraid to leave her, afraid to break the magic spell that held her close to his heart.

As if sensing his frustration, Chrys began to smile. A gentle, teasing smile that started in her eyes and spread to her lips. "Problems?"

"No." Ignoring his boots for the moment, Eric lay beside Chrys on the bed. He watched her for the longest time, silent all the while, his mind asking over and over if loving Chrys, physically, mentally and emotionally for the rest of his life, would even come close to being enough.

The woman she had become was far more enticing than the woman-child she had been.

His hand rose and tangled in her hair. Carefully, he drew out all the pins until her mink-brown tresses lay like a spread of silk across the pale pillows. This was the woman she was. This was the woman he wanted to love.

Unwilling to resist her haunting beauty for even a moment more, Eric lowered his lips to her mouth.

He wanted to tell her how much he loved her, how beautiful she looked, but he couldn't find the words. He wanted to talk to her, to tell her what he was feeling. And yet he didn't dare. She had to know that what was happening here and now, between the two of them, was more special than any words could convey.

At first, Chrys closed her eyes and made no attempt to respond to the persuasive pressure of his lips. She only wanted to savor the feel of his hand slipping from her head to her shoulder. When his hand dropped to linger over her breast, she gloried in her body's eager response.

But still, she lay quiet and quiescent beneath his touch. It had been so long. She just wanted to know, to feel, to experience it all.

As his fingers traced around the dusky edges of her nipple, she could feel her whole breast contracting in response as her nipple grew stiffer and peaked beneath the callused pads of his fingertips. Her breath grew both ragged and shallow as his lips laved a similar trail. The heat in her body grew until a burning fire licked at her veins. A deep, primitive, pulsing need shot through her womb, and her legs moved in restless demand against Eric's practiced patience.

A soft cry, both pleading and distressed, rose into her throat. It was all happening too fast. What she was feeling was too intense. She'd wanted it to be slow. She wanted to have time to savor all the feelings that had been stored inside her. Yet how could she? The scent of his skin, the warmth of his touch, the feel of his body on her were catapulting her into a world that was filled with memories and wondrous new adventures.

Soon, Chrys found that it was no longer enough to let Eric touch her. She needed to participate. She needed to touch him as he touched her.

Her hands rose to his shoulders and pulled him close. His skin was taut and moist. His muscled back, firm and strong.

Eager to feel all of him, Chrys looped one arm around his neck and threaded the fingers of her free hand through his hair. It was soft and silky, crisp and clean. She nipped at his chin, nuzzled his ear and gently bit the baby-soft skin at the side of his neck. Then, her lips settled, hot and urgent, on his and her tongue delved into the moist recesses of his mouth, savoring his masculine flavor.

Groaning, Eric shifted his weight to one side, and his mouth trailed from hers to the soft underside of her breast. His fingers shook as they reached for the snap on her jeans. He couldn't imagine anything more beautiful than being one with her.

In response, Chrys tightened her arms around his neck, sucked in her tummy and lifted her hips, making it easier for him to pull her jeans and panties away.

Lying naked next to him, Chrys reached out and her nimble fingers made short work of Eric's trousers' snap and zipper. Yet once that task was accomplished, she didn't push the material aside. Instead, her fingers slipped beneath the first layer of heavy denim and lingered teasingly over the lighter material of his cotton briefs until he thought he would die with wanting her.

Then, just when he was sure that he couldn't take any more, Chrys's hand slipped away. But the respite, if indeed it was a respite, was all too short. And what Chrys did after that was too good to be true.

Reaching out, Eric shackled her wrist, dimly aware that letting her take control might prove to be a tactical mistake, but the desire he felt was too raw, too powerful. It couldn't be denied.

His words slurred and his voice grated, like a man who was teetering between heaven and hell. "I can't take much more."

"I want to touch you." Her eyes were warm and blue, glistening in a way that he'd never seen before. It was then that he knew he was lost.

He'd wanted to show her what she meant to him, and instead she was showing him. "You want to drive me insane," he corrected gently, lovingly.

"I want to try." She leaned forward and flicked his nipple with the end of her tongue. The feeling of power, the feeling of control, was like a fever in her veins.

"Oh, God," he groaned, pulling her face up to his for a torrid kiss. "You won't have to try very hard."

"Make it easy for me," she urged.

Eric would have given anything to know how she managed to look both arrogant and shy as she demanded his complete surrender. Yet he didn't bother to ask, for the promise in her eyes took precedence over everything else in his life just then.

Sitting up, he pulled off his boots, stripped off his jeans and lay back down in the bed. When she came to him, she came quickly, quietly. And he knew, in that moment, she was completely his.

They touched. A minute that stretched and grew, spinning into hours. Hours that were filled with soft sighs, gentle touches and promises yet unvoiced.

They touched until the moon came up full and bright.

They touched until the stars hid, blushingly, behind the clouds.

They touched until big, puffy flakes of snow began to drift down from the sky outside the windows of their bedroom.

When the storms, inside and out, grew in intensity and bare-limbed trees scraped against the roof of the house, Chrys leaned over and flicked off the bedside light. Then, with the room completely bathed in darkness, she rose above her lover.

Slowly, ever so slowly, she shifted her hips and Eric lifted his until, together, they merged their two bodies into one.

When their union was complete, Eric's arms tightened convulsively and he knew that he'd never be able to let her go. He wanted to hold her—and the moment—forever. But Chrys had grown bold beneath his loving hands and she wasn't content to remain still for very long. Pushing herself up and away, she laughed softly when Eric groaned in a mixture of agony and ecstasy.

"What's wrong?" She teased and nipped at the corded muscles of his shoulder. She hadn't felt this free in years.

Running his hands up and down her spine, he dared to tease her back. "You always did know how to get to a man when he was down."

Chrys gave a little wriggle that was decidedly wicked and reminded him politely that down was hardly where it was at.

In retaliation, Eric rolled over, pinning Chrys to the mattress and kissed her thoroughly. Yet even as he did so, he could feel the slight hesitation that began to seep back into her body.

With an insight into her mind that he'd never known before, Eric suddenly realized that Chrys was, in spite of all they'd shared and in spite of her charming aggression, still very uncertain of him. Slowly, he rolled onto his back and brought her with him until she once again straddled his hips.

When she levered herself cautiously off his chest, Eric's fingers threaded through the tangle of her hair. He pulled her face close for a brief, tight-lipped kiss. "I love you, Chrys. More than you can ever know, and I will never, ever, knowingly harm you."

Chrys sat up, her eyes wide and dark as she studied the solemn look on his face.

Smiling warily, Eric reached up and pushed her long, brown hair back away from her face. She looked beautiful bathed in the black light of night. Her skin was pearly and light. His own hand looked dark and threatening by comparison. "I do frighten you, don't I?"

The briefest flicker of concern showed in her face. "You scare me to death," she answered honestly.

He was glad when she didn't attempt to lie, but it hurt to know. "Why?"

Hands braced against his shoulders, she told him. "Because I know you and I don't. Because it would be so easy to lose myself inside of you. And because I want so very, very badly to have someone warm and loving in my life."

"Chrys—"

"Shh. It's too soon for promises." Then, just as quickly as it had come, Chrys shook off her somber mood. She smiled and her whole face took on a brilliant glow. "I may be crazy and I know I'm insane, but I'm going to make love to you, Eric McLean, like no one's ever made love to you before."

And then, caress by delicious caress, she did.

CHRYS DIDN'T REMEMBER dozing off. Yet when she opened her eyes, she saw that the wind had picked up and the snow outside her bedroom window was falling so fast and furiously that it was impossible to see the tops of the trees at the side of the road.

Chrys sighed and closed her eyes again. The whirling snow matched the whirling of her mind. It was bad enough to be feeling it; she didn't want to see it as well.

How could she have let this happen? How could she have been so—so dumb! Eric McLean had been nothing but trouble from the first day she'd met him. And every time she got within arm's length of him, she let it happen all over again.

Chrys kept her eyes tight shut, even when she felt Eric's hand close over the point of her hip. You'd have thought, she told herself caustically, that after all these years, she'd have learned something about letting him break her heart. But no, here she was—fool that she was—letting herself get involved all over again.

Again? A single tear formed behind Chrys's tightly closed eyelids. It pooled in the corner of her eye and swelled until she couldn't stop it from sliding slowly down her cheek.

There wasn't any again to it. She'd never gotten over him. Sometimes—not often, but sometimes—she wondered if everything in her adult life hadn't been done on account of him.

She'd fallen in love because of him. She'd learned to grow because of him. And because she'd been so afraid of losing him, she'd almost lost herself.

She didn't know where or how she'd found the courage to leave him eight years ago. But she had. And the loneliness had been devastating. Then, thank God, she'd found Ken.

In Ken's arms, and only in Ken's arms, she'd been able to forget Eric. With Ken's love, she'd been able to go on.

But now, Ken was gone and Eric was here. A sob caught in her throat and tore at her self-control. Suddenly, frighteningly, she was deeply, intimately afraid. Who was going to be there to help her pick up the pieces again?

Eric's hand ran soothingly from the point of her hip to the top of her shoulder as he sensed a little of what she was feeling. He'd known that he'd rushed her. He'd known that, in spite of everything, what had happened between the two of them had happened too soon.

He'd wanted to show her all that she'd meant to him. He'd wanted to show her all that he'd become. What he hadn't wanted was to strip away her self-confidence or make her a slave to her body's cravings.

Eric sighed. He shouldn't have let her take control. But he'd wanted her so badly, and it had been so long, that he hadn't been thinking, only feeling. And what she made him feel. Oh, God! He hadn't felt like that in a hundred thousand years.

It had been like coming home. Like finding the desert in full bloom. Like standing on the edge of a mountain and watching a stream turn into a river. Like finding a harbor that was safe and sane and clean. And above all else, it was like finding the key to the meaning of his life.

His hand once again on Chrys's hip, he tried to turn her onto her back. She resisted at first, then gave in and let him have his way, throwing one arm up over her eyes to hide her face. "Are you all right?"

No, she thought. *I'm angry, confused and scared. I don't know what to do and I don't know what I've done.*

Eric slid his hand beneath the covers and wrapped his arms around Chrys, pulling her close into his embrace. His chin rested on the crown of her head and his arms were both comforting and strong as they ran soothingly up and down the length of her spine. It worried him that she felt so cold.

He knew they had to talk, but he didn't know where to begin. He didn't even know if she was ready to hear him out or if she would even believe what he had to say.

In fact, the only thing that he did know was that he had to try.

Lifting one hand to the back of Chrys's head, his fingers tangled in the silken length of her hair and he tugged gently until she looked up.

"I've never wanted anyone or anything as badly as I want to love you." Ducking his head slightly, Eric kissed her cheek and tasted the salt of tears.

Chrys closed her eyes and let the heat of his body envelop hers. He was so warm and she was so cold. So very, very cold. When the silence lengthened into minutes, Chrys's tired mind began to relax beneath the soothing pressure of his hands. Her thoughts slowed and her arms moved, of their own volition, to encircle Eric's waist. She was starting to melt all over again.

How was he able to do it? How was he able to make her care? Especially when every instinct for self-preservation in her body warned her against him?

A ragged breath caught in her throat. "No," her voice trembled, answering the question he'd first asked. "I'm not okay. I'm lonely and scared. I'm frightened of the way you make me feel."

She swallowed a clutch of tears and spoke around the ache that was growing in her heart. "I'm frightened that you'll stay. I'm frightened that you'll leave.

"And all I know for sure is that no matter what happens, no matter which way it works out, I'm going to end up being hurt all over again."

He pulled her closer until their legs tangled and their chests were breast to breast. "It's all right, love. I'm not going anywhere. Not without you." Eric's lips were gentle in her hair and his hands were warm against her back.

"I..." Chrys sighed and gave in to the urge that had been building inside her ever since he'd taken her back into his arms.

It was too late to worry about making a fool of herself. She'd already done that and more. Slowly, her arms rose and circled the corded muscles of his neck. Whatever he wanted of her, she would give. And give, knowing that it might not last.

Eric leaned forward and kissed her lips once, asking for nothing in return. "Chrys, we need to talk. There are things I need to tell you. Things I need to explain. But I want you to understand," he added cryptically, "that I'm not trying to make excuses."

Slipping his strong arms around her waist, Eric pulled Chrys closer. "All my life, I've only wanted one thing."

"To please your father."

"Yes. To please Talbot." Eric's shoulders rose and fell beneath Chrys's hands. "When I was in high school, I took the courses he wanted, I dated the girls he approved of, I made friends with the right kind of people. And when, occasionally, I'd made friends with someone who wasn't the right kind..."

His voice dropped away and poignant silence settled between them. They both knew how tricky this subject had always been. It was several minutes before Eric began to speak again. "Things didn't change a lot in college. I joined the right fraternity, took the right courses, you know the routine.

"But it got harder and harder to conform. I started growing up. I started learning about myself. Still, I wasn't strong enough to break away. The best I could do was move into the frat house and make a few changes in my class schedule.

"I was really pleased with myself. I was sure that I was rebelling. Making a stand."

When Chrys reached out to touch his face, he caught her hand in his and brought it to his lips. Then, settling her back against the pillows, he eased out of the bed and pulled on his jeans.

His bare shoulders gleamed whitely as he walked across the room to look out at the snow-covered street below. Finally, he turned his back to the window, and his face was hidden in the shadows of reflected light. "I wasn't strong enough. You know that better than anyone else."

"We were both very young," she answered softly.

"Young," he acknowledged, "and fumbling for our places in life. I wanted you, Chrys. And I loved you the best I could. But I couldn't love you the way a man should. Not when I couldn't even like myself."

Chrys curled her feet up underneath her bottom and pulled the sheets up around her chest. "I understand that now, but it was very difficult for me then. Sometimes it's still hard to accept."

"I guess it would be." Eric shrugged. After a moment, he came over to sit down beside her. "I know what hurt you the most. Thinking that I wanted Talbot's approval more than I wanted your love."

His hand reached out, resting briefly on the side of her face. "It was just that I didn't know which of the two was more valuable at the time. If I had, I'd have made a different choice. I never meant to hurt you, Chrys."

"How can you say that?" Chrys bit her lower lip, trying to keep back her angry words, but they wouldn't be denied.

"When you let me go, I was lost. You had to have known how I felt. You had to have known that there wasn't anyone I could turn to. My father was so wrapped up in his own world that he didn't even seem to know that I existed and I didn't even have any friends. All my free time—every single bit of it—had been spent with you.

"I was like a boat without a rudder. Then when you casually offered me money like I was some sort of..." Her voice caught in her throat and she couldn't go on.

"When I offered you money, it was because it was the one thing I had to give. Nothing else in my life belonged to me." He sighed and looked away. "I would have married you, Chrys, but...I was sure that it couldn't last. Whatever other sins were mine at least I knew we were too young to make a marriage last."

Chrys laid one hand against his bare shoulder, in unspoken agreement.

"I didn't want us to end up like my folks," he continued softly. "Living together and hating each other all the while."

Tucking the thin sheet securely under her arms, Chrys leaned forward as well. "You know, for all that my father grew cold and unapproachable after my mother's death, I've always had a memory of the way a family should be."

"I never did." An impatient snort broke past his lips. "Listen to me, will you? I make it sound like all of this was someone else's fault and that's not what I meant to do. The fault is, and was, my own."

"Maybe the fault was both of ours." Chrys slipped back down under the covers, and tugged Eric down as well. The wind had picked up outside and the room was growing chilled. "What made you leave your father?"

"You mean how did I finally find the courage?" He snorted again, his voice gruff as he continued. "I don't know now. There were so many things involved in deciding to break away, that I couldn't just pick one and say this is the reason why. I guess I just finally realized that no matter how hard I tried, I'd never make him happy."

His lips quirked humorlessly. "Twenty-two years old and I finally managed to run away.

"It's hard to believe that I waited so long, that I was so tied to his apron strings. Yet, leaving him, leaving what was in its own way safe and secure, was one of the hardest things I ever had to do. All my life, I'd been Talbot McLean's son and then suddenly I wasn't anyone."

He shrugged. "I thought the Peace Corps would help me find myself. Doing good. Helping the oppressed."

"Didn't it?" she asked softly, moving closer. She'd known what it was like to be alone and lost. But she'd been lucky as well. She'd found someone strong enough to help her find her way and her own identity. She'd found Ken.

"In some ways, yes." Eric rolled onto his side, one fist propping up his head and the other opening helplessly. "But there were so many things that needed to be done, and whatever you did, it was never enough."

"Why did you go back?"

"Back?" Her question puzzled him. "You mean overseas?" When she nodded, he shrugged again. "Because I was still looking for myself. The Peace Corps wasn't the answer. But it was a start. I thought I'd keep trying."

"Did you ever find the answer?"

"Yeah. In a hospital bed in Dallas."

"A hospital?"

When she looked appalled, he lifted one shoulder in a gesture that was casually nonchalant. "I was there for a long time and there wasn't much else that I could do besides think about who and what I was."

Chrys didn't ask any more questions, she simply put her arms around his neck and tried to make him forget that he'd ever known the meaning of pain. But Eric wasn't finished with his explanations. Lying back, he tucked her beneath the curve of his arm and stared up at the ceiling. "I didn't love you enough, Chrys. Not at first. You knew that the first time we made love all those years ago."

"That night I seduced you."

"You were too innocent to know the meaning of seduction." Eric laughed silently at her self-deception. "Each time I touched you I fell a little further in love with you, Chrys. It was the easiest thing in the world for me to do. It was also the most frightening."

He shifted onto his side once again and looked straight into her eyes. "At the same time, I knew with every breath that I drew and with every word that I spoke that something was going to go wrong, that someday something would happen that would keep us apart."

"You can't build a future when you're full of fear." She sounded very sad and he knew that she meant it both for him then and for her now.

"I couldn't then," he agreed. "But I'd like to now."

One brow raised, questioning her own feelings. "But can I build one with you?"

Eric winced, then leaned forward and kissed her cheek tenderly. "You have to think we have a chance, or you wouldn't have gone to bed with me tonight."

When Chrys dragged the sheets close and started to sit up, Eric touched her face tenderly. "I know I seduced you into this bed, Chrys. But seduction isn't what kept you here. And you *are* still here."

Although she wanted to deny what he was driving at, Chrys couldn't quite bring herself to say the damning words.

"Sometimes," he offered slowly, "I wish we'd never met before."

That Chrys understood. There were times when she had wished that they could have started fresh, with no problems transferred over from the past.

"I've made so many mistakes with you. I've started over so many times. I'm afraid that we'll never be able to meet on middle ground." He sighed. "I want us to meet. I want us to be a family."

He sat up and put his arms around her, drawing her slender body into the shelter of his warm chest. "I want to be your lover. More, I want to be your husband. But most of all, I want to be your friend. I want to be someone you can turn to whenever it gets too hard to stand alone. But I'm afraid," he continued honestly. "Each time I come to you, one or the other or both of us brings along the past."

"I loved Ken," she warned.

"I know. I'm not jealous of him, Chrys. Just grateful that he could be all the things I never was."

Chrys's breath caught in her throat at the sincerity of his confession. "Don't make me fall in love with you, Eric."

"I want you to fall in love with me. That's what this—" his hand made a sweeping arc, taking in the tangled sheets "—has been all about."

"There's too much behind us."

"There's too much between us just to walk away. Chrys," he pleaded earnestly, "we need time together. Time without the distractions of friends or family or work to get to know each other as we are now."

"I don't want to start over," she protested.

"Neither do I." Eric took a deep breath and bared the remaining fears that scarred his soul. "I'm afraid I'll fail. Both as myself and as the man who has to follow Ken in your heart. In some ways, the thought of a relationship with you now is even more frightening than it was in the past.

"I'm older now. I know how rare this second chance of ours truly is. And like you, I know how lonely the past has been and how lonely the future will be if you aren't by my side."

Chrys searched his face, trying to look beneath the surface and deep into his heart. Did he really love her? Could she afford to let herself believe in what he offered? Should she? Was it wise? Or was it emotional suicide?

"I'm not giving up on us, Chrys. Not ever again. In my heart, I know how much I love you. In your heart, you know it too."

"Yes," she whispered, drawn by the honesty of his clear, blue eyes. "I think maybe I do." Lying back in his arms, she drew him down onto the bed. "It's too soon for promises. But I would be willing to try."

"We need some time to ourselves." He insisted even though he knew he was treading on rocky ground. "We need some time to get to know each other as the people we are, not the people we were."

"It won't be easy," she agreed. "I've already taken more time off work than I really should. But if yo wanted, you could move in here with me. Mary Kathlee will be staying with some of her father's relatives until lat Sunday night. As for getting away, we might be able t manage part of this weekend. Maybe we could find som place where neither of us has any past memories—if it' what you still want."

Eric nodded, his voice cracking with desire, as her hands moved from his neck to his waist. "Nothing would please me more."

Chrys studied his face soberly. Then, seeing the growing desire in his eyes, her spirits soared and she laughed as she hadn't laughed in years.

Ken had taught her many things about true love, and for that and the child he gave her she would always love him. But Eric had taught her things as well. Things that were worth remembering long into the night.

Chapter Thirteen

The next few days were magical, almost like a time apart from reality. Both Chrys and Eric seemed willing to settle into a lighthearted, even playful, coexistence.

Each morning Eric got up and fixed breakfast while Chrys got ready for work. Then, while he dressed, Chrys cleared away the breakfast dishes and put supper in the Crockpot to cook while she was gone.

Most of the college's student population had packed up their suitcases and gone home for the holidays. The Karramann Library was practically deserted, and no one, other than a couple of the other librarians, even stopped in the Regional Archives, where Chrys worked. It was a real change from her normal daily routine, but the peace and solitude gave her time to finish her appraisal of Talbot's collection and to set up a retention and disposition schedule based on each individual record's archival value

Monday, Eric had come by at noon and taken Chrys fo lunch, then, after having asked a number of question about what she was doing, he had offered to help. Bu Chrys, knowing that the material had to be judged i terms of the cost of retention as well as on current an future needs, turned his offer down and sent him on h way.

Later that afternoon Eric had shown up again, research notes in hand. He'd smiled, breaking through her resistance, and had taken a seat at the far end of the large, silent room. At first Chrys, both amused and a bit exasperated, had found it difficult to concentrate on her own work. But when she saw that Eric was serious about working on his dissertation and that he didn't intend to interrupt her own work, she quickly got used to having him around.

That evening when they returned to her house, Eric set the table while Chrys served. Then later, after the dishes were done and put away, Chrys brought out a number of Talbot's papers and set about trying to decipher the code.

Tuesday was pretty much a repeat of the day before. But that night, after two hours of working fruitlessly on Talbot's code, Chrys tossed her pencil down and pushed the pages aside. "Drat Talbot anyway."

Eric looked up from the papers he'd been reading and laughed. "My sentiments exactly."

When Chrys wrinkled her nose at him and started to walk out of the room, he leaned forward and snagged a tenacious arm around her waist. Although she made a pretense of trying to get away, Chrys didn't put any real effort into avoiding the inevitable.

After a few minutes of play, Eric lay back on the couch and pulled her slender body down. As her hips settled on his and her long legs slipped between the longer length of his, Eric began to run his hands soothingly up and down her spine.

His palms were warm and firm. Chrys closed her eyes and murmured softly at the pleasurable feel. When he chuckled and nipped at her shoulder, she propped her elbows onto his chest and her chin in her hands. At times, he could be very distracting, but she was learning to be content with her lot. "Keep that up and I think I may just fall in love with you."

"That's what I've been counting on." Eric tossed one jean-clad leg over hers, pinning her hips closer still. His nose buried itself in her hair and his lips sought a sensitive spot that he'd found behind her left ear. "Aren't you glad I've learned to take off my boots as soon as I come into the house?"

"I'm sure my couch is looking forward to putting you on its Christmas list."

"It's not your couch I'm interested in," he teased. "It's the logistics of getting out of my pants and into yours."

When she started to laugh, Chrys's body slipped a little lower between his legs and she was forced to admit that it was fairly obvious that his father's papers were not at the top of Eric's priority list. Still, she decided to give the failing topic one more try. "Maybe your friend will know."

"Know what? And which friend?" he asked absently, slipping one hand beneath the soft cotton of her tailored blouse. He could spend the whole night touching her and still never get his fill. Her skin was as smooth as satin and as soft as silk. And when she let her long, beautiful hair spread across their bodies when they began to make love... A man could die happy like that.

Chrys was not so easily deterred. "The one that's coming on Wednesday."

"Oh, Joe." He wasn't really interested in Joe Beniki at the moment. Sliding his hands out from under her blouse, he tried a different tactic: sliding his hands under her jeans. "Well, if he doesn't you can bet I'm going to encourage you to give up on the whole mess. It's not worth the aggravation."

"Speaking of aggravation..." She wriggled out from under his embrace and tried to stand up.

"Hey," he protested. "Where're you going?"

Half up, half down, Chrys stopped in mid-wriggle. "To get a drink. Would you like one?"

"No. But I might be open to persuasion." Eric grinned and pulled her back down. Rolling onto his side, he pinned her to the couch and his eager fingers began to make short work of the buttons on her blouse. "What have you got to offer?"

Avoiding the obvious coffee, tea or me, Chrys solemnly offered him fruit juice or Kool-Aid. Eric grimaced and asked her if she couldn't think of something a bit more tasty.

"Not if I really want to get a drink." She laughed. "Which I do."

He grimaced again and did up what he'd just undone. "We're going to have to work on your timing."

"Think so?" she teased from her place in the doorway. "I thought it was pretty good. It got me out of here in one piece and fully clothed for the first time in two days."

He waved her away. "Okay, but hurry back. A man could get lonely in here all by himself."

Waltzing playfully back into the room, Chrys dropped Hezekiah onto his chest, but the cat didn't stay for very long. In fact, the uninterested feline left as soon as he heard the refrigerator door open and close.

Eric lay back on the couch, his arms folded to cradle his head. As he waited for Chrys's return, he couldn't help thinking how much he'd enjoyed the past two days. Chrys had always been warm and loving, generous to a fault. Especially in bed. But now, as a woman who knew her worth, and more, who accepted her body's sexuality as easily as she accepted breathing, she was—for lack of a better word—breathtaking.

He smiled and eased his shoulders deep into the sofa's soft cushions. He couldn't believe that she could respond the way she did and not love him as much as he loved her. All he had to do was be patient and wait. Given enough time, she had to come to the same conclusion. She was too honest to do anything else.

After a while, it occurred to Eric that Chrys had been gone quite some time. Getting up, he wandered out into the kitchen, curious to see what was keeping her, and since he was practically barefoot, Chrys, who was using the phone, didn't hear him come in.

"That's right, Gretchen. I'm going away for the weekend with a friend." She shifted the receiver to the other ear.

"Yes, we'll be staying at the lodge. I don't know the number but if Mary Kathleen should need me, you can get it from the operator. Okay?"

Chrys laughed at something the other woman said, answered a couple more questions and then added, "No, and I'd just as soon she didn't know. Not just yet."

A minute or so later she concluded her conversation and hung up. When she turned and saw him watching her, Chrys flushed like a little girl who'd been caught in the act. "I didn't hear you come in."

"I walk quiet," he teased. "Like a cat. And speaking of cats, who should we ask to watch Mary Kathleen's menagerie?"

"I'm not trying to hide anything from my friends and family," Chrys offered guiltily.

"I didn't think you were." His reply was solemn, belied by the twinkle in his eyes.

Chrys continued to chew on her lower lip, not quite willing to let the subject drop. Whatever he thought, she did owe him an explanation. "This has been a good experience for me."

"How so?" He knew what she was thinking. It was written, plain as day, across the mobile features of her lovely face.

Chrys studied the toe of her shoe and missed the amused look that flashed across his face. "This time it's me who wants to be discreet."

Eric shrugged, not the least upset. "You've got Mary Kathleen to think about. I understand that."

"If this had been you instead of me I don't think I would have been so generous. There's a very unkind part of me that would want to say 'I told you so.'"

"You had a bit more cause," he answered easily, then changed the subject. "What about Berta?"

Chrys looked puzzled until she saw that Eric was watching Hezekiah, who was sitting patiently by his dish.

"You've been fed, cat. Now go away." Looking back at Eric, she answered, "Berta won't be back until after this weekend, that's why we've had the evenings to ourselves. When Berta's home, she practically lives here."

"I noticed." He held up his hands, warding off Chrys's playful scowl. "But I'm not complaining. I like the idea of a built-in baby-sitter."

"You would." Her nose scrunched up. "Especially one who dabbles in matchmaking on the side. I think maybe I'll ask Ann Corey. Her kids have almost as many pets as Mary Kathleen."

"Won't Ann gloat when she knows why you need a pet sitter?"

"Probably. But she still owes me one for watching her oldest boy's pet tarantula for two whole weeks last summer."

"I take it you're not fond of spiders?"

The face Chrys made was comical. "Tex was almost as much fun as Pete."

"Pete?"

Chrys shuddered. "Don't ask. You really don't want to know."

Working very hard to hide the beginnings of a smile, Chrys walked across the room and wrapped her arms around his lean, muscular waist. "Eric," she said, trying to muster an appropriately solemn expression, "I think we should have a little talk."

He knew she was teasing, he could feel it in the way she leaned into him and he could see it in the way a glint of humor peeped around the corners of her summer-blue eyes. "Just what did you have in mind?"

"Well, if this works out and we do end up back together..." She paused for dramatic effect and reminded him forcefully of her daughter. "You've got to promise me that no matter how much Mary Kathleen begs and pleads *I* get final approval on all the pets."

Eric was beginning to catch on. "What," he asked suspiciously, "was Pete?"

"I'm not really sure—I mean, not specifically. But he was long and skinny and green."

Eric chuckled deep in his chest. He loved her this way, teasing and light at heart. "Is this something like twenty questions?"

"It could be. Pete reminded me of a poem I read in college. Dickinson's 'A Narrow Fellow in the Grass.'" Fo a moment, she thought she had him with that, but then h refused to be distracted. "Okay." She sounded resigned "But you're missing out on a fun time. I'm very good a twenty questions."

"Mmm." His hands dropped to her waist and he pulle her close. "I can think of better things to do than ta about someone named Pete when I've got you in m arms."

"You think so now." She grinned, looping her arms around his neck. "But there'll come a day when you'll be too old to do anything else."

The fact that she, either consciously or unconsciously, saw them together in the future was very heartening for Eric. He leaned forward and nipped her ear playfully. His lips followed the line of her jaw, searching for her mouth. Then, suddenly, there wasn't any more room in him for play. Only passion.

As Chrys melted under his burning kiss, she wasn't sure just exactly what the future was going to hold, but if the present was any indication, the odds were getting better every day.

WHEN JOE BENIKI WALKED into Talbot's study, Eric saw that the other man had changed dramatically from the youthful-looking fraternity brother he remembered. For one thing, Joe had skipped past prematurely gray and was heading straight for bald, and that, combined with the slight protuberance around his middle, added a good ten years to his overall appearance.

But even as those changes registered, Eric also noticed that in at least two ways, Joe hadn't changed at all. His bearing was militarily straight and his dark brown eyes were as sharp as ever.

"It's great to see you again." Joe's eyes narrowed slightly as they settled on Chrys, before skipping back to Eric.

"I'm not sure I can say the same." Eric answered curtly, ignoring Joe Beniki's outstretched hand.

Once again, Joe's eyes moved quickly around the room, almost as if he were memorizing all the details for future reference. "You got a problem with my being here?"

Eric leaned back in his father's chair, looking every bit as prepossessing as the old man in his heyday. "Just how did you find me so soon after my father's death?"

Joe reached in his back pocket to fish out his wallet. Flipping it open, he tossed it down on the desk for Eric to see. "When you've got the resources the Bureau does, one man isn't so hard to find."

Eric stared at the metal shield for a moment, then let out a deep breath, relaxing completely for the first time since Joe Beniki had come into the room. "So." He handed back the wallet. "You're one of the good guys."

"I didn't think you'd have to ask." Joe's face was a little grim. Once, although it had been a long time ago, he and Eric had been fairly close.

"Normally, I wouldn't. But I'm a little out of my element." Eric moved from behind Talbot's wide desk and motioned Joe to take a seat on the sofa on the other side of the room. When all three of them were seated, he leaned forward. "What's this all about?"

"Well," Joe began, "five years ago the Bureau got a tip about a violation that needed to be developed." When he noticed Chrys and Eric exchanging puzzled frowns, he chuckled. "I forget that other people aren't used to the jargon.

"What I mean is that a fairly reliable source told us that he'd heard about a high-ranking government official who was getting a reputation for using his position in the Department of the Interior to line his own pockets. So—" Joe shrugged "—we decided to investigate. But our individual is a wily old bird and we've had trouble getting anything concrete."

"Maybe he's innocent."

Joe gave Chrys a funny look, then laughed. "No. He' not innocent. There've been too many allegations. Un fortunately they've all come from people who weren' closely involved in the actual illegal activities, so we couldn't prosecute. Not if we wanted Thorndyke to end up with anything more than a slap on the wrist."

Chrys's eyes opened wide in surprise. Her job as an archivist kept her aware of many men and women who were political figures. And Samuel J. Thorndyke was one of the most powerful. His endorsement alone had swung more than one candidate into office. "You can't mean Samuel Thorndyke?"

"I can and I do." Sitting back, Joe reached into his pocket and pulled out a cigarette. "Okay?" he asked, then lit it and took a long drag when neither Chrys nor Eric objected.

The name sounded familiar to Eric also. "Why do I think I know him?"

Joe took another puff on his cigarette. "Probably because you do. He worked on several of Talbot's campaigns back in the late fifties and early sixties. You probably met him right here in this house when you were younger. But that isn't what concerns us.

"We're a lot more interested in what he's been up to for the past fifteen years. One of his most lucrative jobs has been negotiating contracts between the private sector and the federal government. In fact, the allegations range from accepting bribes to fraud against the government."

"What did my father have to do with this?" Eric asked.

"Talbot agreed to help us catch Thorndyke in a sting operation."

"Why use my father?" Eric asked. "Don't you have your own agents for that kind of thing?"

"Thorndyke's careful," Joe explained. "He refused to deal with anyone he didn't know personally. And he never, *never* makes a step until he's got more dirt on his buyers than they have on him. It's taken us nearly two years to set up this deal with Talbot."

"What's going to happen now that my father's dead?"

"We've been waiting for the papers cementing the deal between Talbot's fake corporation and the Department of the Interior to come through. We couldn't move before now, for fear that Thorndyke would pull back at the last minute. For a while, right after your father's death, it was really touch and go. We thought he was going to drop out of the whole deal.

"Fortunately for us," Joe continued, "Thorndyke's greed outweighed his caution this time. The papers came through this morning. Right on schedule, all signed and sealed. We've already gotten a warrant for his arrest and all we need to do now is pick up Talbot's files on the Indian River project."

Both Eric and Chrys frowned. "There aren't any files." Eric shook his head. "At least not the kind you're talking about."

Joe leaned forward, stubbing out his cigarette. "Maybe I didn't make myself clear. Talbot isn't implicated in any of this, Eric. He was working with us."

"I'm not trying to protect my father." Eric went to the nearest file cabinet. The manila folder he pulled out wasn't nearly as thick as Joe thought it should have been.

"Are you telling me this is it?" A deep furrow worried its way across Joe's brow. "There should have been reams of the stuff. We were nearly two years working out the details."

"This is it," Eric assured him.

"What about the papers that went to the university?"

Chrys sat forward. "I work in the archives. Everything came in through me. Eric and I have been looking for references to the Indian River project for a couple of weeks and what we've found is in that folder. I could check the collection for references to Thorndyke, but I don't think there's anything else."

Joe cursed softly.

"If the papers were that important," Eric asked reasonably, "why didn't you have someone come in and pick them up right after Talbot died?"

"Well, for one thing, we thought there would be copies in a safety deposit box downtown. Mainly though, we were afraid that Thorndyke would catch wind of the investigation if we broke Talbot's cover that late into the negotiations. We know he's had someone watching your father's every move for the past three months.

"We weren't too concerned when we found that you'd turned in the keys on the box. We just figured that you'd taken all Talbot's papers back here to the house. But then, when we did a little discreet checking..." Joe emphasized the word discreet, letting both Chrys and Eric know that the checking had been both unobtrusive and thorough. "We started getting a little nervous."

"You thought Eric took the papers?"

Joe grimaced. "We were counting on it. Oh, we can get a conviction and it will definitely amount to more than a slap on the wrist, but if Thorndyke gets himself a good enough lawyer—" Joe shook his head in disgust. "It would be a lot safer if we had every detail nailed down."

Eric leaned forward, propping his head on his hands. "You know," he began thoughtfully, "I don't know what I would have done if I'd found anything like this."

"You'd have turned them over." Chrys leaned over to squeeze Eric's fingers. "It might not have been an easy thing for you to do—you loved your father a lot more than you let on—but you would have done it anyway."

"Maybe." Eric's answer was a little gruff. Not because he disagreed, but rather because he still felt awkward talking about his father in terms of love.

Chrys understood and gave Eric's fingers another reassuring squeeze. "Some of the papers in Talbot's collection have a series of numbers printed on the back of them. Do you know anything about that?"

"Sure." Joe grinned and lit another cigarette. "Don't tell me you thought that was some sort of secret code he'd worked out with the Bureau."

Chrys sent him a black look, then relented and smiled sheepishly. "The thought of secret codes did cross my mind, but I never imagined any of it having to do with the FBI."

Joe started to laugh just as he inhaled and ended up choking over a cough. When he caught his breath again, he apologized. "How much of it have you figured out?"

"Practically nothing." Chrys gave a disgusted sigh. "And I've spent weeks trying to correlate it. I know that it almost always refers to his correspondence. And I can tell when two sets of papers refer to each other, but I can't tell how or why the code works."

"Well..." Joe took a deep drag on his cigarette. "It's a dating system. The first series of numbers refer to the day the letter came in and the second set to the year and the third to the day he sent back a reply."

"But," Chrys interrupted, sounding indignant, "none of the first set of numbers matched up with the day and the month on any of the dated documents. I checked for that."

"Talbot didn't list his dates by day and month. He used the number of the day in the year. You know, ten would be January tenth, thirty-two would be February first, and so on."

"Why would he use something as awkward as that?" she asked.

Joe's shoulders lifted and fell in a wordless gesture.

"What about the letters that came after some of the numbers?" Eric asked.

"Initials of the correspondents. But I think he only did that when he had a couple of letters that referred back to the same document." Joe shook his head. "It was the most awkward thing I'd ever seen, but Talbot got along with it all right."

Chrys groaned. "Don't say another word. Do you know how much time I wasted on trying to figure that out? I thought it was important. Or at least useful."

"Well," Joe drawled teasingly, "if I were you, I wouldn't go into the secret agent business. You'll never make it as a cryptologist."

"Speaking of secret agents," Eric inserted.

"I'm not a secret agent," Joe protested. "Just a cop—of sorts."

"Special cop."

Joe hunched his shoulders. "What can I say? The Bureau always was the best." Then, more seriously, he returned to the subject of the missing papers. "I can't figure it out. Whoever took those papers never leaked a word of it to Thorndyke."

"You said the papers were incriminating," Chrys repeated. "What if the person you're looking for was trying to protect Talbot?"

"That's the logical conclusion. But who, besides Eric, would want to protect Talbot?"

"Maybe Jerome?" she offered tentatively.

"Jerome!" "Weaver?" the men uttered in unison.

"Well," Chrys defended, "it's just an idea. But I know Jerome always admired Talbot."

"Yeah." Joe's eyes narrowed thoughtfully. "If Weaver had a safety deposit box of his own and access to Talbot's keys . . . Yeah, it might just work."

While the men decided to go pay Jerome a visit, Chrys gathered up her coat and purse. "Unfortunately, I have to get back to work." She leaned forward and kissed Eric's cheek. "Let me know what happens. Okay?"

Eric's hand cupped her jaw, holding her face up for a longer, more intimate kiss. "I'll come by just as soon as I can."

As soon as he could turned out to be just fifteen minutes before the library closed. Chrys greeted him at the hall door, rattling off a barrage of questions.

"You should have come with us if you were so curious," he teased.

"Some of us have to work every day." Chrys sounded so disgusted at being left out that Eric laughed.

"Look on the bright side," he said. "At least you can stop dragging bits and pieces of Talbot's papers home each night."

"Don't remind me," she groaned. "I can't believe I wasted that much time on it." Then, seriously, "What about Jerome? Did he have the papers Joe Beniki wanted?"

"Yes. He'd been holding on to them because he was convinced that someone had been trying to set Talbot up."

"Eric?" Chrys started straightening her desk, a tiny frown marring her brow. "Will Jerome get in trouble for any of this?"

"No. Jerome's not in any trouble." Eric leaned forward, kissing Chrys's cheek. "He was just convinced that Talbot had been innocent of any wrongdoing and was afraid that the papers would fall into the wrong hands before he was able to discover who the right hands belonged to. That's why he took them."

"So everything's okay?"

Eric smiled reassuringly. "Everything's perfect. Joe was elated to get all the documentation that Talbot had prepared and Jerome was relieved to be rid of it. In fact, the only one who's not going to be happy is Thorndyke."

Chrys sat down and propped her elbows on her desk and rested her chin in her hands. "You know, it's really depressing to think that someone as powerful and rich as Sam Thorndyke would do something like this."

"Come on." Eric grabbed Chrys's hand and pulled her to her feet. "I've got an excellent idea to keep away the blues."

Chrys came willingly to her feet and wrapped her arms around his neck. "Oh, what've you got in mind?"

"Dinner. Dancing. A little wine." He grinned devilishly. "I thought maybe we'd celebrate breaking Talbot's code."

Chrys groaned. "If you remind me of that dratted code one more time..."

IT WAS QUITE LATE Friday night when Eric and Chrys arrived at the ski lodge. They had had to endure a little teasing from Ann Corey and her husband, Ed, when Chrys had dropped off an extra set of keys to her house, then the long drive north up toward LaCrosse. Both had been looking forward to this weekend together, it seemed as if they'd never make it. But they did and found, much to their pleasure, that the Pine Meadow Mountain catered to a quiet crowd.

While Eric tipped the bellboy, Chrys busied herself putting their clothes in a cedar-lined chest. Then, when the young man had left and everything else had been stored away, Chrys sat down on one corner of the bed and told Eric that she had a confession to make.

"I never learned how to ski."

Eric's laughter wasn't the response she'd expected. "What's so funny about not being able to ski?" She pouted, reminding him very much of Mary Kathleen.

"I don't ski either."

"You don't?" She looked surprised. "I thought you loved it."

"I used to. But I haven't been on a pair of skis since I came back from overseas."

"Because of your back?" she asked sympathetically, remembering all the times she'd seen him rub it unconsciously.

"No. More lack of incentive than anything else."

Eric lay back on the king-size bed, tucking his hands under his head, and grinned. "Just what were you planning on doing while I was out there in the icy cold, burning up the slopes?"

"I planned on having you teach me how."

"Mmm." Eric stretched like a cat, working the kinks out of each muscle in his arms and back. "I think you might be able to talk me into that. Or maybe—" he reached out and pulled her down onto her back "—we'll just stay here, light a fire in the fireplace, order up room service and get cozy."

"Cozy?" One brow rose questioningly. "I don't think cozy means the same thing to you as it does to me."

"I tell you what," Eric agreed easily, "I'll show you what it means to me now, then later, after dinner, you can show me what it means to you."

As it turned out, their definitions of "cozy" were pretty much the same after all.

Later that night, when their bodies were too sated for anything more strenuous than an occasional brush of lips, they lay in each other's arms, talking—of dreams and memories, of the past, of the present and, eventually, of the future and what it could hold for them, together.

For the next day and a half, they went out for meals, skated occasionally on the resort's tiny pond and even used the Jacuzzi once or twice. Neither skied. For the most part, though, both were content to throw open the floor-to-ceiling drapes, light a fire in the gas fireplace, lie wrapped in each other's arms and talk the days and nights away, for once they started they never ran out of things to say.

The weekend away accomplished more than either had hoped. When they returned to Platteville late Sunday afternoon, Chrys felt that they had laid down a foundation that was strong enough to start building a new, lasting relationship on.

Chrys was looking forward to having Mary Kathleen back home. She and Eric had learned how to be a couple, now they needed to learn how to be a family. "We made it back in plenty of time. Gretchen said she wouldn't be bringing Mary Kathleen by until after supper."

Eric was kneeling on the hearth, filling the fireplace with logs and kindling. When the fire caught and began to crackle merrily, he pivoted on one knee and held out his hand for Chrys.

Once they were both seated cross-legged in front of the fire, staring into the flames, Eric sighed. He was looking forward to seeing Mary Kathleen again, but he knew that the little girl's arrival would herald only the first of many changes.

"I'm going to be sorry when the world starts to intrude on us."

"Me too," she whispered, turning her face to brush a tired kiss along the prickly underside of his jaw. She laid her head on his shoulder and smiled reminiscently. "I've enjoyed having you to myself."

"So," he asked, "what do you think the immediate uture will bring?"

Chrys was staring into the fire and missed the vulnerale look that had shadowed his eyes. "Mary Kathleen and Max."

Eric's lips quirked humorously. "Have you forgiven me for the dog yet?"

"Mmm." Chrys turned her head and kissed his shoulder through the fabric of his cotton shirt. "And for the brooch as well. I was unreasonable. The next time I'll accept whatever you give me a lot more graciously."

When Eric started to protest, Chrys sealed his lips the best way she knew how. It was quite some time later before either spoke again.

"Chrys..." Eric hesitated, then unable to resist, he plunged on. "Have you ever thought about getting married again? To me?"

"I think about it," she answered seriously. "I think about it a lot."

Eric rolled onto his side and reached out to tuck a lock of silky brown hair behind Chrys's ear. "Do you think 'yes,' or 'no'?"

Chrys smiled, a small but serious smile.

"My mind," she told him solemnly, "says that it's still too soon to tell." Then, leaning forward, she pressed a soft kiss on his lean jaw. "Just give me a little more time, Eric."

Eric slid his arms around her slender body and hugged her tight. For Chrys he would wait. A lifetime if he had to.

Chapter Fourteen

Eric was dressed casually: boots, jeans and a thick flannel shirt. He'd come bearing gifts. The large package was hidden behind his back, the smaller flatter one tucked under his jacket.

He rang the doorbell once, then slouched indolently against the wooden frame, waiting for Chrys to answer the door.

"Hi," he said softly.

"Hi, yourself." Chrys's cheeks were flushed from the heat of the kitchen stove. She'd been working on a very special meal.

Eric continued to watch Chrys for several chilly minutes, then realized that the house was unusually silent. "Where is everybody?"

Chrys pushed the door open a little wider. "Mary Kathleen got a last-minute invitation to spend the night at the Coreys. Max was invited too."

"That's nice." Eric stepped inside, bringing with him the scent of cold, clean Wisconsin air. "Real nice."

Chrys moved forward, into Eric's arms. She wrapped her arms around his neck and crossed her wrists behind his head. "You don't have to tell me how nice. I've missed spending the nights with you just as much as you've missed spending them with me."

Eric leaned forward into the kiss. Her body was warm and soft. She smelled of spice. "A few hours here and there are never enough," he agreed.

"Mmm." Chrys relaxed against his solid chest and let her fingers play idly along the back of his neck. Playfully, she swirled one fingertip along his collar. "What are you holding behind your back?"

"Am I holding something behind my back?" he asked innocently, wrapping his free arm around her waist and hugging her tight.

Keeping one arm around Eric's neck, Chrys used her other hand to lever herself away from his chest. "I hear something crinkling behind your back," she informed him solemnly.

"What makes you think it's for you? Valentine's Day was two weeks ago," he teased.

"I think it's for me, because today's my birthday."

"Is today your birthday? I didn't know that." Eric opened his eyes wide and pretended to be surprised. "Gee, if you'd been born one day later you'd only get to celebrate your birthday once every four years."

"Don't tease," Chrys admonished with a laugh. "What did you bring me?"

"Flowers." He held the bouquet out like a torch. "I know you like carnations but I couldn't find any that were beautiful enough. I hope these will do instead."

"Oh, Eric." Chrys's breath caught in her throat at the sight of the beautiful long-stemmed roses. Taking the bouquet in both her hands, she buried her face in the silky display of roses and baby's breath. "They're gorgeous." She took a deep breath, inhaling the sweet, floral scent. "And they smell like heaven."

Eric followed Chrys into the kitchen and watched, smiling, as she fussed with the flowers and vase. "I'm glad you like them."

"Who wouldn't?" She took one of the roses and snapped its stem just a few inches down from the half-opened bud. "Come here."

Eric laughed and stayed where he was. "I haven't got any lapels."

"That's all right." Chrys moved forward and tucked the stem in the pocket of his Western-styled shirt. "It's the thought that counts."

"Do you think so?" Eric's hands moved to Chrys's waist and drew her near. "If you feel that way about it, maybe I should confess that I brought you another present as well."

"You didn't have to," she protested. "The flowers are special enough all by themselves."

"I know I didn't have to." He kissed her forehead lightly, wondering if she'd like the pendant. He'd spent a lot of time looking for just the right piece. "But I wanted to. Do you mind?"

"No. Not at all."

"Good." He grinned and turned her around. "Close your eyes."

Chrys obeyed, feeling like a child at Christmas. She could hear the sound of wrapping paper being torn aside, nd she found herself trying to imagine the size of the ackage. A low, solid snap told her that the gift had come a box. When she heard Eric lay part of the gift on the itchen table, she opened one eye to peek.

"Uh-uh," he warned, anticipating her move. "No eking."

Chrys sighed huffily, then closed her eyes again. Hurry up. I want to see."

Laughing at her impatience, Eric took his time. "I'll bet u were the kind of kid who tore up the wrapping paper d the box to get to the present inside."

Chrys shifted from foot to foot until he relented and lifted his arms to encircle her neck. Surrounded by the warmth of his body, Chrys took a deep breath and found it hard to concentrate on the gift. It was easier, and far more pleasant, to picture the two of them together later in the night, with only his cologne and her perfume between them.

Leaning forward, Eric whispered "Happy birthday" into her ear and Chrys shivered deliciously. At that moment, caught up in her own fantasies, she wanted nothing more than to forget about dinner and take him upstairs to her bed.

"You can open your eyes now." His words moved the tendrils of her hair and whispered past her ear, sending another delightful shiver of anticipation up and down her spine.

Turning, Chrys gave Eric a quick hug, then went to the nearest mirror. Her eyes opened wide, taking in the delicate gold filigree and sapphire stones. "Oh, Eric, you shouldn't have."

"Do you like it?"

Chrys caressed the pendant gently, almost afraid that it would crumble beneath her touch. "I've never seen such dainty work. Of course I love it."

Eric smiled broadly, pleased that he'd found something special that she would enjoy. Watching her pree unconsciously, the expression on his face changed as well She was so beautiful, so natural and free.

He wanted to take her into his arms and love her ove and over and over again. No matter how old he lived t be, he'd never get enough of loving her. "We haven't ha much time together lately. I've missed being with yo holding you and telling you how much I care."

Chrys came back to his side and took his hands in hers. "I've missed you too. If you don't mind dinner being a little late, I'd love to show you just how much."

Eric didn't mind at all.

Later, lying beneath the thick, downy covers on Chrys's bed, Eric sighed contentedly. Reaching out, he ran his hands from her shoulder to her thigh over and over again, stopping the slow, repetitive motion only long enough to drop a gentle kiss on one pale shoulder now and then.

"Mmm," she murmured sleepily. "I like that."

A brief smile touched his lips. He was in an introspective mood. The way Chrys had given herself to him, completely and totally, without reservations of any kind, made him wonder if she was ready to admit that she loved him.

"Chrys?"

"Mmm?" She was too sleepy and content to do more than open her eyes.

His hand stopped its gentle stroking and fell to rest on the curve of her waist. "I'm just about finished with the rough draft of my dissertation."

Chrys started to sit up, but Eric gently held her down. 'Does that mean you'll be leaving soon?" Her voice had lost its sleepy quality and had taken on a note of concern.

"Not until Easter. Then I'll have to go back to Albuquerque and talk to my advisor about it. I can't do much more on it until I get his okay."

His answer was reassuring in one sense, but it wasn't what she wanted to hear. Chrys sighed and closed her eyes. "I'd kind of gotten used to seeing you working in the archives." She didn't want him to go. "How long will you ?"

His shoulder rose and fell silently. "That kind of depends on you."

Chrys wriggled closer and wrapped her arms around his waist. "If you're asking me if I want you to come back, I do."

"No." Eric's hand rose to cup her cheek before he lowered his lips to hers. "What I'm asking is for you to come with me. For a week. I'd like to show you where I live."

"To come with you?" A sunny smile broke across Chrys's face. "When do we leave?"

WHILE ERIC MET with his advisor, Chrys explored Albuquerque on her own. Two days later, when Eric concluded his conferences with his advisor, they packed his dissertation away for the duration and headed south toward Sorrento.

The drive took most of the day, since Eric insisted on stopping several times along the way to show Chrys the best scenic sites. By the time they were only an hour away from Sorrento, Chrys was hot—she hadn't expected the March heat—she was impressed—the cacti were alive with bloom—and she was stunned. Nothing, no pictures, no postcards, no television programs, *nothing* had prepared her for the sheer overwhelming impact of the New Mexico countryside.

It was power in its rawest and most natural form.

On the last leg of their journey, only minutes from his house, Eric reached over and squeezed Chrys's hand encouragingly. "They call New Mexico the land of enchantment. From what I've shown you today, you can see why."

Chrys, who had been studying the sparse hills and towering upthrusts of rocks with growing apprehension, didn't know quite what to say. Enchantment wasn't exactly the word that came to mind.

The difference between the lush, rolling hills of snow-covered Wisconsin and the stark, almost treeless terrain of New Mexico, where the temperature was already pushing eighty in mid-March, was just too much. Everything was alien. So strange and unsettling. Even the shadows were different, not soft and concealing, but stark and bold. A world unto themselves.

Several minutes later, Eric crested a tall hill and pulled his pickup over, off the side of the road. Getting out, he pointed toward an expanse of brown land that to Chrys's untrained eye seemed to be little more than cacti, rocks and sage.

"This is mine. From the creek, back to the outcropping of red rocks, and over to that wire fence."

There was so much pride in his voice that Chrys immediately realized that this, for Eric, was what he truly called home.

"I know there aren't many trees, by Wisconsin standards," he continued quickly, when she didn't reply, "but here's a good-sized creek and grass. Lots of good, sweet grass."

Chrys didn't see any grass. Only sagebrush and sand. he grinned and told him as much.

Eric grinned, too. But he was worried as well. He realed New Mexico was very different from what Chrys had ways known. A lot of people never did adjust.

Climbing back into the pickup, Eric dropped the dusty hicle into gear and started down the dirt road. When ey stopped again, it was in front of a Spanish-style use, complete with red tiles on the roof.

"There wasn't anything on this land but a rotting old rn here when I first bought the place," he told her. "I e it down and salvaged what I could to build the leanin the corral. Then I had a local contractor come by and ıgh in the house."

He took her on a tour of the grounds first, showing her where he intended to build a small barn suitable for housing a horse or two and then pointed out where he wanted to put in a swimming pool next year.

"I've been doing as much of the work as I could by myself on weekends when I'm not up in Albuquerque going to school, and it's almost all done."

He held out his hands proudly. "I've learned how to lay tile and carpets and install cabinets and countertops. And I'm a regular whiz at painting."

The house, when Eric finally took her inside, fascinated Chrys. She couldn't believe that he'd done so much of the work himself. The floors, except for the laundry, kitchen and baths, were hardwood, and the thick sturdy walls either ceramic, plaster or tile. Every room was spacious, from the kitchen to the master bath. And every room was sheltered from the fierce rays of the sun by a large overhang that looked out into the surrounding countryside.

It was clear that the man who had drawn up the plan for this house had loved every nook and cranny of th New Mexico countryside. No matter where you sat c stood, you were aware, intimately aware, of the power c the land.

"Did you design this place yourself?" she asked.

"No. A friend of mine is an architect. He did it for m Well?" Eric prompted, lifting his hands to encompass t entire house. "What do you think?"

"I think I'm overwhelmed."

"If it isn't what you like, or if you'd rather live in to we could."

"Eric—"

"I want to marry you, Chrys." Without giving her ti to answer, Eric wheeled and paced to the far end of living room. "I'd rather not stay in Platteville. You kn that. But I will if it's what I have to do to keep you with me. You know that too."

"I want to marry you, too." She smiled and shook her head slowly from side to side. "And I really can't see you living happily ever after in Platteville."

"If you want the truth, neither can I. But I don't want you to have any reservations about living here."

Chrys's brows drew together in amused exasperation. Of course she had reservations. Who wouldn't when they had a child and half the inmates of the Bronx Zoo to contend with?

"With the exception of the one year Ken and I spent in Georgia—a very lush, green Georgia—I've spent all my life in southern Wisconsin. I'm used to trees and lots of rain. What I call a mountain I doubt if anyone down here would even call a hill. Your mountains stand up and dare you to try and ignore them."

"I know a lot of people see this part of the country as a challenge," Eric reassured her quickly. "But it doesn't ave to be. Not if you learn to live with it on its own erms."

"I'm not afraid of a challenge. And I can see that for ll that the land seems overpowering and ruthless, there's omething stable and rock-solid here as well. It's easy to e why you love it so."

She moved forward and laid her hand on his arm. Don't anticipate problems where there aren't any, Eric. e'll have enough of the other kind to go around. Every arried couple does."

Eric's brow clouded with concern. "I guess I'm just rried that you and Mary Kathleen won't adjust."

Chrys took both his shoulders in her hands and held n steady. "Mary Kathleen and I will adjust. We've got ry reason to want to. After all, you're here. And we ong with you."

Suddenly, more serious than Eric had ever seen her, she wrapped her arms around his waist and pressed herself to him. "Eric, I want this to work out as much as you do. I wouldn't have come if I didn't mean to stay with you."

"Are you sure?" Eric kissed her cheek. "I know how different this all is for you. You're going to miss a lot of things that you take for granted back home."

"You make it sound like we're going to be a million miles away from civilization." Chrys laughed and walked across the room to point to the telephone. "Besides, if I get lonely I can always call Berta long distance."

Stepping back into his arms, Chrys looped her arms around his neck. "Besides, I'm not sure that I'll have time enough to get lonely or bored."

"Think I can keep you busy, hmm?"

"Maybe. But if you can't the Western New Mexico University Museum might."

Eric straightened in surprise. "What do you mean?"

She laughed and pulled him over to the couch. "Well I wasn't going to tell you until tomorrow night, but I'v got an appointment on Thursday at three to see the direc tor." A quick grin flashed across her face. "I'm being ir terviewed for a part-time job."

The stunned look on Eric's face made Chrys want t laugh, but she kept her expression very sober and stai "Don't you want your wife to work?"

"Of course you can work if you want to. Half of wha been bothering me is that I've been worried that you miss your job." He touched her cheek soberly. "I saw hc much you loved it and how good you were at it. Bu didn't think there would be much opportunity for y around here. What's the job like? Is it in your field?"

"It couldn't be better. But the competition will tough, and I'm half afraid that someone with twe years' experience will get it instead."

"How'd you hear about it?"

"Fate." Chrys grinned. "I was looking at a copy of the American Association of State and Local History's newsletter just after you asked me to come down here with you, and I saw an advertisement for a part-time staff member. I gave them a call and got the particulars over the phone. I sent the director a résumé that same day, and then, just before you and I left Platteville, I called up and asked if I could come in for an interview since I'd be in the area."

"Why didn't you say something earlier?"

"I didn't say anything, because there's no guarantee that I'll get the job. There're bound to be a lot of applicants. I didn't want either one of us to get our hopes up.

"Eric." Chrys leaned forward, earnest and intent. "Whether I get that job or not, I intend to move down here with you just as soon as Mary Kathleen is out of school.

"You and I aren't children anymore. We aren't lost and alone, trying to find ourselves in a world we don't understand. When I was eighteen, I needed you to make my life better, because I didn't know how to do it for myself. I wasn't strong enough to stand on my own. Neither were you.

"But we're all grown up now. We know who we are. We know that we have a special value all our own."

She bit her lip, trying unsuccessfully to change her words. "This isn't going to sound very romantic, Eric. But I don't need you to make my life better." Lacing her arms around his neck, she grinned. "I only need you to make it complete."

"I understand." He smiled and touched her cheek tenderly. "We don't need each other for what we can get, but for what we can give."

Chrys smiled and pulled Eric down onto the couch. The mountain that had loomed threateningly in the sky earlier had grown black under the cover of the setting sun. Its solid bulk framed the large picture window and highlighted Eric's wide shoulders, even as its jagged, rough-cut edges faded into the darkness of the night.

Eric was a lot like that mountain. Stark, bold and intent. And nothing, absolutely nothing, in her life would ever be the same again. But Chrys didn't care. She was where she wanted to be.

In Eric's arms.

Epilogue

"Eric should be back any minute, Berta. He was supposed to finish defending his thesis this afternoon." It was the twelfth of August, and Berta had come to New Mexico to spend a week with Chrys and Eric.

"Hmm. Looks like you'll have to have a talk with that man of yours," Berta teased. "He's missed a lot of things lately. My arrival. This great ribbon-cutting ceremony back in Platteville."

Chrys grinned and shaded her eyes from the glare of the sun as she watched Mary Kathleen saddle her pony. "I tried to get Eric to change his mind and go back to Platteville for the dedication, but he didn't want to. He said he was afraid that if he did go, the press would spend more time on the fact that it was Talbot's house being dedicated by Talbot's son than they would on the real issue of a need for a shelter for battered women and their children."

"Hey, Berta! Watch me!" Mary Kathleen yelled as she raced the pony around the corral.

Berta waved vigorously as Mary Kathleen and Buckles circled the corral two more times. "It looks like Mary Kathleen's adjusted well."

"Disgusting child!" Chrys laughed fondly. "She's taken to New Mexico like a duck takes to water. In fact, she's almost as crazy about this place as Eric is."

"How about you?" Berta frowned. "You never say in your letters. Do you like it okay?"

"I love it. In fact, I've even gotten used to not seeing trees. Speaking of which," she said, laughing, "why don't we go in out of the sun. Mary Kathleen knows that we can see her from the kitchen."

Ten minutes later, Berta put down her empty glass and sighed, her dark face wreathed in smiles. "Ah, lemonade!"

"Want another?"

"Nope. One's enough. By the way, how's the new job?"

"It's more challenging than my job in Platteville. I've actually got more say in shaping the collection here than I did there. But best of all, I don't work nearly the hours that I did in Wisconsin so I've got plenty of time for my family."

"Hmm." Berta lifted one brow expectantly and ran her finger around the rim of her empty glass. "Are we talking patter of little feet?"

"Not yet." Chrys laughed, then colored delicately as Eric walked in the kitchen door. "But maybe soon."

Eric hadn't heard Chrys's comment, but he'd heard her laugh and had seen the way she and Berta had their heads tucked together. "Just what are you two ladies up to now?" he asked cheerfully as he came forward to give his wife a kiss on the cheek.

"Us?" Chrys smiled sheepishly as she returned his kiss. "What would make you think the two of us—"

"Don't give me that." Chuckling, he turned to give Berta a welcoming hug. Then, shooting a teasing glance over one shoulder, he added casually, "Ph.Ds know these things."

"Ph— Oh, Eric!" Chrys threw herself into her husband's arms and, half dancing with joy, she hugged him again and again. "That's wonderful," she chatted excitedly. "I'm so proud. Are you sure? Is it all set? I can't believe I forgot to ask. I know how much it means to you."

Since Chrys didn't leave him any time to reply, Eric didn't answer. He just laughed and grinned and pulled her closer still. The Ph.D was nothing compared to what he already had right there in his arms.

Harlequin American Romance

COMING NEXT MONTH

#201 PROMISES by Judith Arnold

In the old days it would've been a "happening." When six friends reunited to celebrate the fifteenth anniversary of a college newspaper they founded in the seventies, they renewed old friendships and shared nostalgic memories. For two of them, Seth and Laura, the night held more magic, as their long-term friendship turned to love. Experience the first book in the *Keeping the Faith* trilogy.

#202 DREAM CHASERS by Anne McAllister

Owain O'Neill couldn't pinpoint the urge that led him to Belle River, Wisconsin, to see for himself the child he'd created. A quick look and then he'd be gone—that was what he'd promised himself. But Owain hadn't planned on discovering he was the father of twins—or on falling in love with their mother.

#203 THE HEART CLUB by Margaret St. George

Next to broccoli, Molly hated injustices the most. So when she discovere her gran's Heart Club had been victimized by a patent thief, she solicited the help of part-time inventor Mike Randall and took justice into her ow hands. The situation looked bad, but it was about to get worse....

#204 TO ASK AGAIN, YES by Carolyn Thornton

Men. Where could women find decent ones? Ivy had looked everywhere—from blind dates to the dreaded personal ads—and then took matters into her own hands. The result: an original Date Mate T-shirt. Now that the task was done, would Ivy find the man of her dreams?

ATTRACTIVE, SPACE SAVING BOOK RACK

Display your most prized novels on this handsome and sturdy book rack. The hand-rubbed walnut finish will blend into your library decor with quiet elegance, providing a practical organizer for your favorite hard-or soft-covered books.

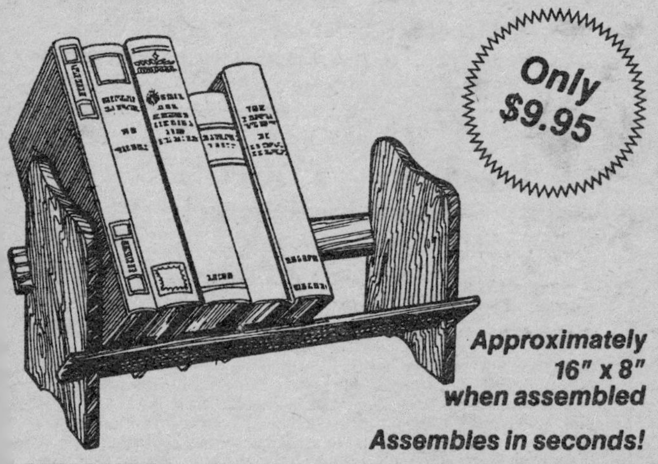

Assembles in seconds!

To order, rush your name, address and zip code, along with a check or money order for $10.70* ($9.95 plus 75¢ postage and handling) payable to *Harlequin Reader Service*:

Harlequin Reader Service
Book Rack Offer
901 Fuhrmann Blvd.
P.O. Box 1325
Buffalo, NY 14269-1325

Offer not available in Canada.

*New York residents add appropriate sales tax.

BKR-1R